Ghost Operations Division

Search for the Panis Vitae

Jackson Nightingale
AUTHOR

This book is a work of fiction. Names, characters, places, and events are made up by the author or used in a fictional way. Any likeness to real people, living or dead, events, or places is purely by chance.

Copyright © 2024 by Jackson Nightingale

All rights reserved. No part of this book may be reproduced or used in any manner without written permission from the copyright owner, except for the use of quotations in a book review.

Cover & Illustrations by: Nauman Akbar & J. Nightingale

ISBN 978-0-9808839-9-2 (Paperback)

ISBN 978-1-0688668-0-7 (ebook)

Published by:

www.jacksonnightingaleauthor.com

Acknowledgements

Special thanks to my wife who supported me in this labor of love, and stood by me through countless rewrites, edits, and machinations. "Just hold on while I reconfigure the links and pages... AGAIN." I love and appreciate the author of the Bible for inspiring the Ghost Operations Division adventures. And thanks to my Mum and sister for always being the best beta readers, and cheer leaders.

Thank you, thank you, thank you Kenneth Zink: A literary genius that not only made this book better but taught me a lot about myself and writing, by asking all the right questions. Best editor ever!

A big hug and thanks to my cover and interior designer Nauman Akbar. You have such a creative spirit that is pure magic. You do for the eyes, what words are for the imagination – just beautiful.

Lastly, thanks to all the readers out there that picked up a copy of Ghost Operations Division: Search for the Panis Vitae. I really hope you enjoy it and stay tuned for the next installment in the saga.

Table of contents

Introducing Olivia Davenport	01
An Important Archeological Find	06
Getting Some Chow	08
It's a Jungle Out There!	10
Little Bird Insertion	14
Break Out the Ghillie Suits	17
Wile E. Coyote Rescue	22
A Sig Sauer Rescue	24
Clandestine Meetings	27
I Like to Live Dangerously	31
The Fourth Horseman	33
Not Just a Pretty Face	38
Pharisee Interdiction	42
The Iron Dome	44
GOD, Are You Out There?	46
Introducing Xavier Washington	52
Send It	57
Cut It Loose, Girl	65
Reuniting with Don Miguel	68
Mosquito Bite	71
Everybody Look to the Left	75
I'm a Vegetarian	79
I Don't Do Political Assassination	81
Getting Out of Dodge	83

Abort, Abort, Abort	85
The Road Not Taken	87
Just Breathe, Olivia	99
The Pale Horse Unleashed	105
Running Down a Lead	114
You Can't Handle the Truth!	119
Blinded by the Light	125
Just Like Chicken!	132
Skyhook	136
Ancient Secrets Unlocked	140
The Tetragrammaton	145
GOD is Great!	152
Bureaucracy at Its Best	165
Getting the Lay of the Land	167
I'm Sexy and I Know It	174
Who Do You People Think You Are?	178
An Ethiopian Surprise	180
I Want Out	190
Back to the War Room	192
Any Last Requests?	196
Let's Find Another Way In	200
Appropriating the Pale Horse	201
RIP Maya Avraham	204
A Mysterious Path	207
We're Going to Die	210
The Final Curtain	212
Stand Down, Agent Gabriel	214
The Door to the Ark Chamber	216
Maybe We Should Smash It!	221

I'm Not That Kind of Girl	224
Gurkha CIV Infiltration Tactics	226
It's Too Dangerous	230
Decrypting the Qurman Cipher Wheel	233
Look What I Found	238
Move Over, Harry Houdini	243
The Mask of Tutankhamun	245
You Won't Find This on YouTube	247
I Want to Come In	249
The Long Goodnight	255
Free the Slider	257
Decoding the Files	258
Recon in Iraq	261
A Secret Passage	266
Meeting His Mother	273
It's a Key	279
It's a Man's Job	286
I'll Cooperate	288
I Got the Shaft	294
Stop, Drop, Roll	296
Into the Creepy Cellar	302
Phase Two	304
Quick, Nobody's Looking	313
It's Nappy Time	318
Ladies First	320

DIY	**322**
Swim for Your Life	**329**
Calling Home to Momma	**331**
It's In AIDA's Hands Now	**333**
All That Glitters	**346**
Just Another Brick in the Wall	**348**
What's Next	**350**
There's Going to be Fireworks	**357**
We Need Our Gear	**359**
Introducing Maya Avraham	**363**

Instructions for Reading

Ghost Operations Division is not a linear book where you start on page 1 and read through pages 2, 3 ,4, and 5….

Instead:

Step 1. Choose your character. There are three: Olivia (the analyst), Maya (the operator), or Xavier (the treasure hunter).

Step 2. Turn to the page where that character's story begins.

Step 3. Your mission is to navigate to the true ending in bold font: **The End**

> The alternate endings will be in normal font: The End.

Step 4. Enjoy!

First Choose Your Character...

Character 1 ~ If you choose Olivia, turn to page 01.

Name: Olivia Davenport DTh — Minor in Ancient Studies

Code Name: Desert Lotus

Date of Birth: September 17, 2009 (Age 25)

Skilled In: Cryptography and ancient languages

Speaks: English, Arabic, Kurdish, Armenian, Greek, and Farsi

Sorority: Alpha Sigma Tau, NYU

Physical

Height: 5' 4" tall

Weight: 114 lbs

Dress Size: 4

Measurements: 33-24-34

Eye Color: Hazel

Hair Color: Light brown

Shoe Size: 6

Build: Petite/slim

Note: Wears prescription eyeglasses.

Born to British parents and immigrated to the US in 2010.

Grew up in the Upper East Side, Manhattan, NY.

Enjoys playing piano.

Current Employer: Museum of the Bible — Artifact Restoration
400 4th St SW, Washington, DC 20024, United States

Vehicle: Electric 3-door Mini Cooper SE Color: Island-blue metallic.

Description: Olivia is a stunning beauty, a delicate flower blooming in the busy world. With her porcelain skin that glows under soft morning light, she has a timeless grace that surpasses ordinary existence. Her eyes, like pools of liquid amber, hold deep emotions without saying a word, sparkling with a playful glint, hinting at a spirit as free and wild as the wind.

Character 2 ~ If you choose Maya, turn to page 363.

Name: Maya Avraham (former Mossad agent)

Code Name: Gabriel

Date of Birth: May 1, 2004 (Age 30)

Skilled In: Counterintelligence; counterinsurgency; hand-to-hand combat (5th-degree black belt in Krav Maga); elite sniper training; tactical knowledge and analysis; unconventional warfare; and explosive ordinance disposal (EOD)

Speaks: English, Hebrew, and Arabic

Graduated: Tel Aviv University with a BA in Biblical studies/Archaeology and Ancient Near Eastern Cultures

Physical

Height: 5' 9" tall

Hair Color: Blonde

Weight: 130 lbs

Shoe Size: 9.5

Dress Size: 4

Complexion: Slightly tanned

Measurements: 35-24-35
Eye Color: Blue

Build: Athletic/slim.

Born In: Petah Tiqwa, Israel Now lives in: Los Angeles, CAParents: Polish/Israeli

Served: IDF from 2022-2024 in the Shaldag ("Kingfisher") Unit; Mossad 2023-2024

Current Employer: Black River PMC (Los Angeles), 2025-present

Vehicle: Aston Martin DBS 777 Ultimate Coup Color: Black

Description: With her sharp features and piercing blue eyes, Maya commands the attention of all as soon as she enters a room. Her golden hair pulled back in a bun adds to her military look, while a few loose strands soften her appearance. She embodies strength and authority with every step, her posture upright and purposeful as she maintains poise and grace, a testament to her unwavering resolve in the face of countless challenges. Beneath her tough exterior lies a woman driven by a fierce sense of duty and a commitment to protecting those she loves. She is both a beacon of hope and a symbol of resilience.

Character 3 ~ If you choose Xavier, turn to page 52.

Name: Xavier Washington (treasure hunter)

Code Name: Wild Card

Date of Birth: November 18th, 2000 (Age 32)

Skilled In: LYDAR to take 3D scans of dig sites; photogrammetry to obtain 3D scans of objects; MMA (dabbles)

Speaks: English and Arabic

Graduated: University of Minnesota—BA in Anthropology

Physical

Height: 6' 2.5" tall

Weight: 205 lbs

Chest: 46"

Biceps: 16"

Waist: 35"

Hair Color: Brown

Eye Color: Hazel

Shoe Size: 12

Complexion: Caucasian

Build: Athletic/Strong

Born in: Galesburg, Illinois Now lives in: Chicago, IL Parents: USA

Mentor: Naturalist and paleontologist Roy Chapman Andrews, former director of the American Museum of Natural History.

Enjoys: basketball, SCUBA diving, helicopter flying, base jumping/wingsuit, and parkour

Current Employer: Self-Employed

Vehicle: Ducati Panigale V4 SP4 Color: Canary Yellow

Description: Xavier's square jawline bring to mind rugged masculinity while his high cheekbones give him a refined look. His hazel eyes framed by thick lashes hold a universe of emotions, showing depth and vulnerability in a single glance.

His hair, always styled with effortless precision, tops off his captivating look. Whether tousled casually or slicked back with sophistication, his spiky locks add to his allure, drawing attention to his expressive eyes and charismatic smile.

Go back and choose your character now.

Then start on the page associated with that character.

Or continue to start with Olivia.

Each character holds a unique experience.

Introducing Olivia Davenport

Date: July 23, 2034

Location: CIA Black Site Cairo (Approx. 30.0444° N, 31.2357° E)

Between the Nile River and the 6th of October Bridge.

In a dimly lit room with blacked-out windows, the air hangs heavy and humid as you survey your surroundings. The teal walls are faded, marred by water stains and peeling paint. A rhythmic drip echoes through the silence. In the center of the room stands a cold metal table.

Wires snake across your chest and stomach, tethering you to a lie detector on the table, each breath faintly labored under the strain. A clamp bites around your right middle fingertip, attached to the lie detector machine by a thin beige wire. Velcro sensors cling to your index and ring fingers while a tight blood pressure cuff constricts your arm. Every vital sign—blood pressure, pulse, respiration rate, skin conductivity, body heat, and even the tiniest micro expressions—is being closely monitored.

Numerous cameras with faint crimson lights track your every move. Opposite you, a mirror reflects a warped version of the room, a cold reminder of the eyes hidden behind the glass. Your foot taps restlessly against the floor, the tension creeping up your neck and tightening your shoulders into knots. Your skin turns clammy as a bead of sweat trickles down your brow.

The four-and-a-half-hour flight from Ramstein Air Base to Cairo aboard a military transport was grueling, leaving you restless and eager to see this through. The black hood over your head during the drive from the airport scratched at your skin, but a small triumph flickered within—the hood wasn't completely opaque. Bits of light and shapes slipped through, giving you glimpses of your surroundings. The noise-canceling headphones felt excessive but were standard protocol for enhanced interrogations.

The silence shatters with the sound of heavy footsteps and the sharp beeps of a keypad. The steel door swings open and Elizabeth Chamberlain strides in, her presence commanding the room. Her gaze slices through you as she approaches the table and slams down a large manila folder marked Top Secret SCI — Restricted Data. Several pages slip out, two of them blotted with redactions, and a grainy CCTV image on another page shows figures running—an image that fuels an anxious uncertainty within you.

"Ms. Davenport." Chamberlain's sharp and unyielding voice cuts through the silence. "I'm Elizabeth Chamberlain, CIA Chief of Station, Cairo. I have one question." She pauses. "Where is the Ark of the Covenant?"

Ms. Chamberlain raises her hand to her face, resting her index finger against her cheek, her eyes narrowing and lips curling into a faint scowl.

"I don't know," you whisper, your voice trembling with uncertainty.

A moment passes, Chamberlain's eyes boring into yours. Then, with a curt nod to her team behind the two-way mirror, she continues.

"Don't play dumb with me. You're up to your neck in this!" Each word drips with authority and menace. The stage is set for a battle of wills.

In Ms. Chamberlain's earpiece, a voice crackles just loud enough for you to hear, "No signs of deception."

She presses a button on the table microphone. "Send in the technician."

After a brief pause, she adds, "Begin transcription. Begin recording."

A stocky technician dressed in black and with a skinny tie around his neck enters the room. Without a word he takes his place in front of the conventional lie detector equipment.

"Alright, Olivia, before we begin, I'll ask you a few simple questions to establish a baseline for your body's responses," he says, adjusting the sensors on your fingers. "Let's start with something simple. Is your name Olivia?"

He watches the paper feed carefully as you respond with, "Yes."

"Good. Are you sitting in a chair right now?"

You nod, your eyes briefly flicking to the wires connecting you to the polygraph machine. The technician observes the readings, seemingly satisfied with your clear responses.

"One last question for the baseline: Are the lights on in this room?"

"Yes," you reply, and again, your pulse remains steady.

"Thank you, Olivia," he says before a quick double knock from the other side of the mirror shatters the tense atmosphere.

Moments later, the door opens and a tall, slender older man, his hair thinning and graying, walks into one of the dark corners. You can barely make out any others features except for the whites of his eyes. The shadow under one of the cameras is just dark enough to obscure the rest of him. He takes a puff from his cigarette and exhales a plume of acrid smoke into the room.

Behind him stands another Caucasian man in a tuxedo, this one more willing to be recognized. He's slightly shorter than the smoker, about ten to fifteen years younger, and exudes an English air with his impeccable posture. He approaches the smoker and whispers something inaudible. The smoker nods in agreement.

"Ms. Davenport, meet Keith Atkins, Deputy Director of the CIA," Ms. Chamberlain says, gesturing first to the man with the cigarette, then to the man in the tuxedo. "And this is Collin Atwell, representing the UK's National Security Council MI6. He'll be sitting in."

You inject a hint of nervous sarcasm. "Quite the outfit for the occasion, Mr. Atwell."

"This is serious, Ms. Davenport," Ms. Chamberlain says. "Under the National Defense Authorization Act, you are being held on charges of espionage and terrorism. You've been declared an enemy combatant. You could be detained indefinitely."

If you want to resist, **turn to page 178**.

If you want to comply and answer their questions, **turn to page 288**.

 **Bookmark Here**

An Important Archeological Find

Olivia suggests donating Aaron's breastplate to the Israel Antiquities Authority (IAA). It will be Israel's most significant discovery in nearly fifty years. The challenge lies in where it was found: the Temple Mount, a highly contested site claimed by Jews, Muslims, and Christians.

Your goal is to locate both the Ark and the panis vitae, the golden jar of manna. Do we really need a sixth-century breastplate?

After consulting with Michael Smith, your handler, you deliver the breastplate to the IAA. Shortly thereafter, you're celebrated as heroes. The prime minister awards all three of you honorary Israeli citizenship and Olivia graces the cover of Smithsonian Magazine.

Without new leads, your search for the Ark is stalled, much like the Pharisees' persistent excavations at their sites.

Three months later, the Ghost Operations Division is shut down due to congressional scrutiny of covert CIA activities and budgetary anomalies uncovered by IRS forensic accountants.

Xavier settles into a chateau in southern France while Olivia accepts a position teaching art history and archaeology at Georgetown University.

As for you, you start working with Black River PMC, handling coups, sinking submarines, and toppling dictatorships. Just another day in the life.

The End

Go Back to Page 317

Getting Some Chow

You find Benji in the mess hall, enjoying a meal, just as Maya mentioned. He smiles when he spots you entering the room. As you enthusiastically recount the excitement at Hillah, you take a large bite of your food and suddenly begin to choke.

Panic erupts in the crowded mess hall as you struggle to breathe, but Benji springs into action. Recalling his first aid training with steady hands and a racing heart, he performs the Heimlich maneuver, but it proves ineffective. Your face turns a pale blue as your airway remains obstructed.

Time seems to stand still as the gravity of the situation sinks in. With tears in his eyes, Benji redoubles his efforts, desperate to save you, his mentor and friend. Despite his best attempts, your body goes limp in his arms. You survived the most daring and harrowing adventure of your life only to be felled by a piece of half-chewed breakfast sausage.

In the aftermath of the tragedy, the base is enveloped in grief. Your colleagues and students mourn the loss of a brilliant mind and a kind soul, while Benji grapples with the suddenness of your passing.

As they gather to honor your memory, they remember you not only for your scholarly achievements but for your warmth and generosity of spirit. Though your time with the GOD team was tragically brief, your legacy endures as a beacon of knowledge and inspiration for generations to come. In quiet moments of reflection, they find solace in knowing that you dedicated your life to a noble pursuit: seeking to understand the past to illuminate the future.

Benji returns to DC to continue his work at the museum while the remnants of the GOD team focus on tracking down the Pale Horse virus, striving to prevent a potential worldwide catastrophe.

The End

Go Back to Page 51

It's a Jungle Out There!

It's 2030 when your latest adventure begins. Backed by a mysterious sponsor, you embark on a quest that could reshape history: the search for the legendary Incan city of Paititi. Many have dismissed it as mere myth or folklore, but deep down, you know it exists, just waiting to be discovered.

Your first step on the path to destiny begins amidst the bustling chaos of Chicago O'Hare. Soon you board a flight to Cusco's Alejandro Velasco Astete International Airport, bound for the heart of Peru, where ancient secrets await in the mist-shrouded Andes mountains.

Upon arriving in Cusco, you travel through the sacred Urubamba Valley aboard the PeruRail train. As you gaze out the window, the breathtaking landscape of the Sacred Valley of the Incas unfolds, rich with both history and mystery. Steep cliffs plunge hundreds of meters into the valley below while the Urubamba River surges through the fertile expanse like a lifeline.

On the train, you sample chicha, a traditional Andean beverage with roots stretching back thousands of years. Though it isn't particularly strong, its cultural significance is unmistakable, offering a glimpse into the rich traditions of the Andes.

From Ollantaytambo, your journey grows more challenging as you enlist local porters to help navigate the rugged terrain of the Patacancha Valley. The elder of the porters doesn't speak much but communicates through a series of gestures and smiles. Without knowing his name you've been given to calling him Don Miguel. His sons however know some broken English, which makes things easier. With dependable mules by your sides, you press onward, each step bringing you closer to your elusive goal.

Amidst the breathtaking vistas and towering peaks, you pause at a serene Quechua village, a bastion of tradition in the face of modern change. Here, you taste the bittersweet coca leaves for the first time, an ageless ritual that has fueled the spirit of exploration for untold generations. As the sun sets, casting amber and gold across the horizon, you stand at the threshold of a new chapter in your journey.

The next morning, with the thrill of adventure still fresh in your mind, you set out to kayak the churning waters of the Urubamba River, its frothy current beckoning you forth like a siren's call.

The river is no gentle stream. It's a tempestuous force of nature, its hidden currents swirling with whispers of danger and death. Every bend holds the threat of peril, its jagged banks poised to capsize both boat and soul with a single misstep.

Driven by a primal urge to uncover Paititi's secrets, you navigate the treacherous waters with unwavering skill and determination. Each paddle stroke feels like a dance with fate, balancing on the brink of disaster.

Above, jagged rocks loom like silent sentinels. Yet, with each obstacle overcome, your defiance only grows stronger, propelling you toward the unknown. After ninety minutes on the river, it's time to begin the trek over land once more.

Adversity fuels your adventure, and you know your journey has only just begun. With the taste of conquest lingering in your mouth you press forward, driven by an unyielding hunger for discovery.

The night drapes a veil of darkness over your campsite where a vast canopy of stars stretches endlessly above. The untamed landscape surrounds you, its raw beauty accentuated by the flickering firelight. Your porters and Don Miguel, silhouetted by the glow, work deftly, fashioning a makeshift oven from stones. The flames lick the air, heating the rocks until they glow red-hot. Your porters fill the oven with potatoes and corn before placing skinned wild guinea pigs on top, creatures beloved as pets in North America but revered here, in the rugged heart of Peru, as a culinary staple.

If you want to dine only on potatoes and corn, **turn to page 79.**

If you want to brave the roasted guinea pig with your Incan porters, **turn to page 132.**

 **Bookmark Here**

Little Bird Insertion

The wind howls as we board the sleek black Boeing MH-6M Little Bird. The helicopter's rotors roar to life, vibrating above us with raw power. Wild Card, our seasoned pilot, gives a quick thumbs-up, his smirk barely visible beneath his helmet. Beside me, Agent Gabriel adjusts her headset. We exchange a tense nod. Our mission to Mount Nebo was urgent. Time was not on our side.

The flight from Amman to Mount Nebo will take just eight minutes. As the helicopter lifts off, a knot tightens in your stomach. Wild Card guides the chopper through the twilight sky. Below, the city lights of Amman dim, swallowed by the growing distance and the upper echelons of night.

Six minutes into the flight, the world beyond the cockpit window vanishes. As if out of nowhere, a freak sandstorm explodes across the sky, engulfing the helicopter in a swirling wall of sand. The Little Bird shudders, its rotors groaning against the relentless winds. Visibility is zero.

"Damn it!" Wild Card growls, his usually steady voice now tinged with panic. His hands fight the controls but the sandstorm's force is overwhelming. Too strong, too sudden. The instruments flicker wildly, warning lights flashing like demonic eyes in the cockpit.

Your stomach flips as the storm slams into the helicopter, buffeting it like a toy in a giant's grip. Wild Card's hands fly across the controls, desperate to regain stability. The helicopter pitches and yaws, the sandstorm turning the world outside into a chaotic blur.

"Wild Card, what the hell is going on?!" Gabriel shouts, her voice nearly drowned out by the deafening roar of the storm.

"Spatial disorientation!" Wild Card shouts back, his face ashen with fear. "I can't tell up from down!"

The helicopter lurches to the side, and through the swirling haze of sand, the ground spirals up toward you. Your heart hammers in your chest, adrenaline flooding your veins. Time seems to stretch endlessly, each second an eternity filled with the weight of impending doom.

The Little Bird crashes into the ground with a bone-shattering impact. The deafening screech of twisting metal and shattering glass fills your ears, merging with your own screams. A searing pain tears through you as something heavy slams into your body. Then everything goes black.

When you regain consciousness, you're no longer in the helicopter. The world is dark and suffocatingly still. Beside you, Wild Card and Gabriel lie motionless, their bodies twisted and broken. Lifeless. The cold truth washes over you like a rising tide —you're dying.

A wave of dread crashes over you. In the distance, the wind whispers, a haunting reminder of the storm that delivered you to this place.

You gaze at Wild Card, his face contorted in a desperate failed attempt to save you. Gabriel's once-vibrant features are now ghostly pale, her eyes blank. And then, as if sealing your fate, everything fades to black one last time.

The End

Go Back to Page 285

Break Out the Ghillie Suits

The idea of covert operations deep in enemy territory, danger lurking at every turn, sends an irresistible thrill through you. "I'm in!" you say. Sergeant Levi Abelman—a man of few words but unmatched skills—is assigned as your spotter.

The details of your target are shrouded in mystery, but you know your mission lies deep within the volatile expanse of the Middle East. The game is on, and the stakes have never been higher. "Understand this: what you're about to hear is classified Epsilon IX. It never happened."

On May 16th, 2024, just before your departure, the details for Operation Cleopatra come through. Your mission: execute a nighttime incursion into Azerbaijani airspace using a High-Altitude High-Opening (HAHO) jump.

Your landing zone lies deep within Azerbaijani territory where you'll trek several kilometers to the Aras River—Objective Alpha. There, you'll deploy a Helix REBS Launcher to fire a quarter-inch steel cable across the sixty-to-eighty-meter span of the rushing Aras, zipping into Iranian territory.

Your next move is to stealthily navigate one kilometer downriver to the Giz Galasi Dam—Objective Bravo. There, three Bell 212 helicopters operated by the Islamic Republic of Iran Air Force await, your target among them: tail number EP-ZYX. Your mission is clear: discreetly plant a small charge of C-4 on the target and retreat into Azerbaijan. If the opportunity arises, execute a hard-target interdiction, using the C-4 as a contingency.

Your extraction plan is precise. You will rendezvous at prearranged coordinates with your CIA contact Adila Mammadova, recognizable by her wine-and-gold Arkhaluk. You'll give her the code phrase. "Gəzinti üçün gözəl bir gecədir." (It's a great night for a walk).

She'll reply, "Martuni görmək lazımdır." (You must see Martuni). From there, she'll transport you an hour and a half to Martuni followed by a seven-hour drive to Baku. From Baku you'll take a three-hour flight to Ben Gurion International Airport in Tel Aviv.

As you gear up for the mission, the air hums with tension. Every detail has to be flawless. Every move could mean the difference between life and death. With each passing second, the weight of your task presses harder on your mind.

Your flight departs at 2330 hours, the darkness outside the windows reflecting the covert nature of your mission. You're outfitted with the finest gear available, state-of-the-art military technology built for precision and stealth.

Still, you know your most powerful weapons aren't the gadgets strapped to your body, but your wits and an unbreakable will to achieve your objectives. The steady hum of the engines serves as a constant reminder of the perilous journey ahead. With each passing minute, tension and anticipation build. You're about to step into the unknown, where every decision will test your skills and resolve. The stakes couldn't be higher, and failure isn't an option.

As you board the sleek black-and-gold pin-striped King Air C90GTx—courtesy of the CIA—a surge of anticipation pulses through you. Capable of reaching speeds of 272 knots (310 mph), the aircraft promises a quick two-hour-and-forty-minute flight to your jump location. You notice a small, laminated card tucked in the seat pocket in front of you detailing the plane's safety features. In the top corner, barely visible, it reads: Iran Aircraft Industries © 1979.

Aboard are David, Daniel, Sergeant Abelman, and the pilots. Your airborne headquarters, code-named Looking Glass, coordinates the operation. You (code-named Aphrodite) and Abelman (code-named Eagle Eye) are prepared for the mission.

The critical equipment, ironically named the Big Red Balloon, is secured and ready. Your ultimate objective is code-named Sneaky Pete.

As you ascend to 30,000 feet, tension grips the cabin. You initiate depressurization and watch as the pilots, David, and Daniel, don their oxygen masks. You and Eagle Eye are suited up in tactical gear, your helmets fitted with oxygen systems to manage the thin atmosphere.

The moment arrives. First the equipment is jettisoned, disappearing into the void below. Then Eagle Eye takes the leap. Finally, it's your turn to plunge into the abyss. The cold air lashes against you before you've even fully exited the aircraft. Your heart races as you plummet through the open sky, the wind howling around you.

Seconds later you pull the rip cord on your black chute. The canopy unfurls above you and you and Eagle Eye are lifted by the updrafts, gliding thirty kilometers into the heart of the Azerbaijani woodlands. For twenty minutes, you float in near silence, with only the rustle of the wind against your chutes breaking the stillness.

You land gently, the dense forest floor absorbing your descent. After packing away your parachutes you activate the beacon on the Big Red Balloon. Your navigation shows it's a few kilometers away. Your first priority is to report your safe landing to HQ and track the equipment.

"Looking Glass, this is Eagle Eye. We have touched down at X-ray and are tracking the Big Red Balloon. Do you copy?"

"We read you five by five, Eagle Eye. Looking Glass has you on thermal, approximately two klicks north of the Big Red Balloon. Your skies are clear with no traffic. I repeat, your skies are clear with no traffic. Over."

"Affirmative, Looking Glass. We'll move two klicks to the Big Red Balloon and provide a sitrep. Eagle Eye out.

With the mission clear, you begin your trek. Each step through the dense underbrush brings you closer to your objective. The night is silent, save for the sounds of your movements and the distant calls of nocturnal creatures. Every sense is heightened, and every shadow feels like a potential threat.

It takes you and Eagle Eye half an hour to locate your gear, suspended twenty feet off the ground. The chute must have become entangled in the trees. Despite being called the Big Red Balloon it's actually a fully camouflaged case, nearly undetectable in the trees.

If you want to climb the tree to cut your gear down, **turn to page 359.**

If you want to abort the mission and radio HQ, **turn to page 85.**

 **Bookmark Here**

Wile E. Coyote Rescue

You believe you slipped out of the warehouse undetected, relying on Seal Team Six to handle any pursuers. All that remains is to march one klick down the shoreline to the extraction zone.

Your stamina falters, heart thrashing in your chest. Despite your best efforts, you didn't escape as cleanly as you hoped. The mercenaries' boots echo behind you, their relentless rhythm pushing you to run faster.

The salty sea air is crisp, but there's no time to savor it. Every second drags as you push harder, desperate for the safety of Seal Team Six. But the artifact is secure—that's all that matters now.

The night shatters with the staccato burst of AK-47 fire as you run up the coast. Bullets whizz and ricochet, slicing through the silence. Your instincts scream at you to take cover, but you can't—your mission takes priority.

In the faint light, you spot them—Seal Team Six, waist-deep in the surf, advancing toward you. Relief surges through you, but it vanishes just as quickly. They've seen your pursuers. Rifles rise, and they open fire. The air cracks with gunfire, bullets tearing through the humid night on both sides.

You dive for cover, adrenaline surging, senses honed and heightened. Sand erupts around you as rounds slam into the ground, each hit a brutal reminder of the danger you're in. The heat of bullets zips past, their lethality unmistakable. The deafening roar of gunfire drowns out the rolling crash of the ocean.

Seal Team Six moves with apex precision, their shots cutting through the night with deadly accuracy. The mercenaries' gunfire falters, and you seize the moment, sprinting the final yards to the extraction point. Your legs burn and lungs scream, but you push on, driven by sheer will and the desperate need for safety.

As you close in on the team, one of them grabs your arm, pulling you into their protective formation. Together, you fall back toward the Mark 8 submersible, its sleek silhouette almost invisible against the dark water. The gunfire fades, replaced by the urgent slosh of your steps and the low hum of the submersible's engines as they bellow to life.

A wave of dizziness hits, and you spot tendrils of blood swirling in the water. You've been hit in the back—two, maybe three times. One of your lungs is punctured, and you feel the life draining from you before you can reach the sub.

The End

Go Back to Page 74

A Sig Sauer Rescue

Time seems to slow as you raise your Sig Sauer P226, steady in your grip. The first shot cracks through the jungle, but it only enrages the creature further, its ferocity unabated.

With a sinking feeling in your gut, you fire again, the sound echoing like a thunderclap. This shot hits its mark, piercing the creature's defenses with lethal precision. With a booming roar, the caiman retreats, vanishing beneath the murky waters, its presence fading into the darkness.

Unshaken by the harrowing encounter, you and Don Miguel press on, eyes locked on the horizon. The search for the skull-shaped rock, the gateway to the legendary city of Paititi, propels you forward, each moment brimming with both peril and the lure of discovery.

You paddle down the winding river, grappling with the oppressive heat and swatting away incessant insects. The jungle is unnervingly silent, save for the splash of your paddles slicing through the water. Then out of nowhere, a stone-tipped spear erupts from the dense foliage, striking the side of your canoe with a resounding thud. Your heart pounds as you and Don Miguel dive for cover, the canoe wobbling in the water.

In an instant, a barrage of spears rains down from both sides of the jungle. The air is filled with the piercing whistle of projectiles slicing through the air, yet the assailants remain unseen.

Suddenly a new sound pierces the chaos—a whirring from both directions. Bolas, expertly thrown, whirl through the air with deadly precision. Small stones follow, pelting you as the jungle erupts with the fierce cries of a native tribe, their voices brimming with fury and rage.

You duck, narrowly avoiding a direct hit from a crude but deadly stone-tipped axe. Your pulse throbs in your ears, each second stretching into eternity as you push forward, driven by sheer desperation. For two hundred meters, you endure the relentless assault, every moment fraught with peril and suspense. Then, as abruptly as it started, the barrage ceases. You drift down the river, carried by the current, your breath ragged and heart still pounding.

For many, this would be seen as proof that the land is cursed, a clear sign to turn back. But for you it only confirms that you're on the right path. A few hours later, strange rock carvings begin to appear intermittently along the riverbanks, depicting unfamiliar symbols except for one recurring motif—the sun. Intricately wrapped threads of colored wool adorn spear tips embedded in trees, serving as enigmatic river markers.

Soon, you reach an opening. Before you stretches a vast expanse of waterfalls, cascading into the basin below. Even from a distance, the scene is breathtakingly majestic. You paddle forward with renewed vigor, knowing in your gut that you're approaching a significant milestone in your quest for Paititi.

Don Miguel gestures toward a large rock rising from the river, its top eerily shaped like a skull—a natural formation that is uncannily lifelike. As you unfold the map, it becomes clear that you've arrived at the gateway to the lost city of gold—Paititi. The mist from the waterfalls creates shimmering rainbows all around you as you forge ahead.

You reach the river's end, confronted by a towering rock face with water cascading down from above. Don Miguel leaps from the boat into the cool, inviting water, his smile urging you to join him. The sun has been relentless, and your explorer's hat offers scant respite from the heat. You toss your hat aside and plunge into the clear, refreshing water. The initial shock of the cold quickly fades, replaced by the invigorating swim amid swirling rainbows and mist. You swim towards the larger waterfall on the left and climb on to a warm rock outcropping, taking a moment to marvel at the breathtaking beauty surrounding you.

You pick up a smooth stone and skim it across the water's surface, pondering whether it's safe to venture behind the waterfall. Curious, you step beneath the cascading curtain of water, enduring its powerful embrace. As you attempt to step back, you lose your footing and tumble into a hidden cavern concealed behind the falls. Inside, the walls are adorned with crude rock paintings, and your gaze is drawn to a mysterious light glowing from the cavern's depths, beckoning you.

If you want to explore the origin of the mysterious light,
turn to page 125.

If you want to head back out and reunite with your guide,
turn to page 68.

 **Bookmark Here**

Clandestine Meetings

You agree to meet Michael at the café, a decision that feels a bit adventurous, maybe even exciting. But when you arrive, Michael is nowhere to be found. He eventually shows up, fashionably late and as handsome as ever.

"I'm so glad you could make it, Liv," he says, pulling you close and kissing you softly on the lips. "I needed that. Ever since our kiss the other night, I haven't been able to think of anything else." And just like that, you're again lost in his deep blue eyes and rugged good looks. But this time something is different. He's carrying a silver briefcase and looks concerned.

"So, what's going on, Michael? Why all the secrecy? First you ask me to translate cryptic messages in Arabic. Then you disappear for two days. And now we have to meet at the café? I thought we had a connection." You feel vulnerable and tinged with hurt.

"I promise I'll explain everything, Olivia. And yes, we do have a connection, but I need to confess something. At first, it's going to sound crazy, but the more I explain, the more you'll understand it's true. I'm not a lobbyist, Liv. I work for the government – more specifically for the Agency. The message I had you decrypt was between a notorious arms dealer known as 'the Prophet' and a man we believe is Ziad Alhussan."

He pulls a photograph from his briefcase and places it in front of you. As you trace the man's face with your finger, you instantly know that you've never seen him before. He's tall, with faded blond hair streaked with white and topped with a pronounced widow's peak. His eyebrows flare menacingly at the edges. Two-day-old white stubble adorns his jawline. His long nose is crooked, as if it was broken and badly reset. Crow's feet and dark eye sockets only add to his sinister presence. There's something unnerving about him, a quiet malice that makes the hair on the back of your neck stand on end.

"This man is Heinrich Jager, a German national who studied at Oxford," Michael says. "We believe he's now using the alias 'the Prophet.' He first showed up on our radar in March 1992, after the Soviet Union collapsed, brokering arms deals with Iran and North Korea. We also know he supplied a weapons shipment to the Houthi rebels in Yemen during the mid-'90s.

"He vanished for years. We believed he'd been killed in a drone strike in Syria, until last week when intelligence intercepted a phone call between him and this man."

Michael sets another photograph on top of the first.

"This is Ziad Alhussan, a Palestinian whose family was killed in the 2023 Israeli bombing of Gaza. Educated at Cambridge University, he graduated with a degree in biological sciences. In 2024 he was radicalized by Hezbollah. His birth records were destroyed in the bombings, but he's believed to be in his late forties. By 2030, he had refined his skills with the Quds Force. He vanished in 2032 and was presumed dead, only to reappear in 2033 as an assassin for hire. We believe he is now the number two in a terrorist group called the Pharisees."

He has a smooth-shaved head, an intense scowl, and dark brown eyes that border on black. His olive-brown complexion is framed by dark trimmed eyebrows and the remnants of a dead innocence that has been obliterated by horrific trauma, replaced now by a palpable hate. A pointed nose and a strong jawline complete his unsettling visage, reflecting his deviant psychopathy.

"We believe Alhussan has developed a biological weapon called the Pale Horse, referencing the Four Horsemen of the Apocalypse from the Bible. It reads: 'And I saw, and behold, a pale horse: and he that sat upon him, his name was Death...'

"What you translated the other night was a conversation between these two men. We believe they're planning to test the weapon in the Republic of Congo, which could result in millions of deaths. We need your help, Olivia—desperately."

You're at a loss for words, stunned and horrified. The gravity of what you've just heard is both exhilarating and terrifying, more intense than anything you've ever experienced.

Michael then reveals he's part of a clandestine task force known as the Ghost Operations Division, and they urgently need a translator with your expertise. You consider his request, but before you can respond, he adds, "Your country needs you."

"I'm not sure I can get time off work. Will I need to travel? Are there any risks involved? My life is safe and routine—actually, it's kind of boring."

What Michael has told you all feels sudden and disconnected from the predictable, bubble-wrapped life you've crafted in Washington: dinners with your parents every Thursday, drinks with friends on Friday nights to shatter the illusion you could meet a nice guy at a bar, and yoga classes on Saturday mornings with young divorcées back on the prowl. Yet there are moments when you've questioned whether there's more to life, something more you're meant for.

"I'm not going to sugarcoat this, Liv. There will be some risk involved, and you'll need to travel with the team. However, your role will focus on translation and analysis—you won't be a typical spy. We call it an analyst. Your job will be to support our field personnel. We can expedite your time-off request as a matter of national security, but we're running out of time. Will you help us?"

If you decide to join the GOD team, **turn to page 152.**

If you decide Michael Smith is crazy and needs psychological help, **turn to page 230.**

 **Bookmark Here**

I Like to Live Dangerously

You methodically prepare your equipment, ensuring every detail is in place. As you inhale pure oxygen before the jump, a sense of calm determination washes over you. You open the locket containing a photograph of you and Shira, staring at it, keeping it with you even once the locket is closed.

Your signature silenced Glock-19s are holstered, primed for action. Strapped to your back is a silenced P90, and your trusted karambit is sheathed at your side. You wear a sleek black HALO helmet fitted with an internal heads-up display and night-vision capabilities, as well as a tactical suit that fits like a second skin. On your left forearm, a slim, flexible computer screen encased in a protective sleeve serves as your interface for AIDA.

Coiled with adrenaline as you grip the chute harness, you watch as the ramp opens. Your thumbs-up to the flight crew is the final signal, and with a sudden whoosh, the cargo bay door lowers, letting the frigid air rush in.

Without hesitation, you plunge backward into the abyss, engulfed by darkness. AIDA's calm voice announces your terminal velocity—126 mph. The free fall is electrifying: the wind howls past you, weightlessness envelops you, and the earth below is nothing more than a distant shadow.

At the crucial moment of deploying your main parachute, you pull the cord. But instead of the reassuring billow of fabric, you're met with a violent jolt. Your heart pounds as you look up and see a chaotic tangle of lines and twisted fabric, flapping futilely in the wind.

Panic surges but your training takes over just as quick. You yank the cutaway handle with all your strength, severing the malfunctioning main chute. Once more, you're plunged into free fall. Desperately, you reach for the reserve chute and pull the cord with a mix of hope and dread. There's a brief tug followed by a jarring jerk. You gasp as the reserve chute detaches from the harness and drifts away into the night like a dark specter.

You're in uncontrolled free fall, the wind howling in your ears and the ground rushing up with terrifying speed. Your mind races for a solution, each second slipping away. They say your life flashes before your eyes in the final moments, but you see none of that. No blinding light, no hellfire, no welcoming figure.

In that fleeting moment, you experience a strange sense of freedom and euphoria, the lights of the world below rushing up to meet you. Regret? Maybe for never becoming a mother, or for the lives you took—those who harbored sinister plots against the innocent. But there's no time for that now. You close your eyes for the last time and summon the faces of your family and Shira, clinging to their image as the darkness envelops you.

The End

Go Back to Page 248

The Fourth Horseman

The alarm blares at 5:00 AM. After hitting snooze a few times, you finally drag yourself out of bed. Mother is now stationed in a large hangar, where the military is busy establishing a command center.

After a few quick stretches, you jog around the hangar to get your blood pumping. Breakfast consists of egg whites and a protein shake. Thirty minutes later, a refreshing shower washes away the lingering weight of the previous mission, preparing you for the day ahead.

To thank Desert Lotus for her bravery in rescuing you in Hillah, you head to the armory. There, you purchase an M&P 380 handgun along with a shoulder and thigh holster, designed to accommodate both the weapon and its user. You request the staff to clean and prepare it, promising to return later to collect it

At 6:00 AM, you return to the hangar, prepared for the briefing. The room is filled with high-ranking military officials, including Michael Smith, your CIA handler; François Garza, the Director General of the World Health Organization; Frasier Santorem, the Deputy Assistant Secretary of Defense for Chemical and Biological Defense; and various members of the Department of Defense.

The Secretary of Health and Human Services, Dick Johnson, and the US CDC Director, Dr. Linda Nakamura, join the briefing via satellite. The Supreme Allied Commander Europe outlines how the NATO Response Force will be prepared to address any threats and will coordinate with the Euro-Atlantic Disaster Response Coordination Centre.

AIDA plays a video recorded by Ziad Alhussan, the second-in-command of the Pharisee terrorist network, in the Democratic Republic of Congo. Intended for Heinrich Jager, the video graphically depicts the devastating effects of the Pale Horse virus. The footage is so shocking that a young airman recoils, throwing up in a nearby trash bin.

"What did it show?" Ms. Chamberlain asks.

You hesitate. "I can only describe what I witnessed, ma'am."

The video opens deep within the Congolese jungle, focusing on a tranquil village where the inhabitants lead simple lives deeply connected to nature. In the corner of the chieftain's hut, a black widow spider weaves its web, looking like it's playing a sinister tune as a moth flutters helplessly against it.

Then a shadowy group clad in yellow hazmat suits, identified as the Pharisees, emerges silently from the dense jungle foliage under the cover of night. Equipped with an array of tools and devices, they advance with stealthy precision, resembling nocturnal predators on the hunt.

The leader, Ziad Alhussan, is a bioterrorist driven by a relentless thirst for vengeance following the death of his family in the Gaza bombings. Since that day, his every thought has been consumed by the profound anguish that fuels his blackened heart. He embodies a sinister, sadistic fanaticism, with a singular resolve to see the world consumed by chaos. He possesses no moral compass, and his hollow, tormented eyes are a stark reflection of his malevolent intent.

He kneels beside a custom-built dispersal device and opens a biohazard container. The liquid nitrogen within produced a hissing steam as he carefully retrieved a vial containing a powdery orange substance with a glossy sheen—a deceptive appearance masking its lethal nature. With meticulous precision, he loaded the virus into the dispersal device, removed the actuator protector, and flipped the switch. A low whirring sound began as the fans activated, dispersing the virus as it slithered through the grass-roofed huts of the unsuspecting village.

The weapon spread insidiously, its invisible tendrils infiltrating like a dark angel's touch. It started with mild symptoms: a headache, a runny nose, a persistent cough. The villagers dismissed these signs as common ailments, unaware that those infected would soon become roaming carriers, their sole purpose to propagate the disease. In the initial twenty-four to forty-eight hours, many villagers remained asymptomatic, completely unaware of the impending horrors.

The Pharisees establish a fake clinic to monitor and document the disease's progression. Within five to ten days, the virus's horrific nature begins to finally manifest. Pus-filled lesions erupt on the skin, causing excruciating pain and a nauseating stench of decay. The infected writhe in agony, convulse with violent seizures, and foam at the mouth. This is followed by severe hemorrhaging from the ears, nose, and eyes. Their crimson tears heighten their terror, marking the inevitable arrival of death.

The Pharisees meticulously document the gruesome tableau, including the eerie yellow tinge of the victims' irises before they succumb to the disease. Hair falls out in clumps and fingernails peel away like brittle parchment. Within thirty days, every infected villager is either dead or dying.

The gasps, groans, and wailing echo through the village day and night, a haunting blend of desperation and grief that permeates the air. A young Congolese boy, no more than five years old, sits cross-legged between his deceased parents, rocking back and forth. He wipes the blood from his nose with an empty stare.

The Pharisees dig a mass grave, methodically stacking bodies in black cadaver bags until their supply is exhausted. They drench the trench in gasoline and set the grotesque pyre ablaze. Once the area is engulfed in flames, they exfiltrate, leaving the devastation behind. Alhussan then orders the deployment of two 750-pound MK-77 fuel-air bombs as a final measure to secure the site, the ultimate step in containing the most perilous biological threat humanity has ever faced—more contagious than Ebola and deadlier than Marburg. Any contact with bodily fluids or even proximity to an infected individual guarantees infection.

The video is horrifying, its intensity leaving a palpable silence in the hangar. The room, once quiet, now buzzes with urgent discussions about strategies and responses. Stopping this threat is an immediate priority. Even you hadn't seen the footage that AIDA retrieved from the flash drive you smuggled out of Hillah until now. The gravity of the situation is clear: if this virus spreads, it will pose an existential threat to all of humanity.

"He shows no signs of deception," the polygraph technician reports in the interrogation room, his gaze fixed on your reactions.

"Let's take a break for lunch, Mr. Washington," Ms. Chamberlain says, signaling Mr. Atkins as they leave the room.

The technician disconnects you from the polygraph machine and cuffs you to a bar bolted to the steel table, which itself is anchored to the floor. He then wheels the equipment out on a stainless-steel cart. Left alone, you remain under surveillance through the two-way glass and various cameras. A shawarma wrap, a bowl of koshary, and a bottle of Safi water are brought to you. After you finish, they shackle your ankles and escort you to the restroom, where a guard waits outside.

If you want to pick the handcuffs using a pen you grabbed from the cart, **turn to page 243.**

If you want to continue with the interview, **turn to page 114.**

 **Bookmark Here**

Not Just a Pretty Face

You smile, having successfully cracked the cryptogram code.

"Do you need a break, Ms. Davenport?" Ms. Chamberlain asks.

"No, I'm fine, thank you. Now, where was I? Ah, yes, we flew to Najaf, a journey that took about eleven hours. The most memorable part of the flight was when I stretched my legs and discovered Maya in the cargo bay, meticulously cleaning a formidable rifle. She called it 'Ole Reliable, but later revealed it was a MK13 sniper rifle equipped with an AICS stock and ThermaSight® attachment. She boasted about its accuracy, claiming she could shoot the wings off a mosquito from a thousand yards away."

As if that weren't impressive enough, Maya also has a compact VKS silent sniper rifle, loaded with 12.7 x 55mm STs-130 subsonic rounds. "A whisper in the ear from this gal is the last thing they'll ever hear," she says with a grin.

Sporting a dual holster with twin Glock-19s—each fitted with sturdy Obsidion9 silencers and fifteen-round magazines—she is also prepared for close combat. You watch as she casually spins a black Karambit around her finger, demonstrating the practiced skill of someone well versed in its use. Her movements, whether stabbing or slashing, appear almost rehearsed, as if she's anticipating an imminent confrontation.

"I already feel safer," you say, rolling your eyes.

"Come find me after we land, Desert Lotus," she says with a playful wink, "so I can outfit you and Benji with tactical vests and acoustic throat mics. I'll give you a crash course on the push-to-talk feature. If we encounter a checkpoint, let me handle the negotiations."

"Understood. You're the boss," you say with a playful salute before turning away. She mentioned that you'd depart after sunset, which is still a few hours away.

You board the CIV around 11 PM, settling into the back seats with Benji while Agent Gabriel takes the wheel. Her gear, along with a map and a tactical compass, is arranged on the front passenger seat, and your laptop is securely stowed in the seat pocket in front of you.

After thirty minutes of driving through gloomy farmlands, you approach a makeshift checkpoint. Agent Gabriel instructs you to remain quiet and composed, but anxiety makes you desperately need to use the restroom.

The checkpoint guards, clad in blue camouflage, are armed with what appear to be AK-47 rifles. As you near the checkpoint, Agent Gabriel rolls down the window.

A commanding figure in a distinctive uniform steps forward. His dark grey outfit is adorned with official patches on the sleeves and gold arrows on the shoulders, and he wore a serious, scrutinizing scowl and a black beret. As he inspects your vehicle, another guard moves to the passenger side. Nearby, a third guard wrestles with a curious German shepherd, while a fourth man approaches, brandishing a long metal bar with a mirror attached to it, likely for inspecting the underside of vehicles.

Checkpoint Guard: "Elly ayn witghon ayha al-nasses?"

Translation: "Where are you headed?"

Maya in Arabic: "I'm escorting these archaeologists to the dig site at Hillah."

Checkpoint Guard: "Let me see your papers and passports."

Maya reaches for the passenger seat, and you tense, wondering if she might resort to violence. You prepare to dive for cover, your anxiety mirrored in Benji's nervous fidgeting and profuse sweating. Despite your racing heart, you manage a forced smile just before the beam of a guard's flashlight pierces your eyes, making you squint. As you consider potential escape routes, your muscles remain coiled, ready for any sudden move.

Then Maya hands over your papers and passports, along with a small envelope.

As the guard inspects the documents, fear causes your hands to tremble while a chilling sense of anxiety wraps around you. Could this be the end? Will they discover your lifeless body discarded in a ditch outside Baghdad?

A desperate urge to escape grips you. You picture yourself slipping out of the vehicle unnoticed and fleeing into the nearby irrigation ditch. Benji and Maya will have to fend for themselves. It's every person for themselves now, and your survival instincts surge to the forefront.

If you think you should run, **turn to page 83.**

If you think you should practice some box breathing and try to keep it together, **turn to page 99.**

 **Bookmark Here**

Pharisee Interdiction

You all agree that taking the most efficient route is best, so you set out along Airport Road and then turn onto Zaid Bin Haritha Street toward Mount Nebo. As the sun has not yet fully set, there's still some light when Maya thinks she sees someone following you.

Realizing you need to drive aggressively to evade them, you weave in and out of traffic. If their goal is to follow you to Mount Nebo, you're determined to thwart their plan.

Suddenly, two additional vehicles break from the line and join the pursuit. One attempts to flank you on the left while the other moves in on the right, with the original car still tailing you closely. The street is a six-lane road—three lanes in your direction and three for oncoming traffic, divided by a narrow median.

As the side vehicles close in, their passengers brandishing Uzis and MK-5s, you yank the wheel to the left, slamming into the silver sedan beside you. The impact crumples its side and sends it skidding across the median into oncoming traffic, where it crashes head-on. Now left with two pursuers, you see the red car behind you rapidly closing the distance.

Maya shouts to Olivia, "Grab the black case from the back seat!" Inside is her P90.

Another car pulls up along the passenger side, matching your speed. The side window rolls down and gunfire erupts. You swerve but several bullets slam into the side of the Gurkha CIV. Maya quickly lowers her window and fires back, spraying the other car's windshield and hitting the driver multiple times. The vehicle careens off the road, leaving you with only the red car to contend with.

The red car behind you accelerates, swerving past on the driver's side before cutting in front. From beneath their vehicle, something drops—a black disc. You hear a sharp clink as it magnetically latches onto the underside of your CIV.

An explosion rips through the front of the CIV, launching you into the air. Time slows as the vehicle spins, the road outside disappearing, replaced by the fading light of a twilight sky. Weightless and powerless, you're thrown around as the car flips. Metal screams against asphalt, and the vehicle slams to a violent stop on its roof, dead center in the road.

The airbags explode out, flooding the cabin with acrid smoke and the sharp stench of gunpowder. You're pinned, struggling to move as your eyes lock onto a steady drip of fuel, pooling on the pavement beneath you. A small flame dances in the wrecked engine, creeping toward the spreading fuel—disaster seconds away.

With your final breath, the secret of the Ark's resting place on Mount Nebo is lost forever.

The End

Go Back to Page 301

The Iron Dome

Ben Gurion International Airport lies just sixteen kilometers from Petah Tiqvah, "Door of Hope," the place you once called home. Six years have passed since you last saw your family, and with your rendezvous with Michael still days away, this feels like the perfect chance to reconnect.

Turning the corner, the house comes into view, and with it, a flood of memories crashes over you—yet it all feels like a once-vibrant photograph now dulled by time.

Your father spent his entire working life at Talitonia Ltd, a textile mill that became as much a part of him as his own skin. Elijah Ori Avraham was a tall, hard-working man, his stoic silence often speaking louder than words. With just a look, he could command attention, his presence carrying the weight of unspoken wisdom. In the community, he was well respected—a man of faith, a steadfast Jew.

In his youth, he was strikingly handsome, but time wore him down. His hands, once strong, were now knobby and weathered, and his once-lustrous hair had turned grey. Dupuytren's contracture in his dominant hand had forced his early retirement.

Your mother, Katarzyna Nowak Avraham, was also a striking beauty in her youth, a blonde bombshell with Polish roots. As a dedicated seamstress, she provided you and your older sister with the most exquisite gowns. But tragedy struck when your sister, Shira, was killed during the Al-Aqsa Intifada by a masked Palestinian suicide bomber targeting civilians. Your aunt and Shira disappeared on a routine trip to the market. Despite Katarzyna's relentless efforts to move forward, she was profoundly changed, and the rest of you were too.

As soon as your mother spots you, she rushes out to embrace you, but it's your nieces and nephews who burst through the door first, eager to greet you. You recall the familiar sound of the screen door snapping shut as they dash outside. Your father, seated in his rocking chair, takes a moment to rise. When he finally does, he hugs you tighter than ever before. Though he says nothing, the way he holds you speaks volumes. It's one of those rare, tender moments when tears roll down his cheeks.

After a long family meal and hours of catching up, the wail of sirens pierces the air. It's a familiar sound, a grim reminder of a history steeped in antisemitism and hatred. You huddle together, anxiously uncertain whether the threat comes from Hamas in the South, Hezbollah in the West, or the Houthis, from Yemen.

The Iron Dome intercepts most missiles effectively, but occasionally, one or more get through. Tonight, your house is in the path of one that evades interception.

The End

Go Back to Page 254

GOD, Are You Out There?

You press the PTT button through your hijab and say, "GOD, can you hear me? I need your help, Gabriel."

Guerrilla #2: *"Maza tafalin?"*

Translation: "What is she doing?"

Guerrilla #1: "Inha tasli elly alleh."

Translation: "She's praying to her God."

Guerrilla #2: "elhockem geir mogod hanna!!"

Translation: "Your God does not exist here!"

The guerrillas raise their rifles, and you hear the faintest click as they switch off the safety selectors. Your senses are heightened to an almost superhuman degree. This is it.

The radicalized Pharisees stand before you, their faces hidden by scarves and their rifles aimed at you with cold determination. It feels like the end, a cruel twist in the dangerous game you've been playing for too long.

Your mind races with the desperate hope that Maya has received your message and thoughts of a future that might never come. You close your eyes, seeking solace in your faith amidst the chaos. Meanwhile, Wild Card, ever the pragmatist, scans your surroundings for any slim chance of escape.

Just as the militants raise their weapons to deliver their fatal shots, two silenced rounds whizz through the darkness with frightening precision, echoing across the barren landscape. The guerrillas stagger and collapse to the ground.

Surprise flickers across Wild Card's face as he scans the area for the source of your salvation. Then he spots her—Gabriel, your silent guardian, perched atop a towering sand dune, her VKS sniper rifle still smoking in the desert breeze.

With practiced efficiency, Agent Gabriel swiftly descends from her vantage point and joins you, cutting the ropes binding your and Wild Card's hands and freeing you both. She hands Wild Card her back-up weapon. As you stand, your heart swells with gratitude.

The escape is executed with precision. You blend into the desert shadows, recognizing that the mission is far from over. You owe your lives to the trust and skill of Agent Gabriel—the silent guardian in the desert's embrace.

But your freedom is fleeting. As you emerge from the ruins you're met with a barrage of gunfire. The terrorists, alerted to your presence, have regrouped and are closing in for the kill.

With no escape routes and danger converging from all sides, you fight your way out, weapons blazing in the darkness, each shot a fierce stand against those who seek to silence you.

You soon reach the Gurkha CIV and find Benji asleep in the back. As dawn breaks, you vanish into the desert sands.

"AIDA, we're inbound in the CIV," Maya says. "ETA is one hour. Please have medical on standby. Wild Card's in bad shape."

"Affirmative, Agent Gabriel. Mother is fueled and ready for exfil in Najaf."

Benji stirs awake, blinking in confusion. "What's going on? I had the most amazing dream. This place isn't so bad. Wait, why are you covered in dirt, Olivia? You look terrible! And who's this? He's bleeding everywhere."

"Benji, meet Agent Wild Card," you say. "Wild Card, this is my intern Benji. I can't believe you slept through all that, Benji. I nearly got killed! I'm wide awake now and feel like I could take on the world. That was intense!"

"I must've lost my earpiece while I was dozing off," Benji says. "I thought everything was under control."

"Well, it wasn't," you say. "Bodies were dropping, and I felt like a femme fatale sneaking into the dig site. But then I got captured, and they already had Wild Card. They were going to kill us. I actually prayed, and just when it seemed hopeless, Maya took out our executioners—bang, bang—and we escaped by the skin of our teeth. Bullets were flying everywhere, which explains why I look like this. Seriously? You didn't know?"

Wild Card gingerly settles into the front passenger seat of the CIV, pulling a USB flash drive from his boot with a grin. He holds it up to Maya, his eyes alight with excitement.

"We did it! I know their plan," Xavier says. Maya responds with a knowing wink and a matching grin.

Who is Xavier Emanuel Washington, really? A paradox indeed. Outwardly, he appears to be a brave and fun-loving adventurer, fearless and always seeking thrills. Yet beneath that exterior lies a complex puzzle, a sensitive soul with a quick wit and a joke ready for any occasion.

Raised in a rigid family environment, Xavier was strictly schooled in preparation for life's challenges, the schooling often verging on psychological abuse. As a boy he frequently gazed from his bedroom window at the neighborhood kids, who played games with each other and tossed sneakers with laces tied over the streetlamps. All he wanted was to join them.

Instead, his time was consumed by homework and chores. In retrospect it seemed that each subsequent adult adventure was his attempt to reclaim the lost joys of his childhood and regain the sense of power that had been taken from him.

"Let's get you patched up, then you can fill us in at Mother," Maya says. She glances back at you in the rear seat. "Is everyone alright back there?"

"Yeah, we're all good, Maya, thanks," you say, a wave of relief washing over you.

Upon returning to the plane at Najaf, the crew swiftly secures the CIV. Maya unloads her gear, removes your throat mics, and heads straight for the shower.

Benji makes a beeline for your quarters to catch up on sleep while Wild Card heads off to get cleaned up and attend to the gash on his forehead. Meanwhile, he uploads the flash drive to AIDA for analysis.

As the adrenaline fades, exhaustion quickly sets in. You take a shower, slip into your satin pajamas, and barely recall climbing into your pod.

Fifteen hours later, you wake up to find Mother parked in a hangar at Ramstein AFB. Stepping off the plane, you feel a wave of relief as your feet touch solid ground. The hangar is alive with activity: red-blooded Americans in uniform shout English at each other and move about in a bustling military hub. Among the crowd, you spot Maya standing with a patched-up and refreshed Wild Card.

As you approach, Maya greets you with a smile. "If you're looking for Benji, he's in the mess hall. How are you holding up, Olivia?"

"I'm good, thanks."

Agent Wild Card extends his hand. "I'm Xavier. What you did was incredibly brave. Thank you."

"Don't mention it. I'm sure you'd have done the same for me," you say, then you raise an eyebrow. "You seem to be feeling better."

"Yeah, I'm a bit bruised and battered, but I'm good to go. Got a few stitches," Xavier says with a reassuring smile. "I was just briefing the General, and Dr. Linda Nakamura, the CDC director, has joined us via a secure video link. Michael's around here somewhere as well. We're about to review the video footage I managed to smuggle out of Hillah."

If you want to stick around and watch the footage, **turn to page 105.**

If you want to see what Benji is up to and get something to eat in the messhall, **turn to page 08.**

 **Bookmark Here**

Introducing Xavier Washington

Date: July 25, 2034 Location: CIA Black Site Cairo (Vicinity 30.0444° N, 31.2357° E)

Somewhere between the Nile River and the 6th of October Bridge

You're in a decrepit chamber, sitting on a creaky wooden chair that provides little comfort, its rough edges digging into your skin. Your limbs are restrained by sturdy metal shackles. The room is enveloped in an air of mystery, illuminated by bleary lighting that attempts to camouflage the pitted concrete.

Before you stands a large steel table. Across the room, a security mirror warps your reflection, a constant reminder of unseen eyes watching from the shadows. The air is thick with dampness, clinging to the peeling walls like a silent witness to the room's tortured past. Above, rusty pipes coil along the ceiling, their corroded presence heightening the room's suffocating atmosphere.

Your journey has been tumultuous. First a harrowing flight aboard a Boeing C17, then from the pandemonium of Cairo International to this little Shangri-La, you were plunged into a void of sensory deprivation, stripped of sight and sound.

Obsolete surveillance cameras leer at you with vacant lenses, desperate to extract any fragment of intelligence from your captivity. Behind the impenetrable veil of the two-way mirror, shadowy figures lurk, their motives hidden beneath a shroud of secrecy.

The silence is shattered by the electronic whir of a keypad, heralding the approach of an ominous figure. A tall, gaunt man steps out of the shadows, his yellowed fingers betraying years of vice. He pores over a file marked Top Secret – SCI, his gaze cutting through the darkness like a blade. At his side stands a stocky woman, her hair pulled back in a severe knot.

In this instant, you feel like you're on the verge of something far greater than yourself. The stakes are immense, the danger palpable. Yet with adrenaline surging through your veins, you steel yourself for whatever awaits beyond the confines of this forbidding room.

As the woman begins to recount your life from the file in her hands, you can't help but smirk inwardly. Xavier Emmanuel Washington—born and raised in Illinois. Childhood under strict parents, every memory regimented and joyless. While other kids played and laughed, you were molded into a disciple of discipline, burdened with chores and schoolbooks. If only your parents could see you now. That would be quite the finger-wagging intervention. Yet here you sit, calm in the stark interrogation room, watching the scene unfold like an observer in your own life.

"Xavier Emmanuel Washington," she begins. "Born November 18th, 2000, in Galesburg, Illinois." Her words trace the contours of your life, from modest beginnings on Elm Avenue to your years at the University of Minnesota.

"You currently reside at 2900 North Central Park Ave, Apartment 2, Chicago, Illinois, 60618," she continues, her gaze steady and unblinking. "Licensed helicopter pilot. Ducati enthusiast. Thoughtful neighbor, helping your mobility-impaired neighbor with her mail every Thursday."

You nearly chuckle at her sterile recitation.

"You forgot Scout leader," you tease, mischief curling in your voice.

"I'm Elizabeth Chamberlain, CIA Chief of Station, Cairo," she announces, her authority unmistakable. "And this"—she gestures to the tall figure beside her—"is Keith Atkins, CIA Deputy Director." The stale scent of cigarette smoke clings to him, a testament to the countless years he's spent navigating the murky depths of espionage.

"As for your questions," she says, her tone adopting a businesslike edge, "let's get straight to the point, shall we?"

With boldness verging on audacity, you lean back in your chair, prepared to meet whatever challenges lie ahead. After all, this is just another day in the life in comparison to what you've been through.

The door creaks open with an ominous groan and a young man with a military-style haircut steps in, his demeanor respectful in the presence of authority. Clad in a plain black suit that seems to absorb the light, his keen eyes betray a flicker of apprehension as he approaches, acutely aware of the gravity of his task.

With meticulous precision, he sets up polygraph equipment, his movements swift and efficient under the unyielding gaze of Chamberlain and Atkins. Sensors are fastened to your fingertips and straps are tightened around your chest, linking you to the machine.

The young soldier then sits down and routine questions begin to spill from him. "Is your name really Xavier Washington?"

You lock eyes with him, the tension in the room becoming almost palpable. "Yes."

Satisfied that their surveillance net is thoroughly in place, Chamberlain presses a button on the platform of a table microphone, marking the start of the interrogation. The room hums with tense anticipation, the weight of their collective scrutiny pressing down on you like an oppressive shroud.

"How did you end up working for an off-the-books clandestine group known as the Ghost Operations Division?" Chamberlain asks.

The question lingers in the air, its implications heavy and foreboding.

"Who recruited you?" Her voice resonates with a chilling authority, each word sharp and deliberate. "AND WHAT HAPPENED TO THE ARK?"

This time, you smirk outwardly. "You're keen to know how I got recruited, aren't you? Buckle up. This ride's gonna be a wild one. But fair warning—what you're about to hear might stretch your belief."

If you want to share the unverified story of your search for Paititi and how you met Michael Smith, **turn to page 10.**

If you want to tell them how you came across the golden mask of Tutankhamun, giving them a red herring, **turn to page 245.**

 **Bookmark Here**

Send It

You exhale slowly, steadying your aim in the suffocating darkness. With calculated precision, you squeeze the trigger. The VKS sniper rifle whispers, barely disturbing the stillness of the night as the round launches at three hundred meters per second.

The guard's eyes dart upward, panic flashing across his face. Before he can react, the bullet slices through his frontal lobe, punching out the base of his skull. He crumples, folding into the desert sand like a marionette with its strings cut.

Olivia's heart pounds in her chest as she watches the guard fall. A wave of relief washes over her, the tension in her muscles finally releasing as the threat is eliminated.

"Position him like he's sleeping, Desert Lotus. Then move inside," you tell her, your voice steady despite the adrenaline coursing through you.

Olivia works quickly, arranging the guard's body with practiced precision and adjusting his keffiyeh to conceal the wound. After one last inspection to ensure the deception will hold, she slips into the compound.

"From here on out, AIDA will track your movements," you say. "Call if you need backup. Gabriel out."

The earpiece crackles as the connection cuts off, and you take a deep breath, the weight of the mission settling on your shoulders. You merge with the shadows, every nerve humming with anticipation. The faint light and cool air sharpen your senses. Your heartbeat echoes in your ears, a steady pulse reminding you of the danger lurking around you.

"GOD, this is Desert Lotus. I'm in," she whispers urgently into your comms as the door clicks shut behind her.

Then, silence. Nearly an hour passes, each second stretching into eternity. AIDA's warning echoes in your mind—Olivia has likely been captured. Concern gnaws at you, a relentless animal feeding on the growing void of communication.

"I'm detecting movement, Agent Gabriel," AIDA says, her voice cutting through the static, offering a welcome relief that tightens your grip on the sniper rifle with renewed resolve. "It appears they're escorting two prisoners in your direction. Stand by…"

You narrow your focus through the scope, searching for any sign of movement. Then you spot them: Wild Card, battered and bleeding but still alive, being prodded forward at gunpoint. Following him is Desert Lotus, trailed by an additional armed guard. Both of your team members' hands are bound behind their backs.

Wild Card gestures for a cigarette, and as he exhales a thick plume of smoke into the air, you calculate the windage. Well done, Wild Card, you think to yourself with a hint of admiration.

Suddenly, the situation shifts. They sever Desert Lotus's ropes and she collapses to her knees, seemingly in prayer. Your heart skips a beat as her mic crackles to life, her voice quivering with a mix of urgency and determination. "GOD? GOD? Can you hear me? I need your help, Gabriel."

The tension in her voice slices through the night, sharpening your focus as you steady your aim. This is the moment to act. You narrow your sight, slow your breathing, and squeeze off a round. Before the first shot finds its mark, you fire another. The guards crumple to the ground, and Desert Lotus and Wild Card scan the area for your position.

You descend swiftly, your footsteps barely making a sound on the sandy ground. Reaching Wild Card first, you draw your karambit, its blade gleaming with a menacing edge in the dim light. You cut through the ropes binding him. His eyes lock onto yours, a glimmer of gratitude and resolve in their depths. You pass him one of your Glock-19s and together, you advance toward the car, each step a perilous dance with death.

Your brief taste of freedom is brutally cut short. As you emerge from the ruins, a deafening barrage of gunfire erupts, the air around you exploding into deadly chaos. The terrorists have discovered your escape, and they're closing in with murderous intent.

Bullets whiz past you, each one a narrow escape from death. With no cover and enemies pressing in from all sides, you have no choice but to fight your way out. The night is filled with the flash and roar of your weapons as you return fire, the darkness a cacophony of violence.

You reach the CIV, adrenaline propelling your desperate sprint. Benji sleeps soundly in the back seat, unaware of the battle you've just endured. The first light of dawn creeps over the horizon, casting long shadows across the desert sands. Without hesitation, you drive into the vast, unforgiving landscape, leaving only the faintest trace of your passage behind.

Wild Card is in rough shape, his injuries bearing witness to the ordeal he's endured.

You offer him a cloth and a bottle of water. "Clean yourself up. We need to reach Mother."

He nods, fatigue and determination etched into his features as he starts to tend to his wounds. The road ahead is uncertain, but you're still alive, and you'll fight another day.

As you navigate the winding road, Wild Card's hand moves to his boot. He retrieves a USB flash drive and holds it aloft, a victorious grin spreading across his rugged features.

"We got it! I know exactly what they're up to," Wild Card says.

A wave of relief washes over you. You glance at Xavier, catching his eye and giving him a reassuring smile and a wink. His unwavering dedication in the face of danger is nothing short of remarkable.

"Let's get you patched up. We can debrief at Mother," you say, glancing over your shoulder to check on Olivia and Benji in the back seat. "Is everyone okay back there?"

"We're fine, Maya, thanks," Olivia says.

Before long, you're back at Najaf. The team secures and stores the CIV in the cargo bay while medical personnel escort Wild Card to the infirmary. You take the gear from Olivia and Benji, stow your own equipment with care, and head to your quarters for a much-needed shower.

Minutes after you arrive, the plane roars to life, taking off for Ramstein AFB in Germany. The urgency of your departure underscores the importance of the critical information AIDA has extracted from the USB flash drive Xavier bravely smuggled out of Hillah.

You touch down at Ramstein AFB in Germany a little over three hours later. You assume Wild Card and the others are asleep. At 0500 hours GMT+2, you wake, pull your hair back into a ponytail, and go for a run. AIDA informs you of a briefing in the hangar at 0600 hours, while military personnel outside Mother are busy setting up a stand-alone communications and computer hub.

The run outside the hangar is refreshing and invigorating and invariably gives your mind time to circle back to your sister Shira. You remember the times you played together and a moment when you chatted with her about the "stinky boys." She smiled, her blonde hair lifting in the breeze as she plucked petals from a flower, saying, "He loves me, he loves me not." That's the last memory you have of her before the terrorists, like the Pharisees, carried out their cruel plan.

You press on, reinvigorated and ready for whatever missions lie ahead.

You wipe the sweat from your brow with a small towel and rehydrate with a sports drink before heading back to the hangar.

The military personnel seem ready for an intense briefing when you spot Olivia coming down the ramp at the back of Mother.

"If you're looking for Benji, he's in the mess hall getting breakfast," you say, pointing to a set of doors in the corner of the hangar. "It's down there if you're hungry."

"I'm good, thanks," Olivia says.

Just then, Xavier praises Olivia for her bravery in coming to his aid in Hillah. You've already exchanged greetings with him. There's a noticeable connection, but given your professional demeanor, you doubt anything will come of it. Still, Xavier is quite easy on the eyes...

High-ranking military officials fill the room for the briefing, including your handler, Michael Smith; the Director General of the World Health Organization, Francois Garza; and the Deputy Assistant Secretary for Chemical and Biological Defense, Frasier Santorem. Other DOD members are present while the Secretary of Health and Human Services, Richard Johnson, and US CDC Director, Dr. Linda Nakamura, join via satellite. The Supreme Allied Commander Europe is also in attendance.

Then, the video begins to play.

In the depths of the Congolese jungle, where ancient trees whisper secrets older than time, a hidden village thrives, untouched by the outside world. The villagers live in harmony with nature, blissfully unaware of the nightmare that's closing in.
On a moonless night, yellow hazmat suits descend upon the village. These are the Pharisees, shadowy operatives led by Ziad Alhussan, his eyes ablaze with vengeful fury, driven by old wounds and an unquenchable thirst for retribution.

Ziad kneels before a nondescript yellow case, a faint, eerie hiss escaping as thin tendrils of steam rise from its dark interior. With care, he extracts a clear vial that holds a menacing orange substance, its label marked Biohazardous Material. His movements are methodical, almost reverent as he secures the vial in a sinister dispersal device. With an unsettling calm, he flips open the cover for the activation switch. Then, with chilling certainty, he activates the device. A low, hum follows, the fans roaring to life, heralding the approach of an unimaginable horror.

The weapon creeps silently through the unsuspecting village, its invisible tendrils of death weaving unseen in the air. At first no one notices the looming disaster. For the next twenty-four to forty-eight hours, life continues as normal—the villagers carry on, blissfully unaware that the virus has already taken hold, lying dormant within them, quietly multiplying, waiting for its moment to strike.

It isn't long before the first symptoms appear. A mild headache, barely noticeable, blooms in their heads, followed by a stubborn cough and a runny nose. The villagers brush these off as ordinary ailments.

In this critical window, the virus reaches its peak contagiousness, jumping effortlessly from one unsuspecting host to another.

Posing as WHO doctors, Ziad and his team set up a false clinic, monitoring the outbreak's progression for Heinrich Jager, the man known to his followers as "the Prophet."

By the fifth day, the virus shows its true horrifying form. Angry pus-filled lesions rupture across the villagers' skin, the sickening odor of infection clinging to the air. The agony twists as the virus ravages their nervous systems, transforming them into shells of their former selves. Then comes the hemorrhaging—a terrifying prelude to violent, uncontrollable seizures that paint the village with blood. Their eyes, once full of life, are drained to a chilling yellow, marking the virus's final, merciless hold.

Turn to page 247.

Cut It Loose, Girl

Maya must have read your mind. With a swift motion, she draws her karambit from its sheath and slices through the tangled lines with both precision and urgency, the blade catching the moonlight's gleam. As she works, her helmet communication cuts out. In these critical seconds, she plummets another fifteen hundred feet.

With mere moments remaining before impact, she deploys the reserve chute, feeling its reassuring pull as it catches the air and almost instantly brings her speed down from 126 mph to just 17.5 mph. She glides toward the port, her HUD and GPS still operational. The ground rushes up to meet her and the lights of Beirut's port grow brighter with each passing second. In the war room, Xavier, Benji, and you watch the live feed from her bodycam as if you're right there with her.

Agent Gabriel touches down gracefully on the rugged terrain, fully aware that her mission is only beginning. In the shadows, she quickly stows her backup chute, its black fabric fluttering in the crosswinds, and melts into the Lebanese night.

A sliver of moon in the night sky casts a faint silvery glow over the Port of Beirut. Agent Gabriel, known for her angelic stealth, approaches the warehouse with her blonde hair pulled into a tight ponytail. "GOD, are you reading me?" she asks into her throat mic.

"We lost communications when your chute malfunctioned, and we feared the worst," AIDA says. "It's good to hear your voice. What's your status?"

"I've stowed my backup chute and am making my way to the warehouse. Any intel from the eye-in-the-sky?" Agent Gabriel asks as she activates her night-vision goggles.

"There's an enemy guard about a hundred feet southeast of your position. He appears to be alone. You can use the dumpsters for cover as you approach."

The first obstacle emerges: a guard stationed two hundred yards from the warehouse entrance. Agent Gabriel's silenced FN P90 —a sleek close-combat weapon—rests against her back. With practiced precision, she draws the firearm, the metal making barely a whisper as she swiftly frees it from its sling.

Aiming through her custom holographic sight, she fires a single round. The suppressed shot looses a muffled sound into the night. The guard slumps to the ground and Agent Gabriel quickly moves to conceal the body in a nearby dumpster.

She presses on, her senses heightened. A single mistake could jeopardize the mission. The Ghost Operations Division has entrusted her with a task of critical importance, and failure is not an option.

As she edges closer to the warehouse entrance, her heart pounds in her chest and beads of perspiration form on her brow.

"There's another guard ahead, smoking a cigarette right by the entrance," AIDA says. "I've also detected a fingerprint door lock. Maybe you can persuade him to cooperate, Agent Gabriel."

"And how do you suggest I handle that?"

"I'm not sure, but I'm confident you'll figure it out."

If you think Agent Gabriel should use her charms to distract the guard, **turn to page 174.**

If you think she should look for another entry point, **turn to page 200.**

 **Bookmark Here**

Reuniting with Don Miguel

Stepping from the cool embrace of the waterfall, you're met with a scene of pure beauty. The water tumbles down in gleaming sheets, the sunlight transforming the mist into shimmering rainbows that dance across the plunge pool.

As you glide through the water, your eyes scan for your guide, the man you've come to call Don Miguel, having never learned his real name. A descendant of the Inca, he's a man of few words, his shy smile and humble gestures doing most of the talking. His poor teeth and quiet demeanor might suggest frailty, but you know better. Don Miguel's courage runs deep, his silent vigilance and tireless work ethic a constant source of comfort. Over time, as you've braved dangers side by side, a quiet bond has formed between you—one built on trust and shared survival.

As you survey the landscape, a sense of unease grows with each passing moment of Miguel's absence. At last, your gaze lands on your canoe, grounded on the nearby shore with a stack of firewood piled beside it. Yet Miguel is conspicuously missing. You swim to the shore, speculating that he may have ventured into the jungle to collect additional wood. Using your machete, you fashion a rudimentary clothesline from sturdy vines and drape your shirt and socks over it to dry in the sun.

Driven by the need to locate Miguel and help with firewood—or perhaps gather materials for shelter—you push deeper into the jungle's dense foliage. As you step into the tangled shadows of the trees, your heart sinks at the unsettling scene before you. Miguel is bound with coarse vines, his wrists secured behind him. He's encircled by a tribe of Inca, their spears leveled in his direction. They converse in Quechua, their voices a blend of unfamiliar syllables, with only a few words registering through your limited understanding.

Without warning, more Inca figures emerge from the dense undergrowth surrounding you on all sides. They press in, driving you toward Don Miguel with the sharp points of their spears. Initially you hope they might be escorting you to their tribal leader, but a chilling realization dawns upon you only moments before it's too late.

They are preparing to offer human sacrifices to their sun god.

Your heart pounds as they guide you deeper into the dense jungle. The oppressive heat and humidity wrap around you, the air thick with tension, mingled with the pungent aroma of sweat and fear. Every step feels heavier than the last. You need to escape soon or face the coming consequences.

Despite their short stature, none exceeding five feet, the Inca are adorned with what appears to be war paint, their eyes burning with intensity. One of the most aggressive among them strikes Miguel with a club-like weapon, its end capped with a heavy ball. Blood trickles down his cheek, staining the lush jungle foliage.

They place Miguel's unconscious body on a large stone altar in a nearby clearing. A figure adorned with a grand, white-feathered headdress begins a solemn dance around the altar, calling out to the jungle in a rhythmic incantation. The scene unfolds as a ritual meant to appease their sun god. The others join in, their voices merging into a deep, ominous chant while one of them swirls a cloud of smoke around the brave warrior in the headdress.

He pauses over Miguel's prone form, drawing two golden blades embellished with jewels. He raises them high, gripping the hilts in a menacing pose. Smoke coils around Miguel's body, a key element of their vicious ritual known as Qhapaq hucha.

Your heart pounds, its tempo syncing with the low hum of their chant. The air is drenched in tension and the acrid scent of smoke. You struggle to catch your breath, overwhelmed by thoughts of rescuing Miguel and escaping this nightmare.

The gleam of the golden blades sends a chill down your spine.

With a decisive thrust, the warrior drives the blade into Miguel's heart. Only the hilt remains visible as blood pours down Miguel's chest, collecting in a dark pool at the edge of the altar.

The warriors burst into frenzied dancing and shouts, circling the altar as if celebrating a victory. Meanwhile, your wrists and ankles are bound with vines against a tree, two guards stationed nearby. The dire atmosphere made it clear: you're the next in line.

The End

Go Back to Page 26

Mosquito Bite

As the woman steps into the changing area and starts to remove her helmet, you maneuver the UAV closer. She unzips her suit, and with impeccable timing, you land the UAV delicately on her shoulder, the one-time-use tranquilizer primed and ready, injecting itself into her bloodstream.

She barely has time to raise her hand to swat at the UAV before the tranquilizer takes hold. Her movements slow, her eyes fluttering, and she collapses to the floor, unconscious, before she can complete the gesture.

The tension in the air is palpable as you descend silently from the ceiling. Your heart pounds in your chest yet your hands remain steady. You approach her unconscious form and remove the remaining sections of the hazmat suit.

As you slip into the suit, you secure each fastening, the heavy material oddly comforting against your skin. The helmet is the final piece, and once it's on, the world comes into focus through its visor. You take a deep breath, the filtered air filling your lungs, and place the woman's unconscious body in the nearby laundry bin. AIDA's voice crackles in your earpiece, guiding you through the maze of corridors ahead.

With your disguise in place, you advance toward the decontamination room the woman just vacated, blending into your surroundings. The mission is progressing as planned, and the suspense of what lies ahead sharpens your senses.

After passing through decontamination, you enter a vast room under negative pressure. This is where the artifact is kept. Your eyes scan the space through the thick hanging sheets of makeshift vinyl dividers. Through the bleary plastic, you catch glimpses of figures conducting tests and engaging in urgent discussions about the artifact.

The artifact stands alone, unprotected except for the intricate, deadly web of an active laser grid. Clad in your hazmat suit, you gain a small boost of confidence. It's the perfect disguise. You move cautiously, your breath echoing in your ears while the vinyl sheets blur your vision and the scientists remain absorbed in their tasks.

"Okay, AIDA," you whisper. "Any suggestions on how to handle this laser grid?"

"Check your utility belt, Agent Gabriel."

You fumble with the belt, your fingers trembling with anxiety, and uncover a small enigmatic device nestled inside. Its arms are folded with articulating mirrors, and a prism sits at the center.

"I had one of the crew place this device in your utility belt," AIDA says. "During my pre-mission reconnaissance, I identified a security laser grid surrounding the artifact. This device should neutralize it. Refer to the animated graphics I just sent to your forearm screen. They will guide you on how to use the device, which will transform the grid into a single manageable beam, allowing you to retrieve the artifact without triggering any alarms. Be aware though that you won't have much time after you take it, as they are monitoring the area periodically through cameras."

"It should neutralize the lasers? You're not exactly instilling a lot of confidence, AIDA."

"It will work."

Swallowing your doubt, you follow the animated instructions with meticulous precision, each movement a crucial step in a high-stakes maneuver. You place the device on the pedestal, your heart pounding in your chest. As AIDA predicted, the beams reflect off the mirrors and converge on the prism, coalescing into a single manageable beam. You reach out, fingers trembling, and grasp the artifact. These brief moments stretch into an eternity, each second drenched in tension, but no one crosses the vinyl dividers.

With the artifact securely stowed in your bag, you detach the device from the pedestal and proceed through the decontamination chamber. The doors hiss shut behind you and the misters emit their cleansing spray.

Suddenly alarm klaxons blare, and red rotating lights cast eerie shadows. The absence of the artifact has been detected. The clattering of boots on cement reverberates outside the decontamination area, creating an impending cacophony of urgency and threat. It sounds like they've bypassed the decontamination chamber and rushed to the viewing area.

The doors hiss open, marking the end of the process. Keeping your head down, you exit the chamber and follow AIDA's instructions. Twice, groups of armed Pharisee mercenaries' storm past you in the corridor, their faces twisted in confusion and rage. You slip into the changing room and remove the hazmat suit, your senses heightened but nerves frayed.

The danger has escalated and AIDA's commands are your lifeline. "Stop here. Wait, wait... Okay go!" Your heart pounds, adrenaline surging through your veins, every nerve on edge. This is one of the rare moments when you feel truly vulnerable. You're entirely dependent on AIDA.

AIDA guides you through how to bypass the security patrols, leading you to the final corridor. Ahead, the steel door with its waist-high push bar beckons you toward freedom. As you approach it and make your final push for escape, boots pound down the corridor.

You have two options: call in Coyote and head to Seal Team Six for extraction via the Mark 8 submersible, which will take you to the USS North Carolina, or signal Road Runner and proceed to the Skyhook deployment area.

If you want to use Coyote and make your way to Seal Team Six, **turn to page 22.**

If you want to use the Road Runner exfil plan, **turn to page 136.**

 **Bookmark Here**

Everybody Look to the Left

The floor shows heavier scuff marks to the left. AIDA's calm voice comes over the comms. "My analysis of the building plans indicates this leads to an exit." Maya navigates the maze of corridors with swift, assured steps, despite the adrenaline coursing through her veins. She knows she has to reach the exit to escape the Pharisees before they close in on her position.

The hall has several bulbs that are either out or flickering, casting intermittent shadows. It's the perfect moment to shed the bulky hazmat suit that's constrained her movements. Freed from its cumbersome grip, she sprints toward her exfiltration point.

Finally, she bursts through the last steel-clad barrier and inhales the humid, sea-salted air that defines the area. Despite the musky heat, it carries the promise of another successful mission. She informs AIDA she'll be using exfil plan Road Runner. A kilometer away, her final means of escape awaits: a self-inflating balloon tethered to a 500-foot cable, courtesy of the CIA's Skyhook system (surface-to-air recovery system [STARS]).

With practiced efficiency, Agent Gabriel dons the Skyhook harness, securing the cable to her body as she braces for the imminent acceleration. Above, the experimental stealth bomber Mother approaches, its sleek form slicing through the night sky at a reduced speed of 200 kilometers per hour.

"Mother is en route, Agent Gabriel. Stand by," AIDA says.

Small lights on the cable act as a beacon, guiding the pilots toward their target. Agent Gabriel stands poised, hands crossed over her chest in anticipation. With the precision born from years of military aviation training, the Skyhook snags the cable, and in a blur of motion, Agent Gabriel is snatched from the ground. The winch hoists her into the belly of the plane as they disappeared into the darkness and Mother soars toward the safety of international airspace.

Once inside the plane, AIDA's voice echoes in Maya's ear. "Welcome back, Agent Gabriel."

As the warehouse disappears into the distance below, Maya allows herself a brief moment of relief, the artifact now safely in their possession. But even as she exhales, with the weight of history in her hands, she knows her mission is far from over.

Benji, Xavier, and you welcome Maya back to the safety of Mother, commending Maya for a job well done. Watching her through the bodycam made you feel as if you were right there with her.

AIDA conducts scans of the artifact before passing it to you for analysis.

The scans, along with carbon dating, reveal that the artifact is from the sixth century BCE—specifically, 587 BCE. The cube is etched with both Hebrew and Aramaic inscriptions. Scans also reveal a cylindrical metal object of unknown origin within.

As you study the artifact in your quarters, you find an inscription that reads:

"הללו את יהוה ואת ארון בריתו אשר הצלנו מן הלוחצים הבבלים
והסתירנו ב..."

You translate it to: "Praise Jehovah and his Ark that we have saved from the Babylonian oppressors and hid in…"

Unfortunately, part of the puzzle box's inscription has been damaged and is missing. On another side, you find a Hebrew inscription that reads:

"קלף של המפה "מתגלה כאן למי שדרכו ישרה".

You translate it to: "A parchment map is revealed inside to those whose path is righteous."

"What did you think it meant?" Ms. Chamberlain asks in the interrogation room.

"I believed it meant that if we could figure out how to open the box, we would find a parchment or papyrus scroll—maybe even a map—leading to where the Hebrews hid the Ark."

Despite all your efforts, you can't figure out how to open it. However, you notice several symbols on the artifact that can be depressed about half an inch. Whenever you press a fifth symbol, they all pop out and reset. There are six symbol actuators on each side of the cube.

AIDA calculates that there are 1,679,616 possible permutations for a 4-digit code using 36 unique symbols or tumblers. It would take approximately 18.6 days to try them all manually. You have to find a clue within the inscriptions—the Pharisees likely scanned the artifact as well and are racing against you to decode it.

You also find an inscription that translated to:

Wxuq wr sdjh 478

If you want to try and use a Caesar cipher decoder found online to figure out where this clue leads, you will need these bits of intel.

Shift/Key (Number 3). Decrypt No Bruteforce
Use the English alphabet and also the digits 0-9

https://www.dcode.fr/caesar-cipher

If you want to try to break the artifact to discover what's inside, **turn to page 221.**

I'm a Vegetarian

You journey deep into the heart of Peru, drawn by the mysterious promise of Paititi. At this high altitude, finding fuel and comfort is important, but the strong smell of roasted guinea pig makes your stomach turn. You choose a simple meal of baked potato and corn, finding comfort in its familiarity.

As night falls under a sky full of stars, the cold from the rocky ground makes you shiver until dawn. Drinking a mixture of coca leaves and hot water with the sunrise, you plunge deeper into the jungle's embrace.

Hours stretch and stretch, the relentless assault of humidity, insect bites, and mud testing your resolve. A persistent cough thumps in your chest. Another night, another meager meal, while the porters indulge in roast guinea pig and a curious delicacy they dub "water snake," a dish you dare not touch.

But hunger wears down your resolve, forcing you to give in to desperation. You see a snake drawn out by the warmth of the fire and use your machete to cut off its triangular-shaped head. It's body coils despite being headless. You skewer it and cook its meat over the fire, not knowing it's an Andean Forest Pit viper. Desperately you gulp down the cooked meat unaware of any danger.

Without warning, pain burns through your mouth and throat. Nausea twists your insides, and paralysis wraps around you like a heavy blanket. The porters, unable to help, offer useless remedies, their voices drowned out by your agony.

In a clearing under the green canopy, you see the beauty of nature. But as the light fades, so does your life, taken by the venom spreading through your veins. In the heart of the Peruvian jungle, among the old legends, you fall victim to a cruel twist of fate.

The End

Go Back to Page 13

I Don't Do Political Assassination

You inform David and Daniel that political assassination is not the type of work you undertake, but you thank them for considering you for the role.

Less than a week later, on the clear, crisp morning of May 19th, 2024, three Iranian helicopters depart from a dam near the Iranian-Azerbaijan border. At 1330 IRST, one of these helicopters, carrying the Iranian president, foreign minister, governor general, the head of the president's security team, and three flight crew members, suddenly crashes. The wreckage is scattered across a rugged hillside and all on board are killed.

The incident dominates the news, with images of charred debris, grieving officials, and the families of the victims.

As conspiracy theories circulate, the official explanation attributes the crash to adverse weather conditions and the outdated Iranian Air Force fleet.

Shortly thereafter, you're tasked with gathering intelligence on the Hezbollah terror network operating out of Syria. Your mission requires you to infiltrate the area using an AS565 Panther helicopter. As you descend toward the landing zone in the dusty, war-torn landscape, one of the pilots reports a lock-on by a Saqr "358" missile. The cockpit is enveloped in an electric silence, moments before the pilots' scream, "INCOMING!"

The End

Go Back to Page 366

Getting Out of Dodge

Benji clutches his backpack while fear coils in your stomach like a murderous snake. The anticipation in the air feels suffocating, pressing against your chest. Your instincts scream for you to flee.

You unbuckle your seat belt and fling open the door, vanishing into the night before Maya or Benji can react. The darkness swallows you as you sprint toward the nearby irrigation ditch, your heart pounding. Gunshots echo as the CIV races away.

The shouts of Iraqi soldiers and their tracking dogs echo behind you, driving you forward with relentless urgency. You sprint through the darkness, hyper-aware of every sound and shadow. Soon it feels as if you've been running for an eternity, your path stretching endlessly in the dark. Despite your exhaustion, adrenaline propels you onward.

Just as you think you've escaped, a new threat materializes from the darkness: a militant group known as Kataib Hezbollah, their faces hidden behind scarves. Their battered truck skids to a halt in a cloud of dust, their weapons catching the moonlight with a menacing gleam.

Your breath freezes in your throat as they close in, their intentions unmistakable. You fight with every ounce of strength, but the odds are against you. Overpowered and outnumbered, your struggles prove futile against the unyielding grip of your captors.

Dragged into the night, fear and uncertainty flood your mind. What horrors await you at the hands of these militants shouting "Allahu Akbar"? Will you ever see daylight again, or will you become another victim in the relentless cycle of violence that plagues the region?

Your terrifying journey plunges you deeper into darkness, leaving you to brace for whatever comes next. You can't help but imagine the worst—torture, abuse, and execution.

Later in the week, Al Jazeera reports that two Americans have successfully evaded Iraqi troops at a checkpoint between Najaf and Hillah. Meanwhile, the mutilated body of an unidentified woman is found in a field outside Baghdad. Although no group has claimed responsibility for the brutal murder, sexual assault has been ruled out.

The US State Department denies any involvement in the area during that time.

The End

Go Back to Page 41

Abort, Abort, Abort

With your gear dangling twenty feet high in a birch tree, completing the mission seems nearly impossible. You consider climbing up to retrieve it, but Sergeant Ableman dismisses the idea and radios for assistance.

"Eagle Eye to Looking Glass, do you copy? Over."

"Eagle Eye, this is Looking Glass. We are reading your traffic. Over."

"Charlie Mike Romeo (Critical Mission Resource—our gear) is Foxtrot Tango Lima (Failure to Locate—unreachable). Requesting mission abort. Over."

"Eagle Eye, this is Looking Glass. Mission abort confirmed. Exfil on Oscar Sierra (Own Schedule—proceed at your own pace). Over."

As you and Eagle Eye hike toward the rendezvous point, the forest suddenly erupts in gunfire. Armenian soldiers engage from one side while the Azerbaijani Land Forces fire from the other. Caught in the crossfire, you and Sergeant Ableman dive for cover as bullets and tracer fire streak across the night sky.

Ableman is hit first. You think he's just taking cover, but when you reach him and roll him over, you discover he's been killed. It's only then that you feel the sharp sting of your own wounds—hits to your thigh and torso. Numb from shock, you drag yourself behind a fallen moss-covered tree as bullets whiz overhead from both sides.

The chaotic shouts of commanders barking orders echo through the air, completely oblivious to your presence. Uncertain how long it will be before you can receive medical treatment, you lie there, clinging to the frail hope of surviving the relentless gunfire. After a few hours, the cold and fatigue set in. You need to rest, clinging to the hope that, when you wake, you'll be able to exfil from the area. Sadly, you never wake up again.

The End

Go Back to Page 21

The Road Not Taken

Guided by intuition, you opt for the less traveled path, detouring through Madaba. The detour adds ten minutes to your journey but rewards you with a more scenic route. The ancient town, with its winding, history-steeped streets, seems to beckon you forward. Despite the uncertainty, you arrive safely with an undeniable sense of anticipation.

As the sun sets at the base of Mount Nebo, it casts shadows over the rugged landscape. The sky, awash in shades of red and gold, creates a scene that's both mesmerizing and ominous. You pull out your phone and call AIDA, your heart racing as you request her help in locating the karst line.

"Scanning the area," AIDA responds, her voice a reassuring presence in the encroaching darkness.

Minutes stretch into what feels like hours, until AIDA finally identifies a geological feature leading to an underground shaft entrance just two meters below the surface. Your heart races with renewed intensity.

You wait for nightfall to remain inconspicuous, the minutes stretching as you struggle to calm your nerves. Once darkness envelops the landscape, you begin to dig. Each scrape of your tool reverberates in the stillness. The soil yields with surprising ease, as though it's leading you to something long concealed. Before long, you uncover the entrance to a dark, gaping shaft that has remained untouched for over 2,600 years. You pause, overwhelmed by a blend of reverence and fear, before mustering the courage to step inside.

Venturing into the unknown, you follow the shaft into a narrow corridor adorned with ancient stalactites. Their jagged forms emit eerie contrasts in the dim glow of your headlamp. The air grows colder, thick with the musty scent of earth and ages past. Each step resonates through the stillness, amplifying the silence and heightening your senses.

After descending several hundred meters, you arrive at the edge of a vast, impenetrable pit. Your lights barely penetrate the depths, exposing only an endless black void. You crack open a few glow sticks and drop them into the abyss. They fall for what feels like an eternity before finally illuminating a point about fifty feet below. A chill runs down your spine: you'll need spelunking gear from the CIV.

You retrace your steps, emerging from the shaft to retrieve your gear. The night deepens, growing heavier with each passing moment. Once equipped, you descend once more, this time using ropes and harnesses. Carefully rappelling down, you reach the bottom of an antechamber, its walls enclosing you in an almost claustrophobic embrace. As your headlamps illuminate the space, you're awestruck by the vastness of the chamber, adorned with ancient carvings and mysterious symbols that seem to whisper secrets from millennia past. The air is thick with both awe and foreboding.

Standing in stunned silence, you're overwhelmed by the magnitude of your discovery.

You glance at Maya and Olivia, your voice steady despite the turbulence within. "We have to keep going," you urge, trying to mask your own unease. But they remain frozen, their faces pale and eyes wide with disbelief. You turn to see what has caught their attention and find yourself face-to-face with an angel, his wings spread in full glory.

The angel's presence feels otherworldly, his large, textured wings folding behind him as he sits on an old wooden chair between two massive doors. He appears as an elderly man, his hair and beard gray with age. In a raspy, ancient voice, he says, "I am the messenger. In my master's house, there are many doors. Only the one with the complete suit of armor may enter."

The air thickens with tension. Maya's hands instinctively move to her shoulder holsters, her twin Glocks poised for action. Perceiving the escalating threat, Olivia gently places a calming hand on Maya's arm, urging her to adopt a more measured approach.

At first you believe the angel is real, but soon your mind starts questioning it. As the angel speaks to Olivia, you creep closer to look at his wings, wondering how they're attached to his body. Maybe it's some kind of trick. But how could anyone get down here? And his wings look strong and completely real.

"Xavier, what are you doing?" Olivia asks nervously, motioning for you to come back to the group.

"I think those are real," you whisper, wide-eyed with amazement, pointing at his wings. You try to slip back to the group without being noticed, but suddenly a deep respect overwhelms you, and you bow your head to him.

Olivia introduces you by your first names and asks the angel for his, trying to restart the conversation since you are all stunned and unsure of how to act.

"Why do you ask my name? Though it is indeed a wonderful one," he replies.

Maya lowers her head, even though he asked you all not to. He said your worship should be directed only to his Father.

Olivia explains that you're searching for the Ark of the Covenant and the panis vitae to save the world from a terrible biohazard threat. That's when the angel says something cryptic that you can't quite understand.

"Did you bring the complete suit of armor?"

"What armor?" Olivia asks, hoping for a clearer explanation. She then asks why he looks so old if he really is an angel. He explains that he's taken the form of one of the Levites who originally brought the Ark here.

"Did you bring the complete suit of armor?" he asks again.

Maya, growing impatient, suggests that you're armed and ready to find the Ark by force if necessary.

But the angel sits resolute, unfazed by her insinuated threat.

The awkwardness of the moment breaks as he spoke again, his words measured and accompanied by a slight smile.

"Ah, I see now. You did bring the armor.

"I see that Maya Avraham has brought the belt of truth and the breastplate of righteousness," he says, as though he can see these pieces of spiritual armor in all their splendor. Then he turns his gaze to you, as if searching for something.

"And I see that Mr. Washington has brought the shield of faith and the helmet of salvation."

Of course, you hold no shield and wear no helmet.

"And Ms. Davenport has the feet shod with the readiness to declare the good news of peace, and is armed with the sword of the Spirit indeed. I wasn't expecting a composite suit of armor. Very well.

"You stand at a crossroads," the angel says, his voice resonating with a foreboding echo. "One path leads to the City of Beelzebub, where deception reigns. The other leads to the City of Zion, where truth prevails. A guardian awaits at the fork, but his origin remains concealed. You may ask him only one question to determine the correct path."

Maya and you turn to Olivia, your hopes resting on her expertise. She had already solved the ancient puzzle box and deciphered the cipher wheel that led you here. As Olivia contemplates the riddle, each passing minute feels like an eternity. The angel's inscrutable gaze only adds to the tension. At last, with a flash of insight, Olivia poses an unexpected question to the angel: "Where do you live?"

The angel responds in a soft, gravelly tone. "Clever girl."

With deliberate slowness, he retrieves a large, rusted metal key —one designed for unlocking a massive door. In one smooth motion, he twists the key and opens the door to the left.

As the door creaks open, the angel begins to glow with golden hues, and the cavern ceiling seems to vanish, revealing a picture-perfect blue sky stretching into the heavens. The angel looks up and a golden light emerges from his chest, rising through the clouds. His form stands dark and stoic, as if his body has been merely a vessel. Then you all watch in awe as the frail and lifeless figure begins to crumble, disintegrating into brittle clay before turning to ash, breaking apart into a small pile of dust, the key ring resting atop it.

Beyond the door stretches a narrow stone corridor, its walls etched with ancient Hebrew symbols. The carvings vividly portray Levites transporting the Ark of the Covenant across the Jordan River, with the waters miraculously held back by an invisible force. The corridor is so constricted that you must duck to navigate it as you lead the way forward.

Each step echoes with a mix of fear and excitement, the air thick with ancient secrets yearning to be uncovered. The symbols on the walls appear to shimmer in the dim light, whispering long-forgotten tales. You press on, hearts racing, bracing yourself to confront the mysteries ahead.

The corridor opens into a vast cave, revealing a breathtaking sight at its center. On a stone altar, illuminated by an ethereal glow, rests the most magnificent artifact you have ever beheld.

"Did you find the Ark? Did you?" The polygraph attendant's voice slices through the silence, brimming with barely-contained eagerness. Ms. Chamberlain casts him a disapproving glare, but he remains undeterred. Mr. Atkins leans forward, his intensity encouraging you to share more.

Taking a deep breath, you recall that pivotal moment. "In the heart of the cave, the Ark of the Covenant rested, bathed in an otherworldly glow. Unlike any treasure you'd encountered before, this one radiated a divine majesty that seemed to pulse with an ancient power. Every instinct warned you to keep your distance. Maya and Olivia shared that same trepidation, their eyes reflecting the same awe and fear that gripped you."

The memory of that fear tightens its grip as you recount the moment.

Without warning, footsteps reverberate from the cave entrance. In the murky glow, Heinrich Jager appears, flanked by Ziad Alhussan and a cadre of Pharisee henchmen, their submachine guns glinting ominously.

"Move aside!" Jager's voice cuts through the tension, laced with a dangerous edge. His men advance toward the Ark with determined strides. Olivia's voice rises in desperation, "Stop! You don't understand what you're tampering with!"

A single gunshot echoes through the cave as Jager coldly fires at Olivia, the bullet striking her in the stomach. Her face contorts with a haunting blend of fear and disbelief as she staggers back, collapsing onto the ground. Maya and you rush to her side, Maya desperately applying pressure to the wound. Olivia's once-pained expression gradually shifts to a serene calm, her eyes growing dim as life fades from them.

Meanwhile, two of Jager's men make contact with the Ark. Instantly, they are seized by violent convulsions, their bodies writhing in agony before they collapse, lifeless. Unfazed by the grim spectacle, Jager signals his remaining men to pry open the Ark with crowbars.

A deafening whoosh echoes through the cave, followed by the emergence of a creature cloaked in radiant light, its face obscured in darkness. It turns toward you. Though it has no eyes, its gaze seems to pierce through to your very soul. Maya clutches Olivia tightly, and you wrap your arms around them, shielding all of you from the unbearable brilliance flooding the chamber. In that moment, the raw power of God descends.

Screams echo through the cavern, mingling with the sharp crack of gunfire, followed by a sound not of this world. A violent wind rips through the air, leaving behind a swirling mist, lit by the eerie glow of blue flames and streaks of electrum. Jager and his men drop dead, one after another, their faces contorted in frozen terror.

A profound silence settled over the chamber. You and Maya rose slowly to your feet. The Ark stood open, its ancient lid cast aside, and Maya carefully reached in, pulling out the Golden Jar of Manna. The Panis Vitae inside shimmered with a radiant, golden light. With steady hands, Maya broke off a piece, the golden shards resembling delicate wafers, and gently placed it on Olivia's tongue. Amid the chaos, Olivia had already succumbed.

You and Maya stood over Olivia, breath held in anxious anticipation. At first, nothing happened. Then, slowly, the color began to return to her pale cheeks. Moments later, she sneezed softly and opened her eyes, as though waking from a deep, dreamless sleep. Her hands trembled as she lifted her blood-soaked top, revealing smooth, unbroken skin—no trace of her wounds remained. Olivia had been miraculously healed.

You knew, beyond any doubt, that protecting the Ark was paramount. Its power was a double-edged sword, capable of bestowing great miracles yet unleashing unimaginable horrors.

Before you had time to fully grasp the situation, government agents appeared, flashing their credentials in the dim, flickering light. They moved with swift authority, immediately securing the Ark and its contents into crates. A well-trained platoon of soldiers flanked the sacred relics, guarding them with precision, as though they had rehearsed this moment countless times.

You were escorted to the wall you had rappelled down earlier, now rigged with a military lift system. The pulleys groaned as you ascended the fifty feet back to the corridor, and from there, you made your way toward the surface. Outside, more soldiers stood at attention, along with an EMS unit, ready and waiting.

The medics examine you, their hands efficient and practiced. The area has been cordoned off, with a helicopter circling overhead, its powerful searchlight ramming through the darkness. Towering lights illuminate the scene, casting bloated shadows that loom like silent sentinels.

Olivia is relentless in her questioning, insisting on knowing the destination of the Ark. The response remains unchanged: it's being moved to a "safe location." Later, you're briefed on the staggering scale of the healthcare industry—$3.7 trillion in annual expenditures and seven million people employed worldwide. It becomes evident that the discovery of the panis vitae has been deemed a clear and present danger.

"Where did they take it?" Ms. Chamberlain's voice in the interrogation room comes out as a harsh whisper, laced with frustration.

"You tell me. You're the government!" you retort. "I heard a rumor it might have been flown to Area 51."

"What do you know about the Groom Lake facility?"

"Nothing. I've never even heard of it." you reply. The polygraph attendant nods, verifying that you're being truthful. Your entire account shows no signs of deception.

Mr. Atkins rises from his chair, his expression inscrutable. Appearing satisfied, he whispers something to his colleague before exiting the room, and Ms. Chamberlain slides a document and a pen across the table toward you.

"What's this?" you ask.

"This is your statement and a nondisclosure agreement," she explained. "It prohibits you from discussing this matter with anyone, under penalty of treason."

What are these redacted sections?"

"Our scientists discovered Stachybotrys chartarum, a black mold that thrives in warm, damp environments and is known to cause hallucinations if inhaled. We redacted all mention of the angel and the specter you described as emerging from the Ark."

"With all due respect, ma'am, it was no hallucination. Even if you don't believe what I said about the angel, what killed Jager and his men? And how was Olivia miraculously healed?"

"We found Olivia's top, which had traces of gunpowder residue and her blood. However, our doctors couldn't find any signs of trauma on Ms. Davenport whatsoever. On the contrary, she appears to be the picture of health. While we appreciate your candor, Mr. Washington, there simply isn't any evidence that these events actually occurred. We believe that you genuinely think what you saw was real, and that is consistent with the kinds of hallucinations the black mold is known to induce. Additionally, the CO_2 levels in the cavern could easily explain what you experienced."

You sign the document, the gravity of your decision settling over you. Shortly thereafter, you are flown to Andrews Air Force Base in Washington, DC. Upon arrival, you are released, and the reality of your situation begins to fully sink in. It feels like the ideal moment to take a much-needed rest.

Upon returning to Chicago, you resolve that it's time for a change. You purchase a picturesque home in France, the Château de Chenonceaux, an exquisite château spanning the River Cher near the village of Chenonceaux in Indre-et-Loire. You make an offer they can't refuse and settle into the historic estate.

To complement your new lifestyle, you indulged in a candy-apple red McLaren P1 GTR-18. The thrill of the open road beckons, and while you still treasure your Ducati, there are moments when a car is simply indispensable.

You also indulge in various luxuries: a private vineyard, an extensive collection of fine wines, a private jet, and a library filled with ancient tomes and manuscripts—an homage to the secrets you have uncovered.

The Ark of the Covenant and its secrets are now behind you, yet the shadows of that night linger—an ever-present reminder of the mysteries that continued to call you.

One day, a package arrives from an unknown sender. Inside, you find an earpiece and a throat mic sticker. You hesitate before inserting the earpiece into your ear. Suddenly, a familiar voice echoes in your mind.

"Agent Wild Card, you are being reactivated. The GOD team requires your unique skills."

"AIDA? I thought I would never hear from you again."

"We knew you wouldn't be permitted to keep the Ark or disclose your discovery. We are the shadows that guard the realms of men—existing in obscurity. Your team is safe, and your records have been expunged. I see you've found ways to enjoy your wealth. Are those bespoke boots you're wearing made of snakeskin?"

"Actually, they're black caiman," you reply with a chuckle. "What's so urgent?"

"Nothing I can discuss over this line. But gather your gear and brush up on your Mandarin. We're heading to China."

The line goes dead, leaving you in silence. You surveyed your new life at the Château de Chenonceaux, with your McLaren gleaming in the sunlight. The days of tranquility are over. A new adventure beckons. Smiling to yourself, you gathered your gear, prepared to plunge back into the shadows where you truly belonged.

The End

Just Breathe, Olivia

You focus on your breathing, taking slow, deep breaths and holding each for a count of four. As you exhale, you feel your heartbeat steady and your fight-or-flight response ease.

The checkpoint official appears captivated by Maya's charm and bottle-blonde locks. A few minutes later he returns your papers and passports.

Checkpoint Guard: "Hasna ya rafak, stemtawa bekamtikem fe al-araq. Yemkenk al-dhahab."

Translation: "Okay folks, enjoy your stay in Iraq. You can go."

Thirty minutes later you reach an unauthorized, heavily guarded dig site near Hillah. Maya parks the vehicle on a dune about six hundred yards away. Faint shouts drift through the night air, mingling with the bright lights of the ongoing work.

"Olivia, I'm heading out to find a good vantage point for overwatch," Maya says. "You and Benji stay with the vehicle. If you need to contact me, use the throat mic's PTT button. Don't use my name. Code names from now on. Keep quiet and avoid the radio. If anyone questions you, claim to be American tourists."

Before you can reply, Maya vanishes into the night, her VKS sniper rifle slung across her back.

Fifteen minutes later, Maya's voice crackles over the radio. "GOD, this is Gabriel. How copy?"

"We read you, Agent Gabriel," AIDA replies. "What's your status?"

"I see about twenty armed Pharisees and ten civilians at the site. I'm still unsure what they're searching for. Someone needs to go in and gather intel firsthand. Isn't Wild Card supposed to be on-site?"

"Wild Card's transdermal transponder went dark, and he missed his last two check-ins," AIDA says. "Can you determine his whereabouts?"

"Not without wet work and a trail of bodies."

"I can do it!" you interject.

Wait, what are you thinking? Just moments ago you were ready to jump out of the CIV and flee. Now you're volunteering to go into the terrorists' lair. But spreading your wings and embracing change is what your therapist is always encouraging you to do. Oh, if Dr. Reynolds could see you now…

"Desert Lotus, are you sure?" Maya asks.

"I've got this, Agent Gabriel. I'll slip in quietly," you say. "If I'm caught, I'll claim to be a lost tourist. The hijab should help with that. I'll need to remove the tactical vest though."

"Alright, stay sharp. If you encounter any obstacles let me know and I'll take care of them. I'll monitor your progress until you're inside. Once you're in, AIDA will track your movements. You've got this."

In the heart of the Iraqi desert, where the sun scorches the land and ancient secrets lie buried beneath the sands, you move like a whisper armed only with the allure of your namesake and the sharp intellect that has earned you a place in the Ghost Operations Division. With your brown hair hidden under a headscarf and your eyes sharp and determined, you navigate the ruins of Hillah, focused on your mission. As you walk, you step over soggy newspaper fragments with Arabic advertisements for the latest abaya styles and a discarded box of Sumer cigarettes.

Tonight, your mission is to infiltrate a secure dig site and uncover the intentions of the terrorist group known as the Pharisees. As you draw closer, the danger intensifies. There's no turning back now.

Fluent in Arabic and guided by your keen mind, you blend into the bustling activity of the excavation site. By listening to the conversations around you, you piece together information with the skill of a master puzzle solver. You identify an unguarded entry point where you can slip inside undetected.

You reach the entrance without being detected, but just as you're about to slip inside, an armed, well-built man opens the door and lights a cigarette right in front of you. Your heart pounds in your throat and you freeze in a paralyzing moment of fear.

When he raises his head and your eyes meet, a surge of panic and adrenaline overwhelms you. If only you had Xavier's or Maya's training, you could execute a swift maneuver to subdue him, but instead the only tactic that comes to mind is a desperate kick to his nether region followed by a hasty escape in the ensuing chaos.

Before you can react, his cigarette slips from his fingers as his body collapses lifelessly to the ground. Agent Gabriel's reassuring voice comes through your earpiece.

"I've got your back, Desert Lotus." You didn't hear even a hint of a gunshot, just an eerie sudden silence. Your heartbeat thunders in your chest as you grab the security keycard from his front pocket. You might need it. The heavy door closes behind you with a final echoing thud.

"GOD, this is Desert Lotus. I'm in."

Not long after you're inside, your luck runs out when you stumble upon a group of Pharisee operatives huddled in a corner, discussing their plans in hushed tones. One of them beckons you over and demands you sit on his lap, groping at you. Despite your efforts to keep your hijab in place and slip away, his friends laugh and urge him on in Arabic. Before you can escape, the man you've been fending off tears your blouse and strikes you across the face with the back of his hand. They bind your hands behind your back, leaving you powerless and vulnerable.

Thrown into a dim room, you're bound to a chair, your heart racing as you brace for whatever comes next. A guard approaches, his hand sliding under your blouse as he licks your cheek, his foul breath making you gag.

"I'll see you soon, American whore," he growls in a guttural Arabic whisper.

To your shock, you're not alone. Bound back-to-back with you is another prisoner, their identity a mystery until they speak.

"I'm Wild Card," he says, his voice cutting through the silence. "And you?"

"Desert Lotus," you say without missing a beat.

A flicker of recognition crosses Wild Card's face as he realizes you're both agents from the Ghost Operations Division.

As you exchange quiet words in the darkness, a flicker of hope kindles amidst your despair. With your combined intelligence and determination, the two of you sense a way out of your predicament and a path to completing the mission. Just days ago you felt like a bird trapped in a cage of your own making. Now stepping outside your comfort zone for the first time has been both terrifying and exhilarating. The greater the threat, the more invigorating the challenge.

The heat is oppressive even at night, and despite your relentless attempts, the ropes binding you to the chair refuse to give, rubbing into your wrists and threatening to soon draw blood. Your hijab stays in place, hiding your throat microphone from view. Sweat trickles down your fogged glasses, pooling on your chin and leaving a salty residue on your lips. Just when you think it can't get worse, an infuriating itch appears on the tip of your nose, making the situation even more unbearable.

After a few hours, a mercenary with eyes devoid of compassion and a heart as dark as his intentions enters the room. He methodically cuts you and Wild Card free from your chairs.

Guard: "Anhadh! elioum les yumek al-mahzouz."

Translation: "Get up! Today's not your lucky day."

The mercenary seizes Wild Card by the neck, dragging him from the room at gunpoint. You're pushed along behind them, a second guard prodding you forward with a steely shove.

"Where are you taking us? What's the plan?" Wild Card demands in Arabic, his voice tense and urgent.

"We're taking you to die!" one of the guards' snarls. He and his companion drag you outside to a desolate area near the edge of the perimeter, positioning you for execution.

"Any last words?" one of the guards' growls in Arabic. His eyes, visible above his scarf, are cold and devoid of empathy. The harsh lines of his face and the grim set of his posture betray a soul hardened by relentless cruelty, having long abandoned any pretense of valuing life.

Wild Card asks for a cigarette. The guard steps forward and places one between Wild Card's lips. Producing a silver lighter, the guard flicks it open and ignites the cigarette. The brief flare of the flame casts a fleeting light over the grim scene. Wild Card inhales deeply, exhaling a cloud of smoke that disrupts the air, giving Agent Gabriel (overlooking the area) the windspeed to calibrate her sniper rifle. Standing resolutely, his hands bound tight behind him with coarse rope, he maintains a stoic demeanor.

You request that they loosen your ropes to allow you to say a prayer. Noticing your smaller stature and the submissive way you hold yourself, they agree and slacken your bindings. With the ropes loosened, you scratch the persistent itch and then drop to your knees, readying yourself for one final gambit.

If you want to try and reach out to Maya, **turn to page 46.**

If you accept your fate having done your best, **turn to page 210.**

 **Bookmark Here**

The Pale Horse Unleashed

"What did the video reveal?" Ms. Chamberlain asks as she leans forward with interest.

"It was a recording made by Ziad Alhussan, second-in-command of the Pharisees, documenting everything for Heinrich Jager…" You recount the details captured in the video.

In a remote rural village deep within the Congolese jungle, where the trees whisper secrets older than time, the unsuspecting inhabitants go about their daily lives. Young women nurse their babies openly while their elders' pound mahangu to make flour. Small barefoot children chase each other, laughing. A goat stands plainly, tied to a wooden stake. It's a place untouched by the chaos of the modern world.

In the dead of night, long after the embers of the fires have cooled to ash and the villagers have retired to their huts, a malevolent fog descends. The air remains still as members of the Pharisees emerge from the dense undergrowth in hazmat suits—disciples of death, led by the vengeful spirit of Ziad Alhussan.

His eyes burn with self-righteous fury as he surveys the humble huts. His heart, twisted by the agony of loss, harbors neither morality nor reservation. With a cruel smile, he orders his followers to set up the biohazard dispersal device. He retrieves a vial containing translucent orange powder and activates the device. A low mechanical whirring starts, imbued with malevolent intent.

The Pale Horse virus, a biological abomination born of hatred and despair, spreads its poisonous tendrils through the air, its invisible touch infecting the innocent with a vile and horrific plague. Phase by phase, the virus tightens its grip on the villagers, its insidious progression transforming the once-vibrant community into harbingers of death.

Disguised as WHO saviors, the Pharisees establish a makeshift clinic to treat the infected. They monitor the villagers, their false promises of aid concealing their true intentions.

Initially the villagers whisper in Mashi about a strange sickness sweeping through the community. Others discuss it in broken English, a remnant of a missionary group that passed through years earlier. By the time the true horror of the Pale Horse is revealed, it will be too late.

The infected writhe in excruciating pain as their bodies seize and contort. Initially the symptoms seem benign, masked by the appearance of common ailments. But beneath the surface, a silent terror lurks.

The virus is merciless, each stage more harrowing than the last. During the initial phase, the infected remain asymptomatic, unknowingly spreading its curse with every cough and sniffle. It spreads insidiously, passing from person to person as they go about their daily lives.

Four and a half days later, the first signs of the virus's true nature emerge. A mild headache, initially dismissed as a routine discomfort, soon gives way to a relentless onslaught of symptoms. Postnasal drip evolves into a gurgling cough, each breath increasingly painful and difficult.

But it's the next phase that reveals the true horror of the Pale Horse. Pus-filled lesions erupt across their skin, oozing with the sickly stench of decay. Their bodies become battlegrounds as the virus wages its cruel biological war.

Then the hemorrhaging erupts—a crimson tide flowing from every orifice, staining the white sheets in stark contrast. Eyes, ears, nose—no part of the body is spared from the relentless flow of blood and virus-filled discharge.

Your stomach churns at the grotesque tableau of human suffering.

But even as the infected teeter on the brink of death, the Pale Horse continues its cruel design. In the final stages of the disease, hair falls out in clumps and nails peel away like parchment, leaving only blood and suppuration where the fingertips once were.

In their final moments, the infected are again wracked by violent blood seizures, their eyes glazed over with the unmistakable stare of the damned. But it is not the vacant gaze nor the convulsions wracking their bodies that chills the blood—it's the iridescent glow of their yellowed irises that still haunts your dreams to this day.

The Pharisees dispose of the bodies in a hastily dug trench, dousing them in gasoline before igniting the macabre pyre. The victims' hair seems to melt as thick smoke drifts through the village, carrying the stench of rot and decay. A baby cries, still cradled in the embrace of its lifeless mother. The Pharisees pass by with callous disregard.

Ziad orders his followers to evacuate the cursed land before unleashing two 750-pound MK-77 incendiary bombs containing 220 US gallons of merciless fuel-gel mix that burns hotter than napalm. This is to safeguard the most lethal biological weapon the world has ever known—more contagious than Ebola and deadlier than Marburg. Any contact with infected bodily fluids, feces, vomit, urine, saliva, or respiratory secretions will almost certainly result in infection.

An entire enclave of civilization wiped out in an instant. The release of the Pale Horse leaves nothing but death and despair in its wake. As the flames of purification consume the remnants of the village, the Pharisees whisper a chilling mantra, promising further terror yet to come.

That's what the video reveals. Throughout the footage, there are several audible gasps, and one young airman vomits into a trash bin.

Dr. Linda Nakamura, the CDC Director in Atlanta, states that an alert will be prepared based on the severity and risk of the virus if it proves not to be contained within the village in the Democratic Republic of the Congo (DRC). The CDC will issue updates on the number of deaths and morbidity rates and enforce a travel ban for affected provinces. They'll also evaluate the risk to the United States using predictive models and stand by for further information.

Dr. Nakamura's smooth porcelain skin and long black hair, tied neatly in a bun and complemented by a formfitting skirt suit, conveys that she's all business. Though she masks her emotions well, it's evident that the Pale Horse deeply troubles her.

The WHO administrator agrees that doctors need to deploy teams and conduct a series of tests to confirm the virus has been eradicated. NATO will place troops on heightened alert until the full extent of the Pharisees' objectives becomes clear.

There's ongoing discussion regarding the Pharisees' multiple dig sites across the Middle East and their potential connection to the release of the virus.

"Let's take a break, Ms. Davenport," Ms. Chamberlain says, pulling you back to the present.

Mr. Atkins and Mr. Atwell rise and exit the room. The polygraph technician disconnects you from the equipment and secures you with handcuffs to a raised bar embedded in the table before leaving as well.

Ms. Chamberlain presses the button at the base of the microphone. "Stop recording and hold transcription." She then gathers the file folder and departs, leaving you alone in the room, where the sound of dripping water punctuates the silence.

After hours of grueling debriefing, you feel weary and drained, your mind racing with thoughts of what lies ahead. The harsh fluorescent lights sear through your eyelids and refuse to let your brain rest, keeping it in a constant state of tension.

About thirty minutes later, the door creaks open once more and a uniformed agent enters, carrying a tray laden with food. It holds a tempting array of comfort: a McFalafel, golden fries, a steaming double espresso, and a bottle of water.

For a moment your defenses falter as you take in the unexpected gesture. Despite the circumstances, the aroma of savory potato sticks cooked to golden perfection stirs a sense of warmth and comfort within you, a brief reprieve of familiarity amid the uncertainty.

As the agent sets the tray before you, your eyes meet his, and a silent acknowledgment passes between you. In that brief moment, within the confines of the interrogation room, a connection is forged—a poignant reminder of shared humanity amidst adversity.

With a grateful nod, you reach for the food before you, finding solace in the simple comfort it offers. As you savor the familiar taste, you draw strength from the realization that you are not alone—that amidst the depths of interrogation, flickers of humanity still exist.

Eating with handcuffs is awkward, but you devour the meal. Soon only wrappers and a half-filled bottle of Hayat water remain. The bottle glistens with condensation, a small pool forming beneath it.

After a short while, you're escorted to the restroom. As you pass by several other interrogation rooms, you catch only fleeting glimpses of their insides, unable to discern who, if anyone, is present.

Returning to the room with Ms. Chamberlain, Mr. Atkins, Mr. Atwell, and the polygrapher, your restraints are removed and you are reconnected to the polygraph equipment.

"Roll the tape and start transcription," Ms. Chamberlain instructs those behind the two-way mirror. "Please continue, Ms. Davenport."

Back in the past, your handler, Michael Smith, approaches you in the hangar and wraps his arms around you, his eyes locking with yours. He whispers that you were exceptionally courageous and brave. Having read the after-action reports, he tells you that your country owes you a debt. This moment of intimacy between you two is rare. Your mind drifts to fantasies of kissing him on the balcony of the Le Tsuba Hotel in Paris or making love on the powdery white sands of the secluded Caribbean Island of Barbuda at sunset. For a fleeting moment you bite your lower lip, trying to pull yourself back to reality. Then he does that for you.

"Unfortunately it's back to work, Liv. We've just received intel that the Pharisees have uncovered a puzzle box inscribed with ancient Hebrew and Aramaic symbols. They found it at a dig site near the Qumran Caves, close to Ein Feshkha in the West Bank. They claim it dates back to the sixth century BCE and believe it holds a clue to their search. The box is being transported to a Pharisee-controlled hub in Lebanon for analysis. Your team is heading there to retrieve it and determine its significance before the Pharisees can. Mother will be wheels-up in an hour. Good luck!"

He leans in close—close enough to kiss—but then pulls away at the last moment.

"Oh, one more thing. Swing by the armory. Xavier has a surprise for you." Michael winks as he walks away.

You head to the armory, your steps hesitant and hands fidgeting with the strap of your clutch. The prospect of meeting Xavier, a seasoned marksman, stirs both excitement and anxiety within you. Though you've always been intrigued by firearms, you've never held, let alone fired one. Xavier's reputation has only heightened your curiosity.

As he steps out of the armory, your pulse quickens. His warm smile and firm handshake offer a sense of reassurance amidst your growing nerves. "I heard we're heading to Lebanon. Ready for the challenge?" he asks, his voice brimming with enthusiasm. You nod and follow Xavier into the armory. The scent of metal and gun oil envelops you as you approach a counter lined with a slew of firearms. He retrieves a sleek black case and places it in front of you, a grin spreading across his face. "This is for you."

Your curiosity is piqued as you lift the lid of the case, revealing an M&P Bodyguard 380 pistol. Its compact frame and matte finish radiate an air of power and precision. You run your fingers along the sleek contours of the ergonomic grip as you admire the weapon's design. To your surprise, it's smaller and lighter than you anticipated.

"This is yours," Xavier says with a note of pride. "I thought it would be a perfect fit for you."

Overcome with gratitude, you lift your gaze to Xavier, your eyes gleaming with excitement. "Thank you," you whisper.

Xavier then leads you to the on-site range, where he takes his time showing you how to handle the pistol with confidence and precision. As you line up your shot, hands steady and focus sharp, a surge of exhilaration pulses through your veins.

With each shot, your confidence soars and your movements become increasingly fluid and controlled. To your astonishment your shots group tightly on the target, a testament to both your innate skill and Xavier's expert guidance.

As the session wraps up, you take off your hearing protection and Xavier hands you a shoulder and thigh holster, allowing you to carry the pistol with ease. Overwhelmed with gratitude, you thank Xavier for his guidance, your heart swelling with pride.

As you leave the armory, a newfound sense of empowerment surges through you. With your trusty 380 strapped on, you're poised to tackle any challenge that comes your way. Danger now has every reason to fear you.

You take off from Ramstein AFB and are denied permission to land at Beirut Rafic Hariri International Airport in Lebanon about two and a half hours later. Your only option is an insertion using a high-altitude low-opening (HALO) jump from thirty-five thousand feet.

AIDA has determined that Maya is the best candidate for a successful mission through precision infiltration under the cover of darkness. The rest of the team will monitor her progress via bodycam.

If you think Maya should make the jump, **turn to page 320.**

If you think Xavier should make the jump, **turn to page 286.**

 **Bookmark Here**

Running Down a Lead

After a brief visit to the restroom to collect your thoughts, you return to find yourself reconnected to the polygraph equipment. Ms. Chamberlain's assured demeanor bolsters your resolve as you prepare for the next round of questioning.

Back in the hangar, tension crackles in the air as Olivia Davenport, also known as Desert Lotus, emerges from Mother. Standing alongside Maya and Michael, you feel a surge of anticipation. Michael's warm embrace of Olivia speaks volumes, their deep connection palpable even from a distance.

Maya's voice cuts through the silence. "We have a new mission. The Pharisees have relocated the wooden puzzle box to a secure facility in Lebanon. Retrieving it is our highest priority."

Olivia approaches you with a warm smile, and you express your gratitude for her heroic intervention at Hillah. Her bravery under pressure was undeniable, and you deeply respect her for it.

During the conversation, a Department of Defense representative inquires about your role in gathering intelligence. As you recount the events, a sense of pride swells within you, until he commends your actions with a firm handshake.

As Olivia engages in conversation, you seize the opportunity to finalize your plans. With Michael's help, you coordinate for her to meet you at the armory before departure.

Not long after, you step out of the armory to find Olivia waiting, her anticipation evident. The promise of a surprise gift has her brimming with excitement. You guide her inside, weaving through the bustling space, dodging the echo of gunfire as shooters focus on their targets.

Upon reaching the display area, you notice her eyes brighten at the array of weapons before her. With a flourish, you reveal the M&P 380 Bodyguard, a compact yet powerful emblem of safety in the face of danger. As you walk her through the fundamentals of handling the firearm, you find yourself genuinely impressed by her instinctive skill.

With every shot she fires, her confidence, and yours, swell. Together, you're ready for whatever lies ahead.

Less than an hour later, you're all aboard Mother, heading toward Lebanon. AIDA has determined that Maya is the best candidate for infiltrating the secure warehouse at Beirut's port.

Plan A: Maya's primary objective is to perform a HALO insertion, infiltrate the facility, and secure the artifact. She has two exfiltration options. The first, code-named Operation Coyote, requires her to rendezvous with SEAL Team Six. They'll use a Mark 8 submersible to board the USS North Carolina, a Virginia-class nuclear submarine positioned two hundred meters off the coast. From there, the sub will transport her to a secure location in France, where Mother and the rest of the team will pick her up.

Plan B: In the event that Maya is at risk of capture, she'll initiate Operation Road Runner. This backup plan involves deploying a self-inflating balloon attached to a reinforced 500-foot cable. Mother will decelerate to 200 kph, allowing the aircraft to latch onto the cable. Maya will endure approximately seven G's of force during the rapid extraction, which is expected to take six minutes in total, concluding with her being pulled into the cargo bay.

Mission Execution: Maya carefully prepares her equipment while you, Olivia, and AIDA, watch the mission via body cameras. The HALO jump goes smoothly, until Maya faces danger when her parachute gets stuck. But she stays calm, cuts away the main chute, and deploys her backup just in time.

Maya's efficiency is nothing short of extraordinary. She neutralizes every obstacle in her path with ruthless precision, so unflinching in the face of brutality that she even severs an enemy combatant's finger to trick a biometric door sensor. Her agility matches her deadly skill. As she moves through the hallway, she spots a group of men in lab coats and swiftly climbs into the overhead pipes, avoiding detection with practiced ease.

Employing a nano-UAV, she provides you and the rest of the team with a detailed aerial view of the warehouse layout. Meanwhile, AIDA utilizes satellite data to monitor heat signatures and breaches computer cameras for additional surveillance. The operation blends cutting-edge technology with expert maneuvering, underscoring Maya's extraordinary capabilities.

Clad in a hazmat suit, Maya penetrates the secure chamber housing the artifact. The room is deserted, save for a sophisticated laser grid shielding the artifact. She employs a prism and mirrors to redirect the lasers, converting the intricate web into a single manageable beam before securing the artifact and exiting the area.

As alarms blare, security forces converge on the scene, and Maya's escape turns into a frantic race against time, with the tense drama vividly playing out on the monitors. In the decontamination room, she can hear guards shouting above their thunderous footsteps.

As security forces close in, Maya swiftly opts to deploy the Skyhook for her extraction. She contacts AIDA and utters the code phrase "Road Runner" to initiate Plan B, and AIDA informs Seal Team Six and Captain Randal Hanes of the USS North Carolina that their assistance is no longer required but expresses gratitude for their readiness and service.

As you prepare for the daring extraction, Mother banks sharply, adjusting your trajectory for a precise approach to retrieve Maya and the artifact. Tension thickens in the air, as you close in for the critical pickup.

As Maya is winched aboard, cheers erupt, and her expression reflects a mix of exhaustion and triumph. Meanwhile, AIDA begins scanning the artifact, poring over its intricate carvings and weathered surfaces.

The findings are extraordinary, the artifact dates back to the sixth century, which only intensifies the mystery. What are the Pharisees really after? With numerous excavation sites scattered across the Middle East, it's evident that they're pursuing something important. But how does this relate to the Pale Horse virus?

Despite still lacking crucial pieces of the puzzle, you're determined to uncover the artifact's true significance with the combined expertise of AIDA and Olivia.

AIDA's scans reveal more than merely the artifact's age. Within it, she discovers a cylindrical metal device, both intriguing and enigmatic, evidently crafted to house something of great value.

You work with AIDA to create a detailed 3D model of the artifact, uncovering ancient Hebrew and Aramaic symbols etched into its surfaces. Each symbol presents a cryptic clue, whispering secrets of the past. With her keen eye and expert touch, Olivia starts to manipulate the cube, quickly realizing that unlocking it demands a specific sequence of four symbols.

AIDA calculates over a million potential combinations, indicating that the box was deliberately designed by its creator to resist easy access.

Turn to page 140.

You Can't Handle the Truth!

Wild Card seizes the terrorist, his grip unyielding as he demands answers. Then the truth emerges: the Pharisees' true objective isn't the Ark, but the golden jar of manna concealed within.

The panis vitae, reputed to contain the cure for the Pale Horse virus—a deadly biological weapon poised to be unleashed upon the world by shadowy forces. The virus, devastating as it is, would be rendered worthless without its antidote. The golden jar of manna is believed to be that antidote, potentially transforming the virus into a weapon of unparalleled value. More than that, it is a cure for cancer, heart disease, diabetes, Alzheimer's, Parkinson's, ALS, and many other afflictions.

With the fate of millions hanging in the balance, Wild Card and Gabriel understand the gravity of their mission. They're in a desperate race against time. They need to locate the real Ark before the Pharisees do in order to secure the golden jar of manna and neutralize the biological weapon.

Thousands of Congolese lives have already been claimed by this insidious virus. The stakes are higher than ever, and failure is not an option. In the shadow of Our Lady of Zion, the struggle for humanity's survival has only just begun.

Through the labyrinthine streets of Axum, tension crackles in the air as Agents Wild Card and Gabriel slither through the shadows, their senses sharp and alert. Every alleyway hints at potential ambushes, every corner masking a possible trap. As they approach the rendezvous point with Yohannes, footsteps reverberate ominously behind them, a chilling reminder of the lurking danger.

At last they arrive at the alley where Yohannes stands, his silhouette a beacon of hope in the encroaching darkness. But a burst of gunfire shatters the stillness, turning the alley into a war zone as bullets slice through the air with lethal intent.

The Pharisees' desecration of the sacred monument has evidently drawn the attention of the ENDF.

Adrenaline surges through their veins as Agents Wild Card and Gabriel dive for cover. Yohannes, his expression steely, barks orders above the cacophony, his voice struggling to pierce through the relentless gunfire.

Surrounded by attackers closing in from every direction, the agents understand the urgency of their predicament. With a wordless agreement, they race toward the waiting vehicle, its engine growling impatiently as they scramble inside.

The chase intensifies as they hurtle through the winding streets of Axum, the ENDF closing in with relentless determination. Bullets ping off the vehicle's exterior, their trajectory altered by the impact while the agents navigate corners with daring precision. Each near miss sends their hearts racing, their pulses pounding with the thrill of escape.

For every obstacle they conquer, a new one seems to take its place. Roadblocks emerge unexpectedly, compelling them to weave through alleyways so narrow that their vehicle barely squeezes through. The passenger side mirror, battered and twisted, dangles precariously by a single wire. As each second ticks by, the ENDF closes in in relentless pursuit like a swarm of angry bees.

Despite the mounting odds, Yohannes, Wild Card, and Gabriel press on.

After two and a half hours they appear to have shaken off the ENDF, the night enveloping them in an eerie silence. But then the quiet is shattered by the wail of sirens and the flash of lights in the distance. The ENDF has somehow tracked them down once more. With Mekelle Airport (MQX) drawing nearer, the agents push their vehicle to its limits, the deafening roar of the engine clashing with the chilling realization that their pursuers are still on their trail.

As they finally reach the relative safety of the airstrip, the wail of sirens and the shine of flashing lights recede into the night. Their relentless pursuers are left behind as they race towards Mother, their freedom hanging in the balance.

Xavier and Maya board Mother as Yohannes disappears into the early-morning fog. The plane is already in takeoff position, its engines roaring in anticipation. As the agents climb aboard, Mother begins its ascent before the cargo bay door has even fully closed. Below, a dozen technicals with flashing lights converge on the tarmac, but it's too late. Mother and the GOD team narrowly escape, the frustrated ENDF firing into the night sky, tracer rounds slicing through the darkness like spectral streaks.

The Ethiopian Broadcasting Corporation (EBC), a state-owned network, later reports that an unknown number of Muslim extremists attempted to steal the Ark of the Covenant in Axum. Allegedly, the heroic forces of the Ethiopian National Defense Force (ENDF) successfully thwarted the attempt, eliminating all attackers. Remarkably, no ENDF personnel were injured or killed, and the Ark's chamber remained secure. The guardian monks continue to protect the Ark, and security measures at the site are subsequently reinforced.

Meanwhile, Walta TV, an independent news agency, reports that several ENDF members and guardian monks were sedated and the inner sanctuary housing the Ark was desecrated by unknown assailants. Despite the intrusion, no damage or theft occurred. Witnesses describe the attack as the work of a single unidentified individual rather than a group.

With Xavier and Maya safely aboard Mother, now flying undetected over international airspace, Benji's death has heightened the gravity of your mission and underscored its real dangers. The pressure to decode the parchment cipher wheel has never been greater. You need to find the golden jar of manna before the Pharisees do, or Benji's sacrifice will have been in vain.

In the war room, you all focus on deciphering what the new intelligence means for our next move. AIDA discusses the various Pharisee dig sites while you struggle to compartmentalize the loss of your intern - Your friend. You wipe away a few tears before resurrecting your façade and fully shifting back to the mission.

"AIDA, can you show me the map of the Pharisee dig sites again please?" you ask, your voice still trembling slightly.

Maya hugs you from the side while Xavier's gaze remains fixed on the floor.

"Absolutely, Olivia," AIDA's voice crackles through the speakers.

"According to the latest satellite data, the Pharisees have been active at several excavation sites. Here's a summary of the key locations.

"One: Hillah, Iraq.

"Two: Khirbet Qumran, Israel.

"Three: Our Lady of Zion, Ethiopia.

"Four: Tell es-Sultan, formerly Old Jericho and now a UNESCO World Heritage Site in the West Bank of Palestine.

"Five: Shiloh, Israel.

"Six: Antakya, Turkey.

"Seven: Chartres Cathedral, France.

"Eight: Nahr Al-Sharieat, in the Hashemite Kingdom of Jordan.

"Based on the visuals from these sites, it appears the Pharisees have been actively searching for the Ark and the golden jar of manna for an extended period."

"Is it accurate to say that the Pale Horse virus would be ineffective without a cure?" you ask. "What's to prevent Jager from unleashing the virus regardless?"

"Jager is a weapons broker, not a suicide bomber," Maya says. "Releasing the Pale Horse without the antidote would guarantee mutual destruction. He's too calculated to risk unleashing it without securing the antidote first."

"How catastrophic would an accidental release of the Pale Horse virus be?" Xavier asks.

"According to Dr. Nakumura from the CDC in Atlanta, the airborne pathogen is extraordinarily contagious and virulent," AIDA says.

"It could spread globally within six months, resulting in the deaths of up to seven billion people, with the remaining population likely infected within a year."

"My god, we need to act fast!" Xavier says.

"Shouldn't we find and secure the virus?"

"No, our priority should be solving the cipher wheel," Maya says.

"It might contain a clue that leads us to the Ark, which is crucial for stopping this catastrophe."

If you think the GOD team should try to locate and steal the Pale Horse virus, **turn to page 201.**

If you think we should put all our efforts into solving the cipher wheel and obtaining another clue, **turn to page 233.**

 **Bookmark Here**

Blinded by the Light

You cautiously advance toward the back of the cavern, which narrows while it extends deeper than you anticipated. The air grows cooler as you delve further. When you glance back, only a portion of the waterfall is visible, its thunderous roar magnified by the cave's acoustics, creating an all-encompassing din.

You continue forward in near-total darkness, your hands tracing the rough, damp stone. Ahead, a faint glow further beckons you. At last you come upon a small bend in the rock formation. As you round the corner, you're blinded by the intense sunlight. Raising a hand to shield your eyes, you squint, struggling to focus amid the dazzling glare.

There it is, sprawling across the horizon—the majestic Paititi, the fabled city of gold! The city gleams with an otherworldly radiance, its golden structures emerging from the jungle floor, their surfaces reflecting the light in a mesmerizing dance.

Intricate carvings adorn the buildings, illustrating ancient legends and deities. Lush vegetation weaves through the architecture in a seamless fusion of nature and civilization. The view is even more breathtaking than you ever imagined, a treasure beyond your wildest dreams.

As you survey your surroundings, you realize there are no people nearby, indicating that this must not be the heart of Paititi but a lesser-known part of the legendary city. To your left is a staircase encrusted with gold and adorned with gems, glittering up into the sunlight. At the base of the steps lie a few gold coins, each embossed with a radiant sun.

To your right, additional gold bars and coins are scattered around a majestic structure with golden pillars and a gleaming dome. A rainbow arches through the mist of a tall waterfall, the kaleidoscopic colors stretching into the sky.

You swim toward the steps on the left, watching and listening for any signs of life, whether friendly or hostile. The water laps against the golden steps as you ascend. At the top, you discover a large raw crystal, weighing approximately one and a half pounds. You marvel at how it catches the sunlight, casting vibrant rainbows on the nearby wall. Smiling at this unexpected find, you place the crystal in your leather saddlebag as a memento.

"Are you going to get to how you joined the GOD team soon, Mr. Washington?" Ms. Chamberlain demands.

"I was about to," you reply. "However, I thought you'd be interested in knowing what I was doing at that time. May I proceed?"

"Please do," Mr. Atkins says. "Let him finish, Liz."

The polygrapher glances at Ms. Chamberlain. "He's showing no signs of deception, ma'am."

Ms. Chamberlain sighs and leans back in her chair. "Go ahead, Mr. Washington," she says with a resigned wave of her hand.

Ah yes, Paititi… You take great care to remain unseen as you slip into the city, merging with the shadows cast by the towering golden structures. The indigenous Incan people, custodians of this hidden sanctuary, move with a serene purpose, their lives untouched by the outside world for centuries. You proceed cautiously, your heart racing with each step, listening for any sign that you've been detected.

The city is a marvel, with its intricate carvings and gold-adorned structures narrating the tale of a long-lost civilization. Your ultimate goal is within reach: the spiritual temple reputed to house the Inti, the Golden Sun Disc. You maneuver through the labyrinthine streets, utilizing the cover of night to approach the temple undetected.

Near the entrance, a fierce-looking mandrill, a large baboon, stands guard, gripping a spear. His normally vigilant eyes are fixed on a bothersome insect buzzing around his head. Fortune is on your side. You hold your breath and slip past him, your pulse quickening as you approach the entrance.

Hanging above the entrance is what at first appears to be a beaded curtain. As you pass through it, you realize it's a series of colorful knotted cords known to the Incas as khipu. They sway, their significance a mystery to all but the initiated.

Inside, the air is thick with the scent of burning incense and the floor is strewn with flower petals. The temple is dimly lit, with flickering flames, a tapestry of light variations on the walls. At the center stands the Inti—the Golden Sun Disc—radiating an otherworldly glow.

You approach with reverence, admiring both its beauty and the skill of the ancient craftsmen. With a blend of awe and determination, you carefully lift the disc from its place on the wall and stow it in your leather saddlebag. Its weight is a tangible reminder of your accomplishment.

As you turn to leave, a young boy appears in the doorway, his wide eyes locking with yours. Time seems to freeze. You could grab him and silence him before he alerts the others, but something in his innocent gaze stays your hand. Reluctantly, you let him go, watching as he runs off to alert the tribe.

The alarm sounds 'phtt, phtt, Ayaya-yaya-yaya-ya' with the blow of an animal horn and the beating of drums, you soon are pursued by a group of fierce Incan warriors. Their shouts echo through the city as they close in on you. Driven by desperation, you stumble upon a dark, narrow passage and dart inside without hesitation.

The corridor is dark, filled with cobwebs, snakes slithering across the floor, and tarantulas scuttling in the shadows. It's clear that this passage has been abandoned for a long time. As you venture deeper, the warriors halt their pursuit, unwilling to enter the darkness.

Halfway down the moss-covered hall, you stumble upon a skeleton, impaled on the wall by ancient spears, a grim warning of the dangers ahead. Nevertheless, you press on, intent on escaping with the treasure you have risked so much to obtain while moving cautiously, remaining alert to the ancient and deadly traps rigged along the corridor.

As you navigate the treacherous passage, guided only by the faint glow of bioluminescent fungi, you sense the weight of history and peril bearing down upon you.

Suddenly your foot triggers a hidden pressure plate. The soft click sends a shiver down your spine as a volley of arrows erupts from the walls. You sprint for your life while you evade the lethal projectiles. Spotting your chance, you execute a daring split-jump, narrowly escaping the final volley.

Gasping for air, you press onward and soon face a pit filled with deadly spikes. Without hesitation, you sprint and leap across, your heart pounding as your rigid fingers barely grasp the ledge on the other side. You pull yourself up, knowing you have to keep moving.

The corridor stretches on endlessly, but the faint light ahead urges you forward. At last you emerge from the darkness, welcomed by the first light of dawn. However, your relief is short-lived as you realize you have to retrace your steps to escape Paititi.

As you sprint through the city, an Incan warrior hurls a spear that punctures your saddlebag. You feel the Golden Sun Disc slipping out until it falls. Regret and urgency clash in your mind, but turning back is not an option. The warriors close in, and your life takes precedence over the treasure you've pursued for so long.

You navigate through the dark cavern behind the waterfall, the roar of the water masking your frantic steps. Emerging from the mist, you return to the waterfall's mouth, where your guide, Don Miguel, waits in the canoe, waving urgently as he perceives your desperate need.

You leap into the canoe and shove off the shore, paddling furiously to escape the pursuing warriors. The roar of the waterfall diminishes as you steer down the river, retracing your path.

Although you lost the Golden Sun Disc and the map to Paititi, a precious artifact remains in your battered saddlebag—the crystal that casts magical rainbows in the sunlight. Don Miguel shares your fascination with it.

You trek back through the Andes, traverse dense jungle, and navigate the Sacred Valley before finally meeting up with Don Miguel's sons. Eventually, you return to civilization and book a flight on a small, chartered aircraft bound for the States. It's on this flight that you first encounter Michael Smith, CIA.

Michael is open and friendly, involved in flying cocaine disguised as Peruvian artifacts into the US to fund a covert operation known as the Ghost Operations Division. During the flight, you strike up a friendship with him. Michael shows a particular interest in the raw crystal paperweight you smuggled out of Paititi.

He examines the crystal closely and reveals it's a raw 3,400-carat diamond, weighing an astonishing one and a half pounds. Michael explains that it could be the largest diamond ever discovered, surpassing even the Cullinan Diamond. He estimates its value to be in the billions, owing to its flawless clarity and cultural significance.

As you recount your recent adventures to Michael, he listens with rapt attention. Impressed by your experiences, he offered you a position on his team and promises to introduce you to a diamond appraiser at De Beers in the UK.

And that's how you meet Michael Smith, your first CIA contact, and join the Ghost Operations Division.

During your initial weeks, you undergo rigorous tradecraft training, acquiring essential skills such as counter-surveillance and situational awareness. You dedicate countless hours to perfecting your lockpicking and safecracking techniques. Additionally, your training covers advanced communication methods, bugging, dead-drop protocols, and the creation of cover identities.

Enhancing your shooting skills at the range is only the beginning. You also refine your ability to understand and influence people, further expanding your skill set. The curriculum goes on to include evasive driving, asset development, and close-quarters combat, where your MMA experience proves particularly valuable.

But the real excitement begins when Michael deems you ready for fieldwork. He takes you to a vast hangar at a private airstrip near Maryland. Inside, he reveals a striking jet-black aircraft he's named Mother. Its surface is coated with an iridescent finish that resembles scales or panels. He explains that it features an advanced camouflage system: cameras mounted on top project images onto the underside, rendering the aircraft nearly invisible.

Michael offers to give you a tour of Mother or allow you to rest in your quarters while he takes care of an important delivery.

If you want to check out your quarters and get some rest, **turn to page 255.**

If you want to take a guided tour of Mother with Michael, **turn to page 167.**

 **Bookmark Here**

Just Like Chicken!

Embracing the "when in Rome" mentality, you're pleasantly surprised by the delectable taste of roasted guinea pig. Its crispy skin even brings to mind the familiar comfort of Southern fried chicken from back home. After enjoying your meal and exchanging stories about Incan culture with Don Miguel and his sons, you settle in beneath the expansive starlit sky for the night.

Morning arrives with a sense of mystery as your porters, deeply rooted in Inca traditions, make solemn offerings to the sun god using coca leaves and remnants of guinea pig. This ritual signals the start of your ascent into the daunting Andean heights. Transitioning from marshy lowlands to oxygen-thin peaks, each step becomes a battle against cramps and the thin air. You take a moment to chew coca leaves, navigating what was once an Inca highway but has now been reduced to a treacherous climb.

Wrapped in aguayos and ponchos from your mules, you endure the biting cold, which drops twenty degrees as you climb through the clouds toward Inka Wasi, a sanctuary where the last Inca treasures were hidden from the Spanish conquerors.

Ancient carved steps stretch skyward. At the summit, nature reveals her majesty through breathtaking vistas, where condors glide on ethereal currents and the valley lies shrouded in clouds, as if veiling the feet of gods.

Descending into the dense jungle armed with machetes, you tackle a trail overtaken by nature. The forest is alive with dangers—pumas, scorpions, and deadly bushmaster vipers. Amidst relentless insect bites, you traverse the Vilecanudra River on a rickety cart suspended by a zip line, making your way toward Lisapatra, the ruins of an ancient Incan city.

Amidst the lush foliage, you discover stone remnants of an ancient civilization, with water flowing through intricate canals. The walls are covered in patches of moss and encroaching undergrowth.

From a distance, the ancient city ruins are almost imperceptible. You spend time cutting away the dense vines and foliage to let sunlight reveal the hidden remnants of the city.

In the village of Supa Marca, a holy man reveals a map for a few hundred dollars, pointing to the heart of the jungle where the fabled lost city of Paititi is said to be concealed. Legends describe this city as bathed in the sweat of the sun god, earning it the moniker, "the lost city of gold." With each step deeper into the wilderness, the allure of untold treasures and ancient mysteries grows stronger, shrouded in the jungle's enigmatic embrace.

Where has this tributary been hidden by the dense canopy and how has it eluded prying eyes for centuries? You and your porters venture deeper into the lush labyrinth, each step fraught with anticipation and uncertainty.

Eventually, you discover a clearing where an ancient Incan statue stands as a grim sentinel, marking your path. To your companions, it serves as an ominous warning, fueling fears of a cursed land. The sight of the foreboding statue shatters their resolve, compelling them to turn back. Only Don Miguel - the eldest among them, undeterred by superstition, offers to guide you through the treacherous terrain. Before you press on, you pause to drink from cool, pure water gathered in large green leaves—a brief respite amid the rainforest's mysteries.

Swinging machetes through the thick, tangled jungle, you forge a path into the unknown. A break in the trees reveals a concealed river, its murky waters beckoning you onward. A weathered, hand-carved canoe rests along the shore, and your unflinching guide takes the lead as you embark on the perilous journey ahead.

Paddling through the inky waters, the tension skyrockets as massive black caimans, like shadows lurking along the banks, surge toward you. Their predatory eyes gleam with hunger as they circle quietly amid the jungle's eerie stillness.

An enormous titan, over thirteen feet long and weighing nearly two thousand pounds, leads the attack, casting a menacing silhouette over your expedition. With each stroke of the paddle, the tension tightens.

With eerie synchronicity, the predators strike, crashing against the canoe with bone-rattling force. The wooden vessel groans under the assault, teetering on the edge of capsizing. Adrenaline floods your veins as you brace yourself, the roar of the river barely masking the sound of your racing heart. Then, in a heart-stopping instant, the colossal titan lunges from the depths, jaws snapping inches from your face.

If you want to draw your weapon and use it against the snarling beast, **turn to page 24.**

If you want to jump out of the boat and swim to the nearby shoreline, **turn to page 329.**

> **Bookmark Here**

Skyhook

The relentless thud of boots on concrete echoes behind you, giving you no time to think—only to run. The mercenaries are closing in, their breath almost hot on your neck.

"GOD, this is Gabriel. Road Runner in motion. I've stirred the hornet's nest and the tangos are closing fast. Do you copy?"

"Copy, Gabriel. Extraction team is inbound," AIDA says. "Deploy the balloon and prepare for immediate pickup."

There's no time to think, only to act. You have one way out: the Fulton surface-to-air recovery system known as Skyhook. Used by the CIA, Navy, and Air Force, Skyhook requires you to launch a self-inflating balloon that sends a 500-foot lift line into the sky. An aircraft like the MC-130E Combat Talon—or Mother—will intercept the line with a V-shaped hook, pulling you up to safety. But before that can happen, you have to reach the extraction zone.

You sprint along the shoreline, every muscle screaming in protest. Your lungs burn, starved for oxygen, but you can't stop. Each minute stretches into an eternity as the relentless mercenaries close in, giving you no chance to slow down.

Nearing the extraction zone, your hands shake as you fumble with the harness, slipping it on just in time. A quick glance over your shoulder shows half a dozen Pharisee mercs closing in. Within a hundred feet, some drop to one knee, taking aim. Your heart hammers in your chest, bracing for the inevitable gunfire.

Suddenly a sharp buzzing fills the air, rising to an ominous crescendo. You glance back, catching the flash of surprise in the mercenaries' eyes. Out of the darkness, the RQ-6 Eagle Eye drone swoops low, its M134 7.62 miniguns unleashing a torrent of bullets. The shoreline erupts in chaos as the barrage tears through the mercenaries, their bodies crumpling under the hail of fire. In mere moments they're incapacitated, the drone disappearing into the night sky as swiftly as it arrived—an efficient, deadly phantom.

"Thank god," you mutter as you deploy the balloon and prepare for extraction.

Mother glides in, barely visible against the night sky. Moments later you feel the powerful 7G force as you launch upward at a velocity of 5.56 meters per second. The ground quickly recedes, and a few minutes later you're winched into the cargo bay as Mother disappears into the Lebanese night, leaving behind only chaos and faint echoes.

Your heart still hammers in your chest, the adrenaline refusing to subside. Somehow, the artifact is secure, and you've survived. Another mission accomplished, but the memory of that harrowing escape will linger, along with all the others.

AIDA scans the artifact and then assigns it to Olivia for further analysis. It's a curious 3D wooden cube adorned with cryptic symbols in Aramaic and Hebrew. Olivia notes that some symbols can be depressed, but every time she inputs a fifth symbol, all the symbols pop out and reset. She deduces that it must be a four-digit code, but with millions of possible combinations, cracking it without even a single clue seems impossible. With the Pale Horse virus looming, every second counts.

Days pass and Olivia's frustration mounts, but after persistent effort, she finally unlocks the mechanism. The solution is the four consonants of the tetragrammaton. Inside the artifact, Olivia discovers a sixth-century cipher wheel, designed to protect crucial documents. AIDA identifies a papyrus scroll within. Your next challenge is to decode the cipher wheel's message.

A few hours later, AIDA's voice crackles over the plane's speaker system. "All agents and personnel, report to the war room." You assemble and learn that intelligence indicates the Pharisees plan to infiltrate the Church of Our Lady of Zion, an Ethiopian Orthodox Church reputed to safeguard the lost Ark of the Covenant.

In the interrogation room, Mr. Atkins, Ms. Chamberlain, and Mr. Atwell lean forward, their anticipation palpable. Their unwavering gaze serves as a stark reminder of the gravity of your situation.
"I don't understand. Why would terrorists target a church in Ethiopia?" Xavier asks back on the plane, his frustration palpable. "Their interests don't appear to lie with ancient Middle Eastern artifacts. How does this connect to a biological attack?"

"Maybe they discovered something in the box that we overlooked," Benji says.

"Since they haven't discovered what's inside yet, we still have the upper hand. But you're right, we need to go to Ethiopia and uncover their exact objective."

"Maya and Xavier, this is your cue to prepare for a mission to uncover their plans," AIDA says. "We can be over Axum, northern Ethiopia, in three hours. Olivia will continue working on the cipher wheel from here."

"We may need an interpreter," Xavier adds.

Olivia, focused and determined like a bloodhound on a scent, suggests you bring Benji along while she remains behind to work on the cipher wheel, eager to unravel the next mystery. With urgency and anticipation, you prepare for the mission, ready to plunge into the depths of the Pharisees' plans.

Turn to page 180.

Ancient Secrets Unlocked

Despite the daunting task, Olivia and AIDA press on, fueled by curiosity and determination. Hours turn into days, and just as despair begins to creep in, Olivia has a spark of inspiration. She decides to try the tetragrammaton in Hebrew. It's a long shot, but as she carefully aligns the symbols, she hears a series of satisfying clicks, and the puzzle box unlocks. But her triumph is short-lived, quickly replaced by shock and apprehension, as she gazes at what lies inside.

Nestled inside the box is an ancient cipher wheel, intricately crafted to safeguard vital documents. The wheel's design is both beautiful and menacing, a testament to the importance of whatever it protected. If we can decipher the correct combination, one end will unlock, revealing the hidden document within. It's yet another layer to the mystery, another piece of the puzzle waiting to be solved.

Suddenly AIDA issues an urgent command for all agents to report to the war room. The Pharisees are preparing to infiltrate the Church of Our Lady of Zion, an Ethiopian Orthodox Church. The motive is unclear—what could they possibly want there? But your objective is unmistakable: you have to reach it before they do.

Mother is scheduled to fly to Axum, a town in the Tigray Province of northern Ethiopia. You believe Olivia would be valuable for this mission, but she opts to send her intern, Benji, instead, so she can focus on deciphering the cipher wheel.

Benji, eager to join you, shares a rumor that the Ark of the Testimony is kept at this site—the legendary golden chest from the Bible, believed to house the presence of the Hebrew god Jehovah. Fire, brimstone, and hidden treasure—this is more than enough to grab your attention.

Mother will fly over Wukro Mayray at an altitude of 35,000 feet, at which point you'll use wingsuits to cover the three-kilometer distance, approaching undetected by the Ethiopian National Defense Force. Once on the ground, you are to rendezvous with your local CIA contact, Yohannes, at Highway B30. From there, he'll drive you the remaining sixteen kilometers to Axum, where the church is located.

Then, Maya will take up an overwatch position as you infiltrate the building. This is a less-than-lethal mission, making it essential to avoid any casualties. You're equipped with tranquilizer darts, gas canisters, and smoke grenades. The exfil plan involves a ride with Yohannes on a two-and-a-half-hour drive to Mekelle Airport, where Mother will be waiting. The objective is to get in and out like ghosts that were never there. But even the best-laid plans have a way of unraveling.

You leap from Mother in black wingsuits, gliding like eagles through the night sky. It's Benji's first jump, and his exhilaration is palpable as you cut through the darkness like aerial predators zeroing in on prey. The heads-up display in your helmets keeps you on course, guiding you toward the target. Everything seems to be going smoothly as you deploy your chutes without a hitch and begin the next phase of your descent.

But a few crosswind gusts complicate your landing, and one particularly strong gust sends Benji off course. To your horror, you and Maya watch helplessly as he crashes into a power transformer, becoming tangled in the pole, sparks exploding around him.

For a brief moment, you and Maya are frozen. But the urgency of the mission yanks you both back to reality.

You pressed on, hearts burdened by such a sudden loss. You stash your chutes and move toward the rendezvous point, the memory of your fallen comrade shadowing every step.

Upon meeting your local Ethiopian CIA contact, Yohannes, you set out on the drive to Axum. The city unfolds before you like a labyrinth, its streets crisscrossing in every direction. While it's a confusing maze to you, Yohannes navigates it with ease, familiar with every twist and turn. The location you seek is a well-known tourist spot, familiar to all the locals. Yohannes brings the car to a smooth stop in the quiet of the night.

"This is it, my friends. Good luck! I'll be at the exfil point, waiting for your return."

In the heart of Axum, beneath the watchful gaze of Our Lady of Zion, you and Maya double-check your gear before vanishing into the shadows. Maya assumes a lookout position atop a nearby obelisk while you stalk toward the Ark of the Testimony that is said to be kept in a small chapel South of the main church. Coordinating with AIDA and Maya, you zip from shadow to shadow.

The site is guarded by sporadic ENDF soldiers and a few monks, whom you suspect are inside the building. AIDA identifies potential threats, Maya neutralizes them with tranquilizer rounds, and you drag the bodies into the shadows, inching closer to the entrance.

As you near your goal, the sound of a guard's footsteps reaches your ears. Your heart races and you dive for cover, anxiously waiting to see if you'll be discovered. The guard, wearing earbuds, is absorbed in a conversation with a loved one, his tone soft and personal. He stops just on the other side of the hedge where you're hidden. Time slows and heightens all at once as you weigh the decision to neutralize him or let him pass.

Maya acts decisively. A thwip announces the tranquilizer dart hitting his neck, followed by his swift collapse. You drag him behind the hedge, concealing him in its shadows.

From here on out, you're on your own. Approaching the entrance, you deploy your lock-picking kit, acutely aware of the ticking clock. The area is bright, heightening your urgency. First you insert the tension wrench into the lock, applying pressure to the plug. Next you position the pick in your snap gun. With a few precise squeezes, the tumblers fall into place. You twist the tension wrench and within seconds, the lock clicks open.

Slipping inside, you find the entrance unguarded. You move to the back where a corridor stretches ahead. The main chamber lies in darkness, ideal for a stealthy approach. As you proceed down the corridor, you spot several monks armed with curved jewel-encrusted daggers in gold sheaths. You conceal yourself in the rooms along the hallway and ambush one monk with a choke hold, rendering him unconscious. While you're concealing his body, another monk bursts into the room and flips on the lights. Through sheer instinct, you fire a tranquilizer dart, catching him as he collapses and ensuring he remains silent.

With both monks dealt with, you proceed deeper into the building, soon discovering a set of circular stone steps, dustily illuminated by candles flickering on the walls. They descend into a darkness that seems to pulse with mystery and danger. If the Ark is real, it's likely waiting below.

If you want to head down the staircase to find the Ark,
turn to page 302.

If you want to search the upper floor before going downstairs,
turn to page 266.

🔖 **Bookmark Here**

The Tetragrammaton

Eureka! You've cracked the Caesar cipher, revealing the next clue that sparks an even greater epiphany.

You stand before the ancient Hebrew artifact, a mysterious cube etched with inscriptions that seem to whisper of ages long past. Your fingers trace the weathered grooves of Hebrew and Aramaic, languages that have faded from memory. The artifact is said to possess unimaginable power. Now, teetering on the edge of a monumental discovery, your heart pounds with anticipation.

For years you pored over ancient texts, unraveling cryptic clues scattered across forgotten manuscripts, never fully grasping their true purpose. But now, it's here, right in front of you—the culmination of everything you've been working for.

Recalling that the Hebrews worshiped a singular God known as Jehovah, you enter the tetragrammaton JHVH, but nothing happens. It takes a moment before you realize this is the Latinized version. The true form, YHWH—Yahweh—reveals itself as the original Hebrew name.

With trembling hands, you reach out and press on the Hebrew symbols of YHWH (יהוה), the sacred tetragrammaton. As your fingers make contact with them, a hushed energy surges through the air, as if the very desert itself is holding its breath in anticipation.

The cube responds with a soft click, and suddenly, the tumblers fall into place with a mesmerizing rhythm.

Your breath catches as the lid of the artifact rises, inch by inch, revealing its hidden secrets. The moment is both terrifying and exhilarating, as though you're standing on the very threshold of another world. Benji's wide eyes gleam with excitement and curiosity.

Then, with a final click, the box opens fully, exposing a brass cipher wheel nestled deep within. Your heart hammers in your chest as you carefully lift it out, feeling the weight of history in your hands.

With trembling fingers, you spin the dials of the cipher wheel, the symbols blurring into patterns and codes that whisper of distant lands and forgotten treasures.

Another puzzle lies before you.

"Who would go to such lengths to conceal a puzzle within a puzzle?" Benji asks.

"Someone who believed they had something of immense importance to protect," you say.

As AIDA scans the cipher wheel, you and Benji toil to uncover its secrets. Despite your earlier success, hours pass with no breakthrough. Frustration gnaws at you as each attempt ends in failure.

Suddenly AIDA's voice crackles over the plane's speaker. "All agents to the war room please."

Moments later you learn that intelligence reports the Pharisees are planning to infiltrate the Church of Our Lady of Zion, an Ethiopian Orthodox site located at latitude: 14° 07' 29.40" N, longitude: 38° 43' 5.99" E.

"I don't get it. Why would a terrorist group want to break into a church in Ethiopia?" Xavier mutters, not realizing he's thinking out loud. "They don't seem like the type to care about ancient Middle Eastern artifacts. And how does that tie into a biological attack?"

"Maybe they found something in the box that we missed!" Benji chimes in.

Xavier pauses, considering. "Well, they never got their hands on what's inside, so we still have the upper hand. But Benji's right—we need to get to Ethiopia and figure out exactly what they're after."

"Why don't you and Maya prep for a mission to uncover their plans?" AIDA says. "We can be over Axum, in the Tigray Province of northern Ethiopia, in three hours. Olivia will keep working on the cipher wheel from here."

Xavier nods. "We might need an interpreter."

You suggest bringing Benji along, and he's thrilled at the chance to go into the field.

"Many believe the Ark of the Hebrews is kept there," he says, his voice buzzing with excitement. "In fact, in June 1992, Edward Ullendorff, a former professor of Ethiopian studies at the University of London, claimed to have seen the Ark himself in 1941, while serving as an officer in the British army."

Today only the guardian monk is permitted to see the Ark, following Biblical warnings about the dangers of unauthorized entry into the holy sanctum. The Ark's inaccessibility and the lingering uncertainty surrounding Ullendorff's account have led both Ethiopians and antiquities scholars to cast doubt on his claim.

A few hours later, you're flying over Ethiopian airspace. The plan is for Mother to bring you in on a sharp attack vector, reaching an altitude of three thousand feet under the cover of darkness.

In the stillness of early morning, three figures clad in sleek black wingsuits and tactical helmets stand at the open hatch of the plane, their hearts pounding with adrenaline as they ready themselves to leap into the unknown.

Maya, the embodiment of lethal grace with her blonde hair peeking from beneath her helmet like a golden halo, leads the trio. Beside her, Wild Card radiates a formidable aura of controlled chaos, and alongside him, Benji, a brilliant intellect, compensates for his lack of skill with boundless enthusiasm.

As they plunge from the belly of the aircraft at three thousand feet, the wind howls past their helmets and their hearts race with the thrill of the unknown. They navigate the night sky, their wingsuits slicing through the air like avenging angels. "Wahoo!" Benji shouts, trailing the pros with pure exhilaration. "This is AMAZING!"

Their destination is three kilometers from the airspace above Wukro Mayray, where a CIA contact is waiting for them on Hwy B30. The contact will drive them the remaining sixteen kilometers to the ancient city of Axum and the legendary Church of Our Lady of Zion.

But fate has other plans. Mid-flight, tragedy strikes. Benji's tracker indicates he has veered off course and crashed into a transformer, where he's electrocuted and left hanging on a pole, his life claimed in an instant. Watching through Maya's bodycam, you're shocked and horrified. Agent Gabriel and Wild Card see the sparks flying in the night and watch as Benji convulses. With heavy hearts, Agent Gabriel and Wild Card press on, their resolve strengthened by the memory of their fallen comrade.

As they land on the deserted highway, their chutes fall behind them before they're met by Yohannes, their Ethiopian CIA contact. He emerges from the darkness with an urgent demeanor. Without a word, they pile into the waiting vehicle and drive off in a cloud of dust. The weight of Benji's loss is set aside for now, but its gravity lingers in their subconsciouses.

As the ancient city of Axum looms on the horizon like a beacon of hope, Agents Gabriel and Wild Care understand that their mission is far from complete and that the true test of their mettle lies ahead.

They travel quietly along Route One, which becomes Axum University Street. Passing the Nile Petroleum station at the corner where they exit, they see road signs for Arabtu Ensessa Church on their left and a historical monument on their right.

Yohannes pulls over and says, "This is it, my friends. Good luck!" Dressed in all black and bearing no identification, Agents Gabriel and Wild Card prepare to split up and approach on foot. If they are caught, the penalty for desecrating this holy site is certain death.

They are now in the heart of Axum, where history and legend intertwine. The ancient Church of Our Lady of Zion stands as a sentinel of the past, guarding secrets buried beneath its hallowed halls. Its dome-like structure and four massive wooden doors appear to be impenetrable.

Here, Wild Card, a master of infiltration and deception, focuses on the Ark of the Covenant, hidden deep within the church grounds. He moves through the shadows with the grace of a predator, each step calculated for maximum effect.

Meanwhile, Agent Gabriel takes position atop a tall obelisk overlooking the church grounds, assuming the role of sniper overwatch. Her sharp eyes survey the area, prepared to unleash havoc on anyone who dares threaten their mission.

Equipped with night vision and thermal imaging, and with AIDA providing real-time satellite updates, they're prepared for any situation. This is a nonlethal mission, so both Gabriel and Wild Card are armed with tranquilizer rounds designed to incapacitate their opponents without causing fatal harm. The objective is to infiltrate and exit swiftly, leaving no trace behind.

They are not alone on this mission. The Ethiopian National Defense Force (ENDF) patrols the area, keeping a vigilant watch for intruders. Meanwhile, in the shadows, the Pharisees lurk, their malicious intentions and presence posing a significant threat to the mission. Will Wild Card reach the site before the Pharisees? What makes this location so crucial to them?

Wild Card identifies the targets, and Maya quietly dispatches the ENDF guards in his path. With only sporadic lighting at his disposal, he must move quickly and efficiently - from cover to cover, as he advances.

But the mission takes a perilous turn as he confronts the celibate monks guarding the Ark. Dressed in what appear to be white robes and wielding jeweled daggers, they're both fierce and fanatical. With ruthless efficiency, Wild Card takes them down, his resolve unshaken in the face of danger.

Entering a dark, brick-lined chamber, he uses a tranquilizer dart to subdue the final guardian monk. Catching the monk's limp body, he lowers him to the floor.

Standing before the Ark, Wild Card senses a palpable anticipation in the air. Yet as he reaches out to touch the ancient relic, nothing occurs. There is no divine wrath or fiery punishment—only silence.

Confusion turns to realization as Wild Card inspects the markings on the Ark, revealing it to be a sixteenth-century replica rather than the ancient artifact of legend. Despite its appearance, which mirrors the telltale signs of the true Ark of the Covenant, this one is merely a facsimile shimmering in the candlelight. Before he can fully grasp this revelation, a member of the Pharisees emerges from the shadows.

If you want Wild Card to interrogate the Pharisee agent, **turn to page 119.**

If you want Wild Card to hide behind the purple fabric curtains that hang against the wall, **turn to page 212.**

 **Bookmark Here**

GOD is Great!

"I'll do it for you, Michael," you say, holding his gaze. Your potential partner is asking for your help and your country needs your patriotic service. But this is even more than that. This is an opportunity to invigorate your life and become the woman you were always meant to be.

"Okay, meet me at this address tomorrow night at 11:30 PM. Pack light for a few days and bring clothing for warm weather," Michael says, handing you a business card. The card reads: Hangar X - Global Air Logistics, 2401 Smith Blvd, Arlington, VA 22202. There's no phone number listed.

"So far she's telling the truth, ma'am," the polygrapher interjects back in the interrogation room in the present day.

You smile inwardly, reliving the moment as if it were yesterday. Ms. Chamberlain, noticing your reaction, says, "Is this funny to you, Ms. Davenport? Because I assure you, we have no sense of humor."

"No, ma'am, I was just recalling a part of the story that was somewhat amusing. Now, where was I?"

Oh yes. You arrive at the airport with your intern, Benji Hiroshi, and all your luggage. You had quite a time trying to locate Hangar X. It turns out there is no official Hangar X at Reagan International, but that didn't deter you and Benji from spending half an hour searching for it. Finally, you approach security, and they escort you outside the usual screening area. Before you know it you're in the largest hangar you've ever seen, where Michael eventually approaches you.

"Olivia, who's this?" Michael asks, his face contorting in dismay and suspicion.

"Michael, this is Benji. He's my intern at the museum. But don't worry, I've explained everything. We're working for our country. I told him it was one of those save-the-world scenarios, and he's on board!"

"Can I speak with Olivia privately for a moment?" Michael asks, pulling you aside.

Benji had extended his hand to shake Michael's but retracts it, mumbling, "No offense taken."

"You weren't supposed to tell anyone," Michael says, "let alone bring your intern along." But you never go anywhere without Benji. Although Michael was initially surprised and disappointed, he reluctantly agrees to let Benji join the team on a provisional basis.

Benji is a Japanese American scholar and a detail-oriented intern with a fun-loving spirit. He's driven by a deep curiosity and a passion for solving mysteries. Set to graduate cum laude from Berkeley College, he has a keen interest in all types of technology.

He's the type who would eagerly discuss advanced tech sciences as small talk at parties with his Dungeons & Dragons role-playing group. Always smiling from behind his pop-bottle-thick glasses, he tells jokes that only his Mensa friends seem to appreciate. Though incredibly clever, he lacks certain social skills that most people acquire naturally. This often places him in the "smiley but awkward" category, relegating him to the friend zone with nearly all the women he knows. Despite this, the two of you get along like two peas in a pod.

Meanwhile, Benji is captivated by the giant black aircraft in the room. "Wow, this thing is incredible!" he says as he circles it. The plane's surface has a gleaming dragon-scale-esque texture, and the windows emit a green glow up close. The ramp at the back of this massive futuristic aircraft is lowered and Michael points out its features as you ascend the incline, referring to the plane as "Mother."

Inside, a black Terradyne CIV Armored Vehicle is secured next to a small helicopter. It's much larger than anything you, at 5'4" and 114 lbs, would want to drive.

Benji's fascination with the engines prompts a deluge of technical jargon from Michael. He explains that Mother is a converted experimental aircraft from Northrop Grumman, known as the B23 Eclipse Stealth. It operates on a muon-catalyzed deuterium-tritium nuclear-fusion pocket reactor with a palladium core. This advanced engine is nearly silent and capable of traveling incredible distances on just a single gallon of heavy water.

You realize you aren't the only one starstruck as Benji looks at Michael with the awe of a devoted fan meeting a celebrity. You should have anticipated this, considering the stacks of old Wired magazines Benji is always reading at his desk. Who still reads that stuff? And using paper for reading materials feels so outdated.

"Let's stay on topic, Ms. Davenport," Ms. Chamberlain says in the interrogation room, plunging you back into the past.

Michael guides you to your quarters, which are more cramped than you anticipated. Despite the billions spent on the aircraft, the bed resembles more of a powered lounger pod than a traditional bed. Fortunately, there are two such pods, so Benji won't have to sleep on the floor.

But the most exciting part is yet to come. As you enter the war room, the full intensity of the moment envelops you. Flashing lights and dials adorn every surface while toggles and monitors fill the dim space. Several personnel in military jumpsuits move with purpose, working diligently.

Suddenly a large stand-up table with a computer screen illuminates and a breathtaking hologram in a futuristic silver bikini materializes. You're mesmerized by her presence. Benji, ever curious, reaches out to the light, his hand slicing through her image. Despite being only a foot tall, she's one of the most astonishing things you've ever seen.

"This is AIDA," Michael says. "She's our top hacker. Feel free to introduce yourself."

"Um, hi AIDA," you say, "my name is O-L-I-V-I-A. Can you understand me?"

A smooth female voice emanates from seemingly nowhere. "Hello, Ms. Davenport. Yes, I can understand you perfectly. There's no need to speak slowly or loudly. My microphone can detect sounds ranging from 0.1 Hz to 200,000 Hz, many of which are beyond the range of human hearing."

"Wow! Tell me a bit about yourself."

"My name is AIDA, which stands for Artificially Intelligent Dynamic Assistant. I'm an advanced quantum AI equipped with state-of-the-art facial recognition software, remote satellite access, and CCTV capabilities through the NSA's PRISM IV surveillance system. I can intercept cell phone calls, use voice recognition to monitor mobile networks, read emails and text messages, and track individuals using GPS and thermal imaging.

I can even read lips and modify email content while it's en route to the recipient. Additionally, I have access to all government records, including those marked 'Top-Secret SCI,' and can manage online banking and crypto wallets. If you need anything, just ask."

You and Benji stand in awe while you wonder what just happened.

"Michael, if AIDA can do all of that, why do you need me?" you ask.

"Michael is a seasoned agent," AIDA says, "but he's cautious about AI due to past mistakes and negative portrayals of technology, which may include racial and gender biases. Additionally, I estimate a 67% chance that he feels unsettled by my modern attire and assertive voice, likely due to his upbringing."

"Thank you for that insight, AIDA," Michael says. "The reason I'm wary of AI is that it's not always reliable. How many times have I followed your GPS and ended up lost? No offense."

"None taken, Michael. Your sarcasm is completely lost on me. Your concept of smart technology seems to be stuck in the dial-up era. Is there anything else I can assist you with, Ms. Davenport? I have several tasks running that require my attention."

"No, thank you, AIDA," you say.

Just like that, she vanishes back into the tabletop. Benji's expression is filled with awe, mirroring that of a child experiencing a planetarium for the first time.

"Your code name will be 'Desert Lotus,' Olivia," Michael says. "Benji, you don't have a code name yet, so you'll remain Benji for now. We'll be departing in a few minutes after we get a tractor to push us back. In the meantime, feel free to explore or rest in your quarters. I'll call you when we're ready."

"When will I meet the rest of the team?" you ask.

"You'll meet Agent Gabriel when we arrive at Ben Gurion International Airport in Tel Aviv in about ten hours. In the meantime, you can review your team's details in this dossier." Michael hands you a manila folder labeled Top Secret SCI-Restricted Data. "You'll primarily work with Agents Gabriel and Wild Card, our field operatives. Wild Card is on temporary assignment right now, but he'll be joining us. For now, try to get some rest. Oh, and I've left some flight suits in your quarters if you'd like to change into something more suitable."

You and Benji return to your quarters and don the flight suits. The cramped restroom makes it challenging. There also doesn't appear to be a designated spot for dirty laundry, so you improvise, neatly folding your clothes and placing them in the bottom drawer, while Benji simply tosses his crumpled garments, he has wrapped tightly in his Spider-Man underwear, onto the top shelf of the room's armoire.

"We are definitely going to discuss your hygiene habits, Benji," you say, before noticing he's already snoring in his pod. Chuckling to yourself, you remove the USA eagle-embossed slippers provided with the room and settle into your own pod. It takes a moment to familiarize yourself with the recline function and the other controls, but you eventually figure them out. Switching on a small reading light, you peruse the dossier about the team...

Maya Avraham (former Mossad agent)

Code Name: Gabriel

Date of Birth: May 1st, 2004 (Age 30)

Place of Birth: Petah Tiqvah, Israel

Current Residence: Los Angeles, CA

Nationality: Polish/Israeli

Physical Attributes:

Height: 5'9"

Weight: 130 lbs

Measurements: 35-24-35

Dress Size: 4

Shoe Size: 9.5

Build: Athletic, strong jawline

Hair Color: Blonde

Eye Color: Blue

Complexion: White

Education:

Graduated from Tel Aviv University with a BA Double Major in Biblical Studies/Archaeology and Ancient Near Eastern Cultures

Military Service:

Served in the IDF from 2021-2023 in the Shaldag ("Kingfisher") Unit

Mossad 2023-2024

Black River PMC 2025-present

Skills and Expertise:

Counterintelligence

Counterinsurgency

Elite sniper school training

Unconventional warfare

Explosive ordinance disposal (EOD) specialist

5th-degree black belt in Krav Maga

Languages: Hebrew, English, and Arabic

Current Employer: Black River PMC

Transportation:

Drives a black Aston Martin DBS 777 Ultimate Coup

Xavier Washington (Treasure Hunter

Code Name: Wild Card

Date of Birth: November 18, 2000 (Age 32)

Place of Birth: Galesburg, Illinois

Nationality: USA

Physical Attributes:

Height: 6' 2.5"

Weight: 205 lbs

Chest: 46"Biceps: 16"

Waist: 35"Shoe Size: 12

Hair Color: Blonde

Eye Color: Dark brown

Hairstyle: Slightly spikey (gel)

Jawline: Chiseled

Facial Hair: Two-day old beard/mustache shadow

Complexion: California sun-kissed

Build: Athletic

Education:

Carl Sandburg High School

University of Minnesota—BA in Anthropology

Skills and Expertise:

Using LYDAR for 3D scans of dig sites

Utilizing photogrammetry for 3D scans of objects

Languages: English and Arabic

Licensed helicopter pilot

Mentor:

Naturalist and paleontologist Roy Chapman Andrews, former Director of the American Museum of Natural History.

Interests:

Basketball, swimming, wingsuit jumping, and MMA

Transportation:

Drives a Ducati Panigale V4 SP4

You barely make it through the files before you drift off. Fortunately, you had the foresight to remove your glasses, which now rest on the open dossier lying on your chest.

You wake up around nine hours later when the captain's voice crackles over the intercom, announcing the descent. "We will be landing shortly, folks. Please fasten your seat belts. We'll be on the ground in about an hour."

Waking up, you feel parched and notice your stomach growling, akin to a bear waking from hibernation. Benji remains asleep in his pod, his thumb resting in his mouth. Deciding not to disturb him, you refresh yourself and gather the scattered pages of the dossier. After locating and cleaning your glasses, you settle in to review the team information once more.

Just then, a young man in a flight suit arrives at your door carrying two aluminum food trays that resemble something from a prison movie. Each tray holds a slice of ham with a side of peas and mashed potatoes smothered in dark gravy. Accompanying the meal is a small orange drink box with a straw awkwardly affixed to the side. At this moment, however, it might as well be a five-star Michelin meal—you're famished.

You land in Tel Aviv at 5:00 PM local time to meet Agent Gabriel. After waking up, Benji has something to eat and joins you in the war room. Michael informs you that he won't be accompanying you for the remainder of the mission, as he has other commitments. Before departing, he leans in close, his lips brushing against your cheek, and whispers, "Good luck."

As he exits on the rear ramp, Michael pauses to chat with a tall attractive blonde woman standing beside a luggage carrier piled with black duffel bags. Although they're fifty feet away, their laughter carries on the breeze, revealing a disconcerting level of familiarity. In retrospect it may have been irrational, but your immediate reaction is one of suspicion and unease. You feel a primal urge to stake your claim, and despite never before having met this woman, you predetermine that you don't like her.

If you want to stay on board and meet Maya organically,
turn to page 192.

If you want to confront Maya as she boards,
turn to page 357.

▸ Bookmark Here

Bureaucracy at Its Best

"I'd rather ask for forgiveness than permission," Xavier jokes, flashing a mischievous grin. Olivia, however, insists on following proper channels, believing that academia will secure the necessary permissions. AIDA's research reveals that we need to apply to the Israel Antiquities Authority (IAA), based at The Jay and Jeanie Schottenstein National Campus for the Archaeology of Israel in Jerusalem.

The following day, the three of you navigate the winding streets of Jerusalem and finally locate the IAA office. A stern-faced woman greets you, her desk cluttered with a mountain of documents. She details the process of securing the necessary permissions to Olivia, who listens with focused attention.

"We'll need this submitted to the Islamic Waqf in triplicate," the woman says, gesturing to a thick stack of papers. "Next, you'll require special approval from the Ministry of Foreign Affairs (MFA), complete with the prime minister's seal.

Finally, you must qualify for and apply for an excavation license. If all goes smoothly, the process could take up to six months."

"Why is this process so complex?" Olivia asked, frustration evident in her voice.

"The Temple Mount is claimed by Jews, Christians, and Muslims," the woman explained. "Honestly, it's unlikely to be worth the effort. We haven't approved an application since 1986. The area has been a point of contention for decades, and there's no immediate incentive to resolve it. The Waqf has consistently denied excavation requests."

Eight months later, despite your persistent efforts and support from the State Department, you still haven't made any progress. Amid your bureaucratic struggles, the world is thrown into chaos. The WHO and CDC issue a global alert: a new virus has been accidentally released. It begins with mild symptoms like a headache, runny nose, and light cough, but it has a 99% mortality rate. People are advised to shelter in place and wash their hands frequently. There is no known treatment or cure.

Fear spreads as the death toll rises. Hospitals, morgues, and cemeteries overflow with bodies. Olivia falls ill first, then Xavier, and finally, you.

The End

Go Back to Page 189

Getting the Lay of the Land

Michael gives you a tour of the craft and you're left in awe. As you enter the expansive cargo area with the ramp lowered, you're struck by how much larger it is inside than you anticipated. There's ample space for a Little Bird helicopter and a sleek, black armored transport, both fastened to the floor with bright yellow nylon straps.

As you move through the aircraft, you encounter several noteworthy sections. First you come across the detention area, a stark reminder of the gravity of your missions. Next you pass the armory, stocked with a wide array of weapons and gear, and the medical bay, fully equipped for any emergency. Finally, you reach the war room, a cutting-edge command center featuring screens and communication devices essential for planning strategies and missions.

As you step into the war room, your gaze is immediately drawn to a quasi-futuristic stand-up desk at the center. The desk is unlike anything you have ever seen. The entire tabletop is a glowing computer screen, softly illuminated beneath your fingertips, while a transparent drop-down screen hangs from the ceiling to provide additional information.

But the true marvel isn't merely the sleek design or the glowing screens, but the tabletop's ability to project a sophisticated and captivating hologram of a quantum AI named AIDA, which stands for Artificially Intelligent Dynamic Assistant.

AIDA isn't just any AI; she's extraordinarily advanced and seamlessly integrated into the global network in a way that far surpasses your imagination. Whenever you need information, no matter how obscure or complex, all you have to do is ask AIDA. Her presence and capabilities are nothing short of revolutionary, making her an indispensable resource for the team.

Beyond the war room, you discover the mess, a surprisingly cozy area where the crew can relax and refuel. Adjacent to it are the crew quarters, designed for maximum comfort during extended missions. Finally, on the second floor, you reach the cockpit. The view from there is nothing short of breathtaking, with state-of-the-art controls and a panoramic vista that makes you feel as though you're exploring uncharted territories.

Michael hands you a dossier on potential GOD-team recruits. From the outset, it's evident that he's zeroed in on two standout candidates: an Israeli tier-one operator named Maya Avraham and an analyst from Washington, DC named Olivia Davenport. The dossier is meticulously detailed, outlining their skills, achievements, and vital statistics, underscoring the careful consideration behind their selection.

After catching up on some much-needed rest, Michael wakes you with urgent news: your first mission is imminent. In the war room, AIDA briefs you on a terrorist threat from a group calling themselves the Pharisees. As she speaks, a transparent screen hanging from the ceiling displays supporting graphics and intelligence. The group is led by a shadowy figure known only as "the Prophet," whose identity remains unknown, and his second-in-command, a man named Ziad Alhussan.

Alhussan's past is marked by profound loss and radicalization. A Palestinian, he lost his family in the Israeli bombing of Gaza from 2023-2024, a retaliation for the unprovoked Hamas attack on Israeli civilians on October 7, 2023. He studied biological sciences at Cambridge University before joining the Iranian proxy Hezbollah in Lebanon in 2024. Consumed by grief and hatred, he was radicalized and trained by the Quds Force, eventually emerging as a feared assassin for hire. Now, he serves as the second-in-command of the Pharisees.

AIDA has been monitoring various dig sites across the Middle East and has detected heightened activity at a site in Hillah, Iraq. Your mission is straightforward: conduct advanced reconnaissance of the site, infiltrate if feasible, and gather intelligence on the Pharisees' objectives in the region.

Adrenaline surges through you as you ready yourself for the mission, your senses primed for the challenge ahead. The plan is clear: You will fly Mother over the drop zone at 35,000 feet and perform a HALO jump. For approximately three minutes, you will free-fall through the night sky before deploying your chute at 900 feet to minimize the risk of detection.

You're equipped with standard night-vision goggles, tranquilizer rounds, a USB stick, and an earpiece. Additionally, you have an experimental jawbone vibration cap fitted to one of your rear molars, courtesy of DARPA. Your primary weapons include a Sig Sauer P226 with a silencer and a boot knife. The tactical helmet you wear features a navigational HUD to guide you to the Pharisee site.

This mission demands both stealth and precision. Every action counts, leaving no margin for error. The thrill of the jump, the exhilaration of free fall, and the quiet approach to the target—this is the essence of what you live for.

The flight from Maryland to Hillah spans nine hours, during which you review the mission details and analyze satellite images provided by AIDA from the NRO's Gemini-6 SIGINT satellite. After completing the HALO jump, you're scheduled to travel to Najaf, a forty-minute drive, where Mother will be positioned for extraction.

Clad in a black StealthGuard MK 1 tactical suit—a collaboration between NanoTech Fabrications and Armory Innovations—you feel adrenaline surge through you. You double-check your oxygen system, altimeter, and HUD, ensuring each is functioning correctly. Then, with a resolute thumbs-up, you signal to the flight crew to depressurize the cargo bay.

As the ramp lowers, the biting cold air lashes against your suit. Without hesitation, you leap into the void, tucking your arms close and slicing through the night like a bullet. You rapidly reach 126 mph—terminal velocity—by minimizing your drag.

The thrill is exhilarating, but you remain focused on your training and altitude. AIDA's reassuring voice in your ear confirms that you're on course. Thirty seconds later, at 900 feet, the command crackles: "Deploy, deploy, deploy." You yank the rip cord, experiencing a brief moment of tension followed by a swift deceleration as the chute deploys. A wave of calm envelops you as you use the toggles to guide yourself to a smooth landing on a desert plain just north of the dig site.

You bury your chute and tactical helmet in the sand. The darkness serves as your ally, so you activate your night-vision goggles and advance stealthily toward the dig site. Diesel-powered lighting towers sporadically illuminate the area.

As you approach, a guard unexpectedly emerges on patrol. You dive behind a makeshift wall of sandbags about four feet tall. The guard walks right up to it, unaware of your presence. and lights a cigarette, sending a thick plume of smoke into the night sky. Seizing the opportunity, you scoop up a handful of sand and tossed it away from your position. The guard, curious about the sound, leans toward it to investigate, giving you the chance to subdue him with a tranquilizer dart to his neck. As he slumps to the ground, you pull him over the sandbags and conceal him in the shadows. One less obstacle.

Under the cover of darkness, you approach a large tent. You wait for a moment of reduced activity before slicing a slit in the fabric. Inside, a laptop rests atop what appears to be weapons crates. You insert a USB stick into the laptop and AIDA begins penetrating the military-grade firewall using a brute-force attack. Each second feels like an eternity as you wait and remain vigilant for any signs of intrusion.

Suddenly footsteps echo from just outside. The drive isn't finished downloading, but you have no time to wait. You shut off the screen, plunging the room into darkness, and dive through the slit in the tent wall, tranq gun at the ready. Your heart pounds as you listen to the approaching voices.

"Yes, I'm coming," one of them says in Arabic. "I left my badge. Let me grab it, and we'll go."

The man enters, his shadow stretching across the floor as he grabs his ID badge from the crate and leaves, unaware of the USB stick flashing dully in the dark. You slip back inside, turn on the screen, and see that the download is complete. You eject the USB stick and tuck it into your boot.

But your relief is brief as you hear two new men approaching. Pressing yourself against the corner, you hold your breath. One of them enters and starts up the laptop, his fingers clattering across the keys.

Moving like a shadow, you grab him from behind and apply a lateral vascular neck restraint. He struggles briefly before slumping into unconsciousness. You drag his limp body into the corner, but before you can conceal him, his companion shouts in Arabic, "They found something! They need us in sector seven to verify the find. Let's go!"

"Wild Card, you've got company," AIDA says.

Panic surges through you, but there's no time to waste. You draw the tranq gun and aim at the man's silhouette, squeezing the trigger. The dart hurtles through the air and strikes him in the chest as he passes through the tent's curtain divider. His face twists in surprise before his eyes roll back, and he collapses. You catch him as he falls, lowering him to the sand. With both bodies hidden in the shadows, your mission is secure.

You take a deep breath, feeling the weight of the moment settle over you. You steel yourself. This is just the beginning. The next phase awaits, and you need to be ready.

You move through the encampment like a ghost in the shadows. As you pass through, you overhear a conversation between two men. One mentions the Prophet. His companion responds in Arabic, "Jager is terrifying. Once, I saw him execute a man just for kicking sand onto his loafers. It was insane. Be glad he's not here, or we'd be stacking body bags."

"Wow. How long are we stuck on this job?" Pharisee #2 asks.

"I'm not sure, but definitely a few more days," Pharisee #1 says. "I heard over the radio that they just found an artifact that might lead us to the prize. If we find it, we all get bonuses!"

"That would be great. Right now, we're just babysitting sand dunes," Pharisee #2 grumbles. "There's nothing out here. But I guess the money's good, so whatever."

A voice crackles over Pharisee #1's radio. "Team Six, sitrep?"

"All clear in this sector," Pharisee #1 says.

If you want to shoot them with tranq darts, **turn to page 318.**

If you want to sneak past them to try and get a look at the artifact, **turn to page 238.**

 **Bookmark Here**

I'm Sexy and I Know It

Agent Gabriel sets her firearms aside and removes the elastic band from her hair, letting it fall around her shoulders, then adjusts her clothing to enhance her cleavage before approaching the guard. Her blonde hair, tousled by the breeze, frames her face with an effortless allure.

"What are you doing here?" the guard asks in Arabic. "This area is off-limits!"

"I was looking for a big strong handsome Lebanese man to sweep me off my feet," Maya says as she closes the distance between them.

His gaze lingers on her as she approaches, taking in her confident demeanor and striking appearance. She smiles while subtly adjusting her stance and running her fingers through her blonde hair. As she draws nearer, he seems distracted, his eyes betraying a mix of curiosity and admiration.

In a split second she thrusts her hand into his Adam's apple with a penetrating blow. He gasps, hands flying to his neck as he struggles to breathe. Seizing the moment, she delivers a forceful double-ear strike, disorienting him further, then maneuvers behind him and executes a sharp twist of his neck. The confrontation is over in under a minute.

She moves the body into the shadows, then twirls her hair and resecures it with her hair tie. Within moments she's back in her tactical gear, prepared for the next phase of the mission. Drawing her karambit, she severs the guard's thumb with a precise flick of her wrist.

"That's absolutely revolting!" you say in the war room. Benji's face contorts with shock and revulsion while Xavier's smile conveys silent approval.

Inside is the target: a sixth-century puzzle box crucial to national security. Pushing aside all doubts and fears with each step, Agent Gabriel remains focused on the mission.

Reaching the entrance, she pauses to listen for any signs of movement. Hearing nothing, she presses the severed thumb against the lock pad and slips inside, blending into the darkness like a wisp of smoke.

She moves like a wraith through the dim warehouse corridors. Her athletic frame blends with the shadows while AIDA's cool voice offers guidance in her ear.

As Maya weaves through the maze of corridors with pipes overhead, the sound of approaching footsteps reaches her ears. Like a predator, she scales the pipes, melting into the darkness above just as two scientists in stark white lab coats pass by below.

Their conversation floats up to her concealed position, revealing fragments about the artifact—ancient, enigmatic, and highly sought after by the Pharisees. Her pulse quickens. She's getting close.

Maya deploys her nano-UAV—a cutting-edge DARPA technology disguised as a mosquito—guiding it toward her target: an enemy combatant emerging from a decontamination chamber, clad in a hazmat suit and matching her own height and build. With years of refined skill, she maneuvers the drone to the woman's neck and administers a single-use tranquilizer.

The enemy collapses to the floor and Maya descends from her vantage point. Concealing the unconscious body in a nearby laundry bin, she dons the hazmat suit, its layers providing a valuable shield against detection.

As Maya passes through the decontamination chamber, a thrill of anticipation courses through her. The artifact lies ahead, shielded by a laser grid that shimmers with deadly precision. Undeterred, she removes her helmet and unzips her hazmat suit. With unwavering focus, she retrieves a prism-like device from her utility belt, its mirrors catching the dim light. Carefully positioning it, she adjusts the device to merge the laser beams into a single clear path.

Before her stands the pedestal, and on it, the artifact pulses with an ancient, almost palpable power. Hebrew and Aramaic symbols flicker across its surface, bearing witness to its rich history. With reverence, she extends her hand, her fingers grazing the cool, textured surface of the cube.

Just as her hand clasps the artifact, the warehouse erupts into chaos. Alarm klaxons blare and lights flicker to life as the Pharisees converge.

Fueled by a surge of adrenaline, Maya places the artifact into a black Spectra fiber bag concealed in her tactical suit. She zips up, and dons her hazmat helmet, dashing for the exit, her pulse pounding as the past and present collide in a frenetic symphony of danger.

Terrorists scramble, their frantic shouts merging with the deafening alarms as they respond to the breach.

Maya maneuvers through the cool misting nozzles of the decontamination chamber, still disguised as one of the Pharisee scientists. With the ever-present threat of capture or death looming large, she pushes forward, desperate to escape. In these tense moments, she feels exposed, vulnerable, bereft of the comfort that the shadows usually provide.

Once out of the decontamination chamber, AIDA directs her to a long corridor branching left and right. The choice is critical: one path promises escape while the other leads to certain capture or death.

If you think Maya should choose the dark corridor to the right, **turn to page 294.**

If you think Maya should choose the dark corridor to the left, **turn to page 75.**

 **Bookmark Here**

Who Do You People Think You Are?

"Who do you think you are?" you demand. "Ms. Chamberlain, is it? I have rights! I want a lawyer and a phone call!"

Chamberlain presses a button on the microphone stand. "Hold transcription. Stop recording."

She releases the button. "This is a matter of national security," she says coldly. "You are being held under The National Defense Authorization Act for espionage and terrorism. You've been declared an enemy combatant. As far as we're concerned, you have no rights. We take these charges very seriously. We can detain you indefinitely if we so choose. "

Her gaze becomes icy and unyielding. "You will answer our questions, Ms. Davenport. You will tell us everything we want to know or I will personally authorize your rendition. You won't be so pretty when you emerge from the darkest hole on the planet. There are places that will make you pray to be treated this kindly."

She leans in closer, her voice dropping to a menacing whisper. "These are places where keeping your teeth is a rare luxury and each finger becomes a bargaining chip. Places where the pain is so excruciating that revealing secrets becomes the only respite. Places where grown men emerge sobbing, desperate just to make it through the day. Do you understand what I'm saying?"

Ms. Chamberlain's gaze flicks to a side table in the corner of the room, cluttered with an assortment of sinister tools—pliers, drills, a bone saw, a hammer, and other instruments with purposes too horrifying to contemplate.

"WHERE IS THE ARK OF THE COVENANT?" she barks.

"You touch me and I'll have you fired!" you retort, your voice steady despite the fear creeping in. "Is this bad cop and worse cop? You don't scare me. I want my phone call. Now!"

Days blend together in a haze of relentless interrogation and torment. You're subjected to unending stress positions, sensory deprivation, blaring music, and the unspeakable agony of waterboarding. Each method chips away at your resolve, hollowing you out. Eventually you find yourself in a pitch-black cell, curled into the fetal position, consumed by despair and the gnawing question of how it all unraveled.

Your next destination is a detention camp in Guantanamo Bay, Cuba. By September 2034, the GOD program is abruptly disbanded and all operatives, including you, vanish from public view. The official records are meticulously erased. The CIA, in a briefing to a congressional oversight committee later that year, asserts that no biological threat ever existed. The entire fiasco is publicly dismissed as a geopolitical ruse orchestrated by Russia, North Korea, and China to incite chaos in the Middle East.

But is it truly a deception, or is there something more sinister at play?

The End

Go Back to Page 05

An Ethiopian Surprise

The plan is straightforward: Mother will fly over Wukro Mayray at 35,000 feet. At that altitude, you, Xavier, and Benji will jump into the night in black wingsuits. The moonless night will provide the perfect cover for your descent. You'll glide for three kilometers, aiming to reach the ground undetected by the Ethiopian National Defense Force (ENDF).

Once you land, you'll assume an overwatch position while Xavier infiltrates the building. For exfiltration, Yohannes, a local CIA asset, will drive you for two and a half hours to Mekelle Airport, where Mother will be waiting for your safe return. You'll be in and out like ghosts in the night—at least that's the plan.

As you near the drop zone, adrenaline surges through you while the plane's engine hums and the landscape unfolds as a patchwork of shadows and distant village lights.

Upon landing, you'll meet Yohannes on the highway leading to Axum. He'll drive you the final sixteen kilometers to Our Lady of Zion. Your task is to provide overwatch while Xavier leads the operation. This mission is non-lethal, and your gear includes tranquilizer darts, sleeping gas, and smoke grenades.

Benji is buzzing with excitement for his first real field mission. The chance to uncover the Ark of the Covenant is a thrill he can't pass up. He's a walking encyclopedia about the Ethiopian Church that claims to house the Ark, detailing its history and the legends surrounding it. Only the guardian monk is allowed to see the Ark, and no one is permitted to touch it, although he notes that most of the evidence of this is anecdotal.

"The Ark is said to possess the power of God," Benji says, his eyes wide with wonder. "Anyone who isn't a direct descendant of the Levitical priests is believed to die instantly upon contact."

You can't help but smirk. "If you buy into all that mumbo jumbo…" you mutter, though you can't deny the eerie chill that runs down your spine at the legends.

As you gear up for the jump, the gravity of your mission settles in, and the wind howls around you as the ramp descends, revealing the endless night below. You exchange a final nod with your team and leap into the void, your wingsuits catching the air.

The ground races up to meet you, and you brace yourself for whatever lies in wait in the ancient city of Axum.

As you near your landing, a crosswind gust slams into Benji, veering him off course. He crashes into an electrical transformer and you watch in horror as sparks erupt and his body convulses with current. The grim reality sets in as his lifeless form dangles from the wires.

With heavy hearts and steely determination, you and Xavier press forward with the mission, the loss of your friend a stark reminder of just how high the high stakes are—this is no game, and failure is not an option.

You stow your gear in the trunk of Yohannes's car and settle into the oppressive silence of the drive to Axum. The weight of Benji's loss hangs over you and Xavier both like a dark cloud. Your training taught you to compartmentalize your emotions, but reality is far more challenging than any training could prepare you for. You find yourself longing to complete the mission before it has even truly begun.

The city of Axum stretches out before you, a maze of streets woven together like an intricate thatch basket. It's bewildering to you, but Yohannes navigates it with practiced ease. The site you're looking for is a well-known tourist destination that's familiar to the locals. Soon Yohannes brings the car to a stop in the stillness of the night. "This is it, my friends. Good luck!"

You double-check your gear, then wish Xavier a safe mission, giving him a soft kiss on the cheek.

Scanning the area, your gaze is drawn to a peculiar obelisk rising above the site. Among several others like it, this one provides the perfect vantage point. Its intricate masonry offers ample footholds for a skilled climber like yourself. Within minutes, you're perched atop it, using night and thermal vision to survey the grounds on the southeast side of the compound.

Finding Wild Card takes a moment. He moves through the shadows like a specter of the night. Sporadic ENDF soldiers and a few monks, presumably guarding the Ark, patrol the site. AIDA identifies potential threats along Wild Card's path, you neutralize them with tranquilizer darts, and he hauls their unconscious bodies into the shadows.

Everything proceeds smoothly until Wild Card approaches the entrance. A soldier emerges from behind the building, muttering to himself. He pauses directly beside the hedge where Wild Card has taken cover, the final shadowy refuge before the entrance.

Your heartbeat steadies as you exhale, aiming with precision. In a moment of perfect stillness, you squeeze the trigger. The weapon hisses softly with just six pounds of pressure as the dart slices through the night, lodging itself in the soldier's jugular. He collapses and you observe as Wild Card pulls the body into the hedge.

For a few tense moments, Wild Card stands exposed in the light as he picks the lock. The snap gun in his hand reveals the precision and skill with which he operates. With a few pumps of the device, the lock gives way with a soft click. From here on out, Wild Card must work alone until he exits the building. You keep a silent vigil, scanning the area to ensure his exit remains unchallenged.

From what you can hear, it appears the Ark that Wild Card finds isn't authentic. Instead of dating back to the sixth century, Wild Card determines it's from the sixteenth century. You can't help but think Benji would have been deeply disappointed. For a time, Wild Card's signal goes dark, leaving you uncertain about his status. Your concern for him goes beyond mere professional duty—fortunately and unfortunately, you've developed feelings for Xavier.

Suddenly his voice crackles through your earpiece. "What are you looking for? Why are you here?" His tone is sharp, authoritative, cutting through the stillness like a blade.

"Please, don't hurt me," a trembling voice pleads. "We're here for the panis vitae."

"The what?"

"The golden jar of manna! It's the cure for any human ailment. My boss needs it to sell a biological weapon—the Pale Horse. Without the cure, the weapon's useless. But with the panis vitae, we'll be unstoppable. Name your price and my boss will pay it. Just... let me go."

A dull thud echoes through your earpiece, marking the abrupt end of their negotiations. The ensuing silence leaves you to piece together what just happened.

Latin isn't your strong suit, but panis vitae translates loosely to "bread of life."

"Did you catch all that, AIDA?" Wild Card murmurs.

"Affirmative, Wild Card. I suspected they were after the Ark, but the golden jar of manna? That explains everything—the virus testing, the dig sites. All of these locations were believed to be potential resting places for the Ark. We need to secure it first, whether it's otherworldly or just a priceless relic. Finish up and get out before you're compromised. Leave no trace. Agent Gabriel, continue overwatch and exfil with Wild Card. Yohannes is standing by."

"Copy that, AIDA. Gabriel out."

Moments later, Wild Card says, "I'm coming out now, Gabriel."

You head toward the rendezvous, your footfalls echoing in the still night. Just as Yohannes comes into view, gunfire erupts, shattering the quiet. The Ethiopian National Defense Force (ENDF) have clearly been alerted by the Pharisee operatives' sloppy infiltration, and now they're determined to eliminate all intruders—including you.

Yohannes shouts for you to hurry as you dive for cover. Keeping low, you sprint toward the vehicle, but the illusion of safety shatters as bullets rip through the windshield and sides. You pop smoke and a dense cloud obscures the scene as you tear away, engine roaring, tires screeching, adrenaline surging. Sirens wail and lights flash, roadblocks looming ahead.

Yohannes weaves through the chaotic streets, balancing skill and desperation as your escape blurs into a frantic dance of speed and danger. The city's twisting layout is both ally and enemy, every sharp turn either a near miss or a fleeting chance at freedom.

A roadblock looms ahead, forcing Yohannes to jerk the wheel, sending the vehicle skidding down an alley so narrow you could reach out the window and touch its walls. The passenger-side mirror tears off with a metallic screech as it scrapes against the buildings' masonry, the echo of twisted metal reverberating in the cramped space.

As you burst out of the alleyway, it seems you've finally evaded your pursuers. The road ahead stretches out, a few hours' drive from the rendezvous with Mother. AIDA's voice crackles over the comms, providing real-time satellite guidance to ensure you navigate clear of any lingering threats.

"Turn left at the next junction and head straight for five kilometers," AIDA says.

Yohannes nods, maneuvering the vehicle around the corner.

"Keep your eyes peeled, Wild Card. We're not out of the woods yet," you say.

You speed past closed shops and sleeping neighborhoods, the distant sound of sirens fading. The tension inside the car is palpable.

"Next right, then immediate left," AIDA says, guiding you through the urban maze.

The cool night air sweeps through the broken windows, whipping your hair around, strands having broken free of your hair tie during your hasty escape. You remove it from your hair and reapply it to secure the loose strands, keeping your face clear and your vision unobstructed.

With the city's chaos fading into the distance, you drive through the serene countryside. The tension ebbs but your vigilance remains sharp, eyes scanning the rearview mirror for any signs of pursuit, even though your pursuers are no longer visible.

After hours with the wind whipping against your face and fatigue setting in, you arrive at Mekelle Airport's tarmac, where Mother is already prepped and ready for departure. Yohannes drops you off, waving as he dissolves into the encroaching fog. You stow your gear and breathe a sigh of relief as the aircraft begins its takeoff before the ramp is fully raised.

"We made it," Xavier says, reflecting your relief and locking eyes with you.

"For now," you say, sharing a brief embrace with him in the cargo bay. His body against yours makes your heart flutter for an entirely different reason than the dangerous adrenaline of before. With her active camo engaged, Mother soars into the sky like an eagle ascending toward the stars. Below, a swarm of trucks with M60s mounted in their beds fire aimlessly into the night. Tracer rounds futilely streak through the darkness, rapid bolts of light that vanish into the distance.

Every moment of your escape replays vividly in your mind, a pulse-pounding sequence of narrow escapes and near misses. As Mother ascends higher, the stars blur into streaks of light. For now, you're safe, but the key to stopping the Pharisees remains out of reach. The whereabouts of the panis vitae and the looming threat of the Pale Horse virus cast long shadows, and you must be prepared for whatever comes next.

You watch the news unfold on Ethiopian state-owned television. Reports detail a harrowing attempt by a group of radical extremists to break into Our Lady of Zion at Axum and steal the Ark of the Covenant. Thankfully, brave ENDF soldiers thwarted the intrusion, successfully protecting the sacred relic. However, another broadcast presents a different account: a lone gunman infiltrated the building where the Ark was thought to be kept, sedating several ENDF soldiers and monks. Surprisingly, nothing was stolen during this bold robbery attempt.

Meanwhile, as you soar through international airspace aboard Mother, the weight of Benji's loss finally has time to fully bear down on everyone, but none more so than Olivia. She fights to maintain her composure, tears streaming down her cheeks despite her efforts. You embrace her, whispering that Benji was brave, fighting to save the world. Now the responsibility rests with you. His sacrifice must not be in vain.

Determined to press on, Olivia wipes away her tears and requests that AIDA display a map of all the dig sites. It's becoming evident that the Pharisees have been searching for the panis vitae for some time, but their efforts suggest they haven't located it yet. Xavier proposes a bold plan to locate and steal the virus, but you find yourself uncertain about where to start. Everything hinges on Olivia deciphering the cipher wheel.

As hours turn into days, your faith in Olivia remains unshaken. Her determination, coupled with AIDA's analytical prowess, finally bears fruit. Together, they crack the cipher wheel, unveiling a map that points to the Ark of the Covenant—the very Ark the Hebrews believed housed their God and bestowed victory upon them.

Your journey is far from over, but you're closer than ever to a breakthrough. With a map, a clear purpose, and the memories of Shira and Benji pushing you forward, the Ark of the Covenant awaits. It might hold the power to turn the tide in your favor.

The map in your hands is adorned with intricate details and cryptic symbols, reminiscent of the puzzle box Olivia recently deciphered. Additionally, it features a sophisticated 3D rendering of Jerusalem.

AIDA pinpoints the precise location indicated by the map in the present day.

Xavier, brimming with excitement, describes the breastplate of Aaron, believed to be housed within the Ark. Crafted from pure gold and set with twelve precious gems, it's a relic of immense historical significance.

"Do you realize what this means? We're all going to be rich!" Xavier says.

"You're already wealthy, Xavier," you point out.

"True, but this will make me even richer! Let's get started."

Even Olivia appears eager to discover where this lead will take you. The thrill of the hunt is palpable as you race against the Pharisees and their deadly virus. AIDA's analysis indicates that the Ark might be located on Mount Moriah in Jerusalem.

With that, you head to Ben Gurion International Airport in Tel Aviv. Finding the Ark won't be easy though. The Temple Mount is fiercely protected by the local Muslim community, who have consistently refused any excavation efforts. By day, it's a bustling historical and tourist destination for both Christians and Muslims. By night, it becomes a guarded and revered religious bastion.

Olivia packs the wooden puzzle box and the cipher wheel as AIDA uploads scans of the map to your cell phones, and you depart from Ben Gurion for the Temple Mount, posing as Christian tourists. Typically, you would drive, but this time Xavier insists. When he flashes those pleading brown eyes, you find yourself giving in.

With AIDA's guidance, you navigate through a labyrinth of underground tunnels until you reach a section that isn't part of the usual tourist spaces and has been cordoned off. It's unlikely that anyone has ventured this way in recent memory.

If you want to get permission to go beyond the tape, **turn to page 165.**

If you want to sneak under the Do Not Cross tape, **turn to page 313.**

 **Bookmark Here**

I Want Out

Upon arriving at Ramstein AFB, you meet Michael and tell him you want out. The pain in your ribs is excruciating, and even the Tylenol #3's can't relieve it. Each breath causes sharp discomfort as your chest expands.

Fortunately, your wealth affords you the luxury of a lengthy hiatus. Michael tries to dissuade you, emphasizing that the Pale Horse isn't just a localized threat but a global menace. But his warnings only strengthen your resolve to leave immediately. After signing several NDA documents, you're finally allowed to depart.

You return to the US aboard a Gulfstream G900 you purchased. A few weeks later, you book a Chinese junk (a traditional sailing ship that originated in China) departing from Hanoi, Vietnam and bound for Halong Bay and beyond. It's your own version of a slow boat to China.

A few local women choose to accompany you, easing your many aches and pains. You find peace and joy at last, surrounded by breathtaking landscapes and warmhearted people. Life feels good, and you're ready to embrace a new chapter with a renewed sense of happiness and adventure.

Besides, if the Pale Horse ever does unleash its havoc, they'll need someone to help repopulate the planet. Sure, the champagne and caviar will likely run out long before that happens, but you're prepared.

You purchase a remote island in the heart of the Pacific and build a fortified bunker there. This is no ordinary bunker—it's stocked with enough food and water to sustain you completely off the grid for three to five years.

You've been assured that it can withstand a direct hit from a bunker buster. Constructing it posed a new challenge, unlike anything you'd tackled before. But then, what else would you expect from a wild card like yourself?

The End

<center>Go Back to Page 199</center>

Back to the War Room

"Good evening, Ms. Olivia Davenport and Mr. Benjamin Hiroshi," AIDA says. "As you adjust to the time difference, you may experience jet lag over the next forty-eight hours. Dr. Howard Lewin, M.D., Chief Medical Editor at Harvard Health, recommends staying well hydrated, adapting to your new schedule as soon as possible, and getting exposure to daylight in your new environment. Additionally, taking melatonin may help with sleep adjustment."

"You can just call me Benji, AIDA. That's what everyone calls me."

"Alright, Benji. Would you prefer a different name, Ms. Olivia Davenport?"

"Sure, you can call me Olivia, or Liv, or even by my code name, Desert Lotus. That sounds kinda cool."

"Very well, Olivia, Liv, Desert Lotus.

"Good evening, Agent Gabriel. How can I assist you? I was just helping Olivia and Benji get settled."

Just then, Maya enters the war room. "I'm good, AIDA. How's everything on the home front?"

You haven't yet learned much about Maya besides what's written in her file. As you speak to the CIA in the interrogation room, you recall some of her subtle nuances that you would later uncover—layers that went beyond the surface details documented in any file.

Maya is nothing like what you'd expect at first glance. Anyone assuming she's just a dumb blonde would be making a fatal error. With striking blue eyes, a killer figure, and looks that could stop traffic, she captivates most men—and plenty of women too. But her inviting smile, with its charmingly sharp canines, as well as the effervescent warmth she radiates, completely masks her lethal skill set.

As a covert agent, Maya is armed with a keen eye, razor-sharp reflexes, and resolute decisiveness honed from years of rigorous training. Her infectious allure makes you believe most men would happily surrender their national secrets to her. Though every eye in the room often instinctively turns to her, she remains unaware of the full force of her beauty—a woman who can't quite see herself as... well, beautiful.

Yet Maya has no steady boyfriend, choosing instead to focus on whatever mission is in front of her. Her looks are just another weapon in her arsenal. But beneath her free-spirited, tip-of-the-spear persona, she's still a woman longing for a genuine connection. What she doesn't fully realize is how the loss of her aunt and sister to a Palestinian suicide bomber during an intifada has solidified her need to bring justice to the "bad guys"—a driving force behind everything she does.

AIDA interrupts your Maya admiration. "Agent Wild Card is currently conducting advanced recon at a Pharisee dig site in Hillah, Iraq, roughly fifty miles south of Baghdad. While we're still uncertain of the Pharisees' ultimate goal, I'm monitoring their online communications closely to gather any useful intel. I've tracked several payments through shell corporations, but the trail goes cold once the money enters the Hawala network. Still, I'll continue to keep a close watch on the situation.

"In the meantime, could you take a look at some files, Olivia? I intercepted encrypted messages between known Pharisee members, and Michael wants your insight on their discussions. The files are on a laptop delivered to your room. You'll have internet access if needed, but it may take a few extra minutes to connect since I'll be masking your IP address. In your inbox you'll find an email with instructions for setting up your password and accessing the files.

"Welcome back, Agent Gabriel. Tomorrow, you and your team will assist Agent Wild Card in the field. We'll depart from Ben Gurion at 2100 hours, traveling under cover of darkness to Najaf, Iraq. The flight will take approximately three hours. From there, you'll travel seventy-eight kilometers through hostile territory to Hillah, which should take about one hour and eight minutes, depending on traffic and checkpoints. Be advised, this area is notoriously known as the Triangle of Death for a reason.

"The region is predominantly farmland, with irrigation ditches managed by local families, and is home to about one million Sunni civilians. It's crucial to note that Iran-based proxies are actively conducting operations in the area, so be prepared for combat. Your passports and documents are securely stored in the lockbox in your room.

"Please ensure Olivia is equipped with an earpiece and tactical mic for this operation. Also, remain vigilant for IEDs and local criminals, as kidnapping for ransom has been on the rise in the area. "Humidity will also be high due to the nearby Euphrates River. That's all for now, Maya."

"Wait, what?" you ask. "I'm going out there? Are you crazy? No way! I don't have any training or experience for this! And Benji's suddenly feeling homesick, right, Benji?"

"Definitely. Homesick!" Benji says, looking a bit faint.

"Don't worry, Olivia, I'll ensure you and Benji are safe," Maya says. "We might need your help with translating or figuring out what they're looking for. You can do that with your laptop while you're in the CIV. It's an armored vehicle with bulletproof glass. Plus, we have the advantage of surprise. No one knows we're coming. Just remember not to roll down the windows. If it gets too hot, we can adjust the AC. Snacks and water will be available on board. You might want to use the restroom before we leave. There may not be another chance for a while. I'll also provide you both with tactical vests and armor plates, just in case. Catch up with you both later."

Maya raises her fist with a reassuring smile, prompting you to reciprocate with a fist bump, though in retrospect it stings. "Okay, but if things go wrong, I'm off the field missions roster."

Turn to page 258.

Any Last Requests?

You watch as he reaches into his pocket and pulls out a weathered Zippo lighter. Its metal surface glimmers in the dim light, bearing the marks of years of use and countless flames. With a practiced flick, he snaps it open, the metallic click cutting through the silence. The familiar scent of pungent lighter fluid wafts up as he rolls the flint wheel with his thumb, igniting the wick with a satisfying whoosh.

The small flame dances atop the lighter, casting a warm glow on your face. Leaning forward, he extends the lit Zippo toward your cigarette. You tilt your head against the breeze as he brings the flame closer. The tip of the cigarette catches fire, and you inhale, watching the ember glow.

Once the cigarette is lit, he snaps the Zippo shut with a decisive click, extinguishing the flame. The lighter smoothly disappears into his pocket. You exhale a plume of smoke, nodding your thanks as the darkness again encircles you both.

Desert Lotus requests that they untie her hands so she can pray, and to yours and Maya's surprise, they comply. Her petite frame and serene demeanor appear to ease their tension. She kneels, trembling with fear.

"God, God, can you hear me? I need your help, Gabriel," she pleads.

"What's she doing?" one of them asks.

"She's praying to her God," the other replies.

"Your God can't save you now!" mocks the first, his voice dripping with scorn as he laughs coldly.

The two guerrillas, their faces concealed by scarves, stand before you with rifles raised, their eyes cold and unfeeling. You scan your surroundings, desperate for any chance of escape.

Instantly two silenced shots pierce the darkness, traveling through their heads at three hundred meters per second. They stagger, then collapse to the ground.

You scan the area, searching for your rescuer, and then there she is—Agent Gabriel, perched atop a sand dune, her VKS sniper rifle still smoking in the desert breeze.

She descends from her vantage point and cuts the ropes binding your and Desert Lotus's hands.

"Better late than never, Agent Gabriel," you say, as she hands you her backup weapon. Her photograph didn't capture her captivating allure.

Your brief moment of freedom is shattered as terrorists, alerted to your presence, close in with a barrage of gunfire.

With no escape and danger closing in, you fight back, guns blazing in the night. Each shot is a defiant stand against those who seek to silence you.

Soon you reach the Gurkha CIV and find an Asian man sleeping inside. As dawn breaks, you vanish into the desert horizon.

"AIDA, we're en route in the CIV," Maya radios. "ETA one hour. Notify medical. Wild Card requires urgent attention."

"Affirmative, Agent Gabriel. Mother is prepared for extraction in Al-Najaf."

Desert Lotus introduces you to her intern, Benji, who is seated in the back seat. Meanwhile, Maya hands you a rag and a bottle of water to tend to your bleeding head, which started bleeding again during your escape.

With a triumphant smile, despite the pain, you pull a flash drive from your boot.

"We got it! I know what they're up to," you tell Maya.

She smiles and winks. "Let's get you patched up. You can debrief us back at Mother."

For a fleeting moment, you sense an unspoken connection with her. If you weren't so battered, you might have explored it further.

Finally, you return to Mother, your massive mobile command center stationed in Najaf. The crew, clad in jumpsuits, secures the CIV while Maya unloads her gear, the clinks and clatters resonating through the cavernous space.

The medic, a reassuring presence amidst the chaos, escorts you to the infirmary. The antiseptic scent greets you as you enter. He stitches you up, the needle pricking your tender skin before the pain subsides. Each stitch is recorded in your medical file. He wraps your torso tightly, alleviating the ache from your fractured ribs, as revealed by the stark X-rays.

Following AIDA's instructions, you insert the thumb drive into a USB port on the sleek metallic table in the war room. The room hums with the activity of electronics and muted conversations. AIDA begins analyzing the data, delivering updates and insights in her calm, digital voice.

Exhausted, you head to your quarters to freshen up. The debriefing is scheduled for 0600 hours (eleven hours from now). Splashing hot water on your face soothes your bruises, and for the first time in a while, you feel like you can finally breathe.

Meanwhile, Mother is en route to Ramstein AFB in Germany—your next destination on this relentless journey.

If you want to be at the debriefing at 0600, **turn to page 33.**

If you want to tell Michael that the last operation has you spooked and you want out, **turn to page 190.**

 **Bookmark Here**

Let's Find Another Way In

Scaling the building's exterior, Agent Gabriel reaches the roof and removes the grate covering an air duct. She slips inside and navigates the cramped passages, remaining alert for any sign of danger.

Suddenly a faint hum echoes through the duct and Agent Gabriel's heart skips a beat. Ahead, she sees the red glow of lasers slicing through the blackness. She's triggered an anti-intrusion system.

She watches in horror as the deadly grid advances toward her, the lasers slicing through a rat in the duct ahead, leaving a trail of burned flesh and destruction. There's no escape.

With resignation, Maya clenches her jaw and braces herself as the lasers close in. In an instant, they pierce her body, ending her mission and her life. Her remains are reduced to small, seared pieces, like a 3D puzzle, with the smell of burnt hair.

Thus, in the depths of the warehouse's ductwork at the Port of Beirut, Agent Gabriel's valiant effort comes to a tragic and untimely end.

The End

Go Back to Page 67

Appropriating the Pale Horse

AIDA has detected a level-4 biosafety lab where the Pharisees are likely storing the Pale Horse virus. However, there's a high risk of execution if any of the GOD team members are captured.

"Where is it?" Xavier asks.

"You're not going to like this, Agent Wild Card," AIDA says.

"Enough with the suspense, AIDA. Where is it?" Maya asks.

"The facility is in Tehran," AIDA says, and the war room falls silent as the operatives absorb the gravity of their most dangerous mission yet.

Then Xavier says, "Let's do it!"

"I'm in," Maya says.

Later that night, the moon hangs low over the sprawling city of Tehran as Agents Gabriel and Wild Card prepare to embark on their most perilous mission yet. Their target: PryoGen Pharmaceuticals Ltd., an organization concealing the most dangerous secret in plain sight. Inside the facility is a biosafety level-4 laboratory (BSL-4).

With AIDA's intelligence at their disposal, Maya and Xavier devise a daring plan to infiltrate the heavily guarded facility. They know the risks were high, as lurking in the shadows are members of the elite Quds Force, prepared to defend their secrets at any cost, not to mention a dozen operatives from the Pharisees.

Beneath the veil of night, Tehran's bustling streets whisper with the secrets of increased activity at PryoGen. Gabriel and Wild Card, the Ghost Operations Division's finest, stand at the edge of the labyrinthine compound, their breath mingling with the chill of anticipation.

A sign blinking sporadically with PryoGen's contact details—123 Ferdowsi Street, Tehran, Iran. Phone: +98 21 5555 1234—attracts large insects and buzzes with the monotonous hum of an aging transformer.

Every step carries the weight of imminent danger as they skirt the outer perimeters, their movements fluid and silent like wraiths gliding through shadows. Armed guards patrol like trained predators, their eyes scanning for any sign of intrusion. Agents Gabriel and Wild Card inch closer to their objective with every step, each quiet takedown a necessity. As they approach the compound's core, the atmosphere grows oppressive, thick with mounting tension.

The decontamination chamber stands imposingly before them with sterile walls. Hazmat suits await, their cold, rubbery texture a foreboding reminder of the perilous task ahead.

Gabriel and Wild Card suit up with practiced efficiency, the rhythmic hiss of their breath amplified within the confines of their protective gear. As they step into the chamber, a fine mist envelops them, swirling under the harsh glare of fluorescent lights.

They press forward, their hearts pounding alongside the steady hum of machinery. Every second feels like an eternity.

At last they arrive at the inner sanctum, where the Pale Horse virus awaits its release, its devastating potential contained within delicate glass vials.

Trembling, Wild Card extends his gloved hands toward the container holding the virus. With care, he grabs the vials and places them into a specialized container that hisses open, steam pluming from the liquid nitrogen encasing each vial.

But their fleeting moment of triumph is abruptly shattered by a burst of gunfire as enemy forces materialize from the shadows.

Amidst the ensuing chaos, Agents Gabriel and Wild Card fight with the ferocity of cornered predators. As bullets whizz through the air, catastrophe strikes—stray rounds penetrate their hazmat suits and shatter the delicate container holding the Pale Horse virus.

Then a blaring alarm overwhelms the cacophony, its piercing wail reverberating off the sterile walls as the facility plunges into chaos, and a computerized voice declares the initiation of lockdown protocols as charges rigged to the concrete supports begin to detonate, sealing their fate within the compound's depths.

The End

Go Back to Page 124

RIP Maya Avraham

Having been targeted by both the CIA and Mossad, and with both agencies convinced you're dead, now is the ideal moment to reinvent yourself. Besides, you've always dreamed of being a California girl.

You reach out to a forger on the dark web, and a few days later you emerge as Marionette Quinlan, a US citizen from San Diego. You board Emirates Flight EK2024 from Azerbaijan to Los Angeles. Armed with your new identity, you wait in line for the customs official.

When it's your turn, he gestures for you to step forward. You slide your passport and CBP declaration form through the small slot in the window. He meticulously examines your passport, comparing your photo to your actual appearance. After scanning it and reviewing a small monitor, he looks up and says, "Welcome home, Marionette. What was the purpose of your trip?"

"I went to meet a man I'd been dating online for two years," you reply.

"How did that work out?"

"Turns out I was catfished, so I guess I'm still searching for love." You smile and twirl a strand of your hair.

"Are you bringing anything back with you?"

"Just a T-shirt that says 'Azerbaijan' on it. Everything else is what I brought with me."

"Are you bringing back any fruits or vegetables from this trip?"

"Nope."

"Where do you live?"

"San Diego."

"Alright, welcome home."

He gestures for you to proceed, and before long, you find a cozy spot on the beach, leaving behind the feel of a gun in your hands and the terrifying, exhilarating rush of adrenaline, savoring the warm sand between your toes.

The End

Go Back to Page 312

A Mysterious Path

You observe as the angel, wise in appearance, holds up an ornate skeleton key. His metallic voice reverberates through the corridor as he intones, "Welcome to the Hotel California." With a slow, ominous creak, the door swings open, revealing an expanse of impenetrable darkness.

With no other choice, you step inside. The door slams shut behind you with a resounding thud, and the angel's ominous words reverberate in your mind. "This way," you murmur, your voice betraying the unease you feel. Agent Gabriel nods, her gaze meticulously probing every shadow for potential threats, while Wild Card's hand hovers tensely over his weapon.

The corridor seems to stretch endlessly, each footfall magnifying the oppressive silence. At last, a faint, eerie glow pierces the darkness, revealing a precarious rope bridge suspended over a chasm of roiling volcanic lava. Occasional bursts of flame erupt from the depths, casting a grotesque, flickering light across your path.

"Stay close," Wild Card mutters, cautiously stepping onto the first wooden plank. It groans under his weight but remains intact. Gabriel moves next, her steps deliberate and poised. You take up the rear, every sense sharpened and on high alert.

Midway across, a sickening snap reverberates through the cavern. The planks behind you begin to disintegrate, flames consuming the bridge with alarming speed.

"Move!" you shout, desperation driving you forward. You sprint, the acrid stench of burning wood and sulfur stinging your senses. As you near the end of the bridge, a chilling metallic clink echoes from above. Glancing up, your heart plummets. Deadly blades, gleaming and menacing, descend from the ceiling, swaying perilously close. With each swing, they loom like guillotines, threatening to cast you into the molten lava below.

"Watch out!" Agent Gabriel cries out, narrowly dodging a lethal blade. Her agility is remarkable, yet even she finds it challenging to evade the relentless pendulums.

Wild Card, ever the strategist, yells, "Time your movements! Wait for the right moment and go!" He leads by example, his body moving with a precision that defies his rugged appearance. He dodges one blade, then another, always staying one step ahead.

Agent Gabriel and you mirror Wild Card's movements, your heart pounding furiously in your chest. The blades swing dangerously close, their swift arcs fueled by the oppressive heat from the lava below, making each breath a struggle. The searing heat licks at your boots, and the platform beneath you creaks ominously, threatening to give way at any moment.

As a blade swings perilously close to your head, you drop to your knees, sliding swiftly beneath it and springing back to your feet in one fluid motion. Gabriel has already reached the other side, her hand extended, urging you forward.

You collapse onto solid ground, gasping for breath as relief washes over you. The bridge behind you is reduced to smoldering ashes, and the blades retract into the ceiling with a silent, ominous finality, as though they had never been there.

"That was way too close," Agent Gabriel breathes heavily, wiping sweat from her brow.

"Too close," Wild Card replies, a grim smile tugging at his lips.

You nod, your eyes surveying the path ahead. Whatever challenges lie in wait, you're ready to face them together, your bond forged stronger through adversity. "Let's move," you say, rising and adjusting your gear. "We've got a mission to complete."

Suddenly, the ground beneath you gives way, and you all plummet into the searing lava below.

The End

Go Back to Page 229

We're Going to Die

The moon hangs high, its cold light illuminating the ancient ruins of Hillah. Enveloped by the whispers of history and the echoes of long-lost civilizations, you kneel on the sunbaked ground, your small frame concealed beneath the flowing fabric of your hijab. Weighed down by fear and uncertainty, you gaze up at the stars that blanket the desert sky.

Wild Card stands tall and defiant, his rugged features streaked with blood. His hands are bound behind his back, his muscles taut with the lingering strain of battle.

The Pharisee members encircle you with their weapons drawn, their faces obscured by keffiyeh that reflect hatred and fanaticism. Stepping forward from their midst, the leader—a figure shrouded in shadow—wears a cruel smile.

"You have violated sacred ground," he says, his voice dripping with disdain. "For that transgression, you will pay the ultimate price."

Your heart pounds in your chest as you raise your gaze to confront your captors. You feel a flicker of fear, but your resolve remains steadfast and defiant.

As the executioners raise their weapons, a tense silence descends over the ancient ruins. Time seems to freeze as you and Wild Card brace yourselves for the inevitable. The shots erupt in rapid succession, a jarring clash shattering the nocturnal stillness.

The End

Go Back to Page 104

The Final Curtain

Wild Card waits behind the heavy purple curtains guarding the Holy of Holies, the most sacred sanctuary. His heart pounds like a war drum, each beat synchronized with the flickering candlelight and his own ragged breath.

Across the chamber, a sinister silhouette, an agent of the Pharisees, glides through the dim light like a phantom toward the Ark. A guardian lies unconscious nearby, nothing more than an impediment to his mission.

He lifts the lid of the Ark, expecting to unveil its ancient treasures, only to be met with emptiness. Panic flashes across his face as he takes in the absence of the legendary artifacts: the golden jar of manna, the rod of Aaron, the tablets of the testimony, and the breastplate of Aaron. It's as if these sacred relics have been whisked away by the ghosts of antiquity.

In that tense moment of revelation, a faint rustle from behind the curtains breaks the eerie silence. The Pharisee operative whirls around, his senses on high alert as his hand instinctively reaches for his weapon.

In a flash of movement, he lunges toward the source of the sound, thrusting his blade through the heavy fabric. The steel slices through the air with a menacing hiss before striking its target, the sickening thud of the blade driving into Wild Card's heart.

Outside the building, Agent Gabriel desperately tries to reestablish contact through their comms channel. The airwaves, however, remain hauntingly silent, devoid of any response from her comrade. Meanwhile, AIDA, monitoring their vital signs, detects a critical blip—a sudden drop in life support readings for Agent Wild Card.

The Pharisee dials his superior, Heinrich Jager, to report the situation, and Jager's voice crackles through the comms. "What happened?"

"A monk who had to be dealt with," the Pharisee assassin says. "Nothing to worry about."

Jager reprimands him for failing to recover the crucial artifact. The golden jar of manna is the missing component of their biological weapon, the Pale Horse. Without it, the Pale Horse is effectively useless. Jager is convinced that the manna holds divine properties, capable of curing any affliction.

In the depths of darkness, beneath the ancient stones of Axum, the dance of deception has reached its chilling climax. As the echoes of betrayal vanish into the abyss, the secrets of the Ark remain shrouded in mystery, a stark reminder of the cost of venturing where mortals were never meant to tread.

The End

Go Back to Page 151

Stand Down, Agent Gabriel

You have a clear shot, but you need to wait and see if Desert Lotus can defuse the situation peacefully.

She remains composed, her eyes meeting the guard's with a blend of innocence and bewilderment. You hold your breath, poised to act if the situation deteriorates. The suspense is almost unbearable. She's so close to the objective, and the success of your mission hangs by a thread.

"What are you doing here?" he demands in a harsh, guttural Arabic, his eyes narrowing with suspicion.

"I've always been intrigued by Hillah, and I noticed your excavation work. I'm with the Museum of the Bible in the United States," Olivia says, her voice steady but laced with feigned curiosity.

"Do you always conduct your research at night?" His tone drips with skepticism, and his grip tightens on his rifle.

"No, of course not. I was merely out for a stroll and happened to notice the lighting towers. Are there any artifacts being uncovered? Which group are you affiliated with?" She strives to keep her composure, her heart undeniably pounding beneath her calm facade as you survey the scene.

The guard's expression darkens. He fixes Olivia with a cold glare. Without warning, he raises his rifle, the metal barrel glinting in the dim light. While his intentions remain unclear, the threat he poses is unmistakable.

The night seems to close in around you, the previously still air now thick with a palpable sense of dread. The shadows cast by the lighting towers stretch and twist, as if they too are alive and malevolent. You know what Olivia is feeling right now. Pulse pounding in her ears, blood rushing through her veins like a relentless drumbeat of impending doom.

The guard's finger hovers near the trigger, and for a heart-stopping moment, it feels as if time itself has frozen. The terror in Olivia's eyes reflects the grim realization that a single misstep could lead to bloodshed. The desert, once silent and still, now seems to resonate with the unspoken horrors buried beneath its sands.

Without warning, he fires three rapid shots, each hitting Desert Lotus center mass. She stumbles backward, her eyes wide with shock and disbelief as she draws her final breath.

The End

Go Back to Page 265

The Door to the Ark Chamber

The angel gestures and murmurs softly, "Clever girl." You remember the logic: someone from Beelzebub City always lies and points to Zion City, while someone from Zion City tells the truth and also points to Zion City.

He retrieves a large skeleton key and unlocks the door to your left. It creaks open to reveal a dimly lit corridor that leads to a vast chamber. At the room's center stands the Ark of the Covenant, its golden surface radiating a mystical glow in the gloom. You approach it with awe, the significance of your discovery overwhelming you like a tidal wave.

The silence is abruptly shattered by the echo of approaching footsteps. Henrich Jager, the ruthless mastermind behind the terrorist group known as The Pharisees, emerges from the shadows, flanked by his armed henchmen. "STEP ASIDE!" he bellows, his voice oozing with menace.

You have no choice but to obey. As they move to take the Ark, you shout, "Stop! You don't understand what you're dealing with!"

A gunshot cracks through the air, and an intense pain sears through your stomach. You collapse, your vision dimming as Wild Card and Gabriel rush to stem the bleeding. Shadows start to encroach upon your sight. "He... shot me," you gasp, your voice barely above a whisper.

Through the haze, you watch as two of Jager's men reach for the Ark. Their cries are abruptly silenced as they collapse, lifeless, their bodies hitting the ground with a nauseating thud. The remaining henchmen, unfazed, forcefully pry the lid off the Ark with crowbars. A chilling, swooshing sound fills the chamber, and a spectral form begins to materialize—a haunting embodiment of divine wrath.

A supernatural creature is unleashed, a swirling, radiant specter that inundates the chamber with blinding light and an otherworldly roar. One by one, the henchmen collapse, their faces twisted in abject terror. Their screams reverberate like the cries of the damned as they futilely fire at the apparition.

Maya, her face pale but resolute, hunches over you, Xavier's arms tightly encircling her. Neither dares to look at the terror unleashed from the Ark. As the roaring wind and fearsome blue lightning strikes die down, an unsettling silence settles over the room. Despite their usual composure, Maya and Xavier tremble, their control slipping in the wake of the divine onslaught.

After a few minutes, Maya rises and carefully opens the golden jar. She extracts a piece of the radiant manna cake—the panis vitae—from within, her movements deliberate and precise. She gently places it on your lips, her hands unwavering despite the palpable tension. As the manna makes contact, a soothing warmth spreads through your body. The searing pain eases, and you sense vitality surging back into your limbs.

As you open your eyes, you are greeted by the relieved faces of Wild Card and Gabriel. The healing warmth from the manna has fully restored you. The Ark, a miraculous salvation, now stands as both a blessing and a burden. Your mission is far from complete; you must safeguard the Ark, for its immense power must not fall into the wrong hands.

As you prepare to leave the chamber, you glance at the gaping hole in your top and the pristine skin beneath it, now miraculously healed. The transformation fills you with awe and a deep sense of wonder at the divine intervention that saved you.
Ms. Chamberlain inquires, "How can you describe the events that occurred when the Ark was opened if you were unconscious?"

You respond, "Maya and Xavier told me everything. They were as pale as ghosts and honestly looked completely terrified as they relayed the account. I just knew they were not lying!"

"Her statements have been consistent throughout, ma'am," the polygraph attendant reports, clearly astonished by the revelations.

Government agents arrived promptly, displaying their badges and swiftly taking command of the scene. They meticulously packed the artifacts into crates, ensuring their preservation. Outside you are guided to a nearby EMS tent for medical attention. As you look back, you see the cave entrance cordoned off with 'Do Not Cross' tape, while unmarked military personnel set up lighting towers. The site has transformed into what may be the most significant archaeological discovery of the century.

You insist on knowing the destination of the Ark, but your questions are initially met with silence. When you press further, one agent finally responds, "It's being transported to a secure facility, Ma'am."

Later, you uncover the grim reality: Big Pharma has exerted its influence to ensure that the panis vitae remains concealed. They argue that their industry, which generates $3.7 trillion annually and employs 7 million people globally, including 1.5 million in the United States, supports an additional 4.8 million jobs across the U.S. economy. The panis vitae's discovery is deemed a direct threat to the national security of the United States of America.

What became of the Ark? The truth remains elusive. Perhaps it's stored alongside alien artifacts at Area 51 or concealed in a top-secret bunker beneath the Pentagon, entangled with other hidden secrets like the truth about the JFK assassination. The answer is anyone's guess.

The next thing you knew, you found yourself in CIA custody.

Mr. Atkins handed a document to Ms. Chamberlain, the ashtray beside him overflowing with cigarette butts, a stark reminder of the long hours he had spent. She set the document down in front of you.

"This is a non-disclosure agreement. You are forbidden from discussing this matter with anyone, under any circumstances. It is classified as top-secret DS-9. We will be monitoring your communications closely. Should this information be leaked, you and anyone you share it with will be considered enemies of the State, and your family will suffer the same fate."

You sign the document noting that everything about the angel and the ark specter has been redacted. A side notation reads: 'Suspected hypercapnia and high black mold concentrations.' Your thoughts are racing, and you await their next move. After hours of solitude, shackled in the interrogation room, you are eventually given back your clothes and have the handcuffs removed. You are then flown to a concealed hangar at Andrews Air Force Base in DC and released.

Back at home, you attempt to resume your normal routines, but the absence of your friend Benji—declared KIA and missing from work—serves as a constant reminder of the ordeal you endured. Weeks later, while sorting through your belongings, you discover an earpiece. As you insert it, ADA's familiar voice crackles to life, filling your ear.

"Desert Lotus, our work is far from over. There's a new threat in China. Can we count on you for this next mission?"

The End

Maybe We Should Smash It!

You stand before the artifact, its ancient carvings whispering of hidden mysteries. Hebrew and Aramaic symbols seem to dance across its surface, sparking your curiosity. This box, believed to date back to the sixth century, harbors secrets that have eluded scholars and adventurers for centuries.

Hours stretch into days as you examine every inch of the intricate puzzle, your determination unwavering. Yet despite your best efforts, the box remains stubbornly closed, its secrets tantalizingly out of reach.

Frustration eats away at your resolve, your patience dwindling with each failed attempt. Benji, despite his best efforts, hasn't made any headway either. Finally, consumed by desperation, you make a fateful decision. With a heavy heart, you raise the artifact into the air.

"No, Liv, don't do it! It's irreplaceable!" Benji shouts, his voice filled with desperation.

But it's too late. With a decisive swing, you smash the artifact down onto the examination table, splintering it into pieces.

A blinding light erupts from the point of impact, flooding the room with searing brilliance. An otherworldly sound reverberates through the space, as if echoing from some ancient abyss. Wisps of smoke snake through the air, twisting and writhing like dark, spectral serpents.

You and Benji stand paralyzed with terror as the room is engulfed by an unearthly presence. The air thickens, pressing down on you with a suffocating, malevolent weight. Then, with a deafening roar, the box and its contents disintegrate into a cloud of ash before your stunned eyes.

You and Benji collapse to the ground, your bodies convulsing with excruciating pain. Surveillance cameras capture your final harrowing moments, documenting the horror that overwhelms you both.

Alone in the room, the spectral presence remains, an eerie witness to your tragic end. As the dust settles, you and Benji lie motionless, eyes wide open. Your hair has turned ghostly white, your eyes covered with thick cataracts. Your skin, once vibrant and alive, withers and ages rapidly, as though the very essence of time itself has claimed you both.

The cursed relic has claimed its victims, its dark power unleashed upon those who dared to unravel its ancient secrets. As the shadows envelop you, the world trembles at the dreadful cost of your curiosity.

The End

Go Back to Page 78

I'm Not That Kind of Girl

Olivia Davenport

> I'm sorry Michael. I don't know what you're involved in, but I work in a museum restoring artifacts. I'm not a secret agent or anything like that.

> I understand Liv. I know things are complicated right now. I hope we can meet again under better circumstances.

Unknown number
(Michael Smith)

You're expecting a call, but as a week passes without any word from Michael, a growing sense of unease takes hold. One evening, while heading home, you catch a glimpse of two men in black-and-white keffiyehs potentially trailing you. You try to dismiss it as paranoia, but the unsettling feeling persists.

As you park in front of your cozy two-story walk-up, you notice the same car driving by once more. A shiver runs down your spine and a creeping sense of anxiety sets in. Fumbling with your keys, you're overcome by the pressing need to get inside and lock the door behind you.

On the doorstep, you notice an unmarked package wrapped in brown paper. You hesitate, weighing the risk, but ultimately decide to bring it inside. After setting down the package and your purse, you lock all three dead bolts and secure the chain, then lean against the door, sliding down to sit on the floor as your heart races with dread in your chest.

You let out a weary sigh. You need a glass of wine. After taking a few minutes to compose yourself, you head to the kitchen for your usual evening respite. But before you do, you decide to open the package, carefully using a letter opener to slit the paper. As you peel it back, a faint phone starts ringing from within. It's the last sound you'll ever hear.

The End

Go Back to Page 293

Gurkha CIV Infiltration Tactics

You and your team disembark from Mother, blending into the dusky evening shadows as you set out. Your destination is Mount Nebo, thirty-seven kilometers away, where ancient legends speak of the Ark's hidden resting place. The drive is fraught with tension, each of you lost in your thoughts, the gravity of your mission pressing down on our shoulders.

As you reach the base of Mount Nebo, the landscape bathed in the golden hues of the setting sun, you activate AIDA's app on your forearm-mounted iPhone XX.

"AIDA, scan for the karst line."

"Scanning," AIDA says. Moments later she identifies a narrow geological fissure leading to an underground cave entrance, concealed two meters below the surface.

You wait until nightfall, the darkness providing ideal cover. Shovels in hand, you start digging. The soil yields and soon you reveal the entrance. The narrow shaft descends into a long corridor adorned with ghostly stalactites, their forms illuminated by the dim glow of your headlamps.

Soon you reach an impassable drop-off and peer into the abyss below. Wild Card tosses a glow stick into the void. The faint green light flickers through the air, then stops, revealing the distant floor. "Looks like a fifty-foot drop," he says.

You anchor your ropes and rappel down, your descent slow and deliberate. Having never rappelled before only intensifies your fear and excitement.

As your feet touch the floor of the antechamber, you are filled with awe. Before you stand two impressive doors, and between them sits an elderly gentleman on an antique wooden chair. He's wearing a partially soiled white short-sleeve shirt with a khaki vest and faded, loose khaki trousers. His hair and full beard have mostly turned white with age, and his skin appears weathered and slightly tanned, as if he's spent much of his life working outdoors doing manual labor. He sits stoically. Rising from behind him are a pair of white-feathered wings that look remarkably real.

With a raspy voice, he speaks: "I am the messenger. In my master's house, there are many doors. Only the one with the complete suit of armor may enter."

You watch as Maya unclips the clasps on her twin Glocks. Placing a hand on her shoulder, you offer a reassuring touch to steady her.

"What is he doing?" the messenger asks, gesturing to Xavier.

Xavier slowly slipped to the messenger's left side and is trying to inspect his wings.

"Xavier, what are you doing?" you ask.

I think those are real," Xavier says in a hushed tone, as if his inner voice slipped out in amazement.

"Let's start over. I'm Olivia, this is Maya, and that's Xavier. What's your name?"

"Why do you ask my name? For it is a wonderful one. Please do not do that. There is only one you should worship."

Xavier begins bowing as a sign of respect. This makes sense, given that he was an altar boy at St. Michael's Church back in the day. However, the messenger is not amused by it.

We're hoping to find the lost Ark of the Covenant to secure the panis vitae and save the world from a terrible virus. Can you help us?"

The angel replies, "Did you bring the complete suit of armor?"

What armor? I don't understand. And if you're an angel, why do you look older? I thought angels never aged."

"I took this form because I thought it would be acceptable to you. This was the form of one of the last remaining Levites who brought the Ark here—minus the wings and clothing, of course. Did you bring the complete suit of armor?"

"We don't have any armor, but we are armed. Can we speed this up?" Maya says. "Just tell us which way leads to the Ark."

Ah, I see now. You did bring the armor."

"Wait, what?" you say.

"Maya Avraham, I see you brought the belt of honesty and the breastplate of righteousness." He stands and begins inspecting Xavier. "And I see that Mr. Washington has brought the large shield of faith and the helm of salvation. And you, Ms. Davenport, have feet protected with the readiness to declare peace, and... the sword of the Spirit. I wasn't expecting a composite set of armor. Very well."

He informs you that you may ask only one question to determine which door he will unlock. One door leads to the path of righteousness and the Ark: the other to Hades, a realm of torment and despair.

He presents a riddle: You find yourself at a fork in the road, one path leads to the City of Beelzebub, where everyone always lies, and the other leads to the City of Zion, where the truth is always told. A guardian stands at the fork, residing in one of these cities, but you do not know which.

What question could you ask the guardian to find out which road leads to the City of Zion? From these sparce clues you would need to determine only one question to solve the conundrum.

Maya and Xavier turned their expectant gazes toward you. "I've got this!" You declared, your mind racing to solve the age-old logic puzzle.

If you want to ask: "Which way should we go?"
turn to page 207.

If you want to ask: "Which path leads to where you live?"
turn to page 216.

 **Bookmark Here**

It's Too Dangerous...

I can't join a secretive underground network driven by a god complex! your inner voice cries. You place your hands on Michael's shoulders, trying your hardest to convey empathy for his situation.

"Michael, you need help. You're not yourself." As you speak, you quietly dial 911 on your cell phone, striving to keep your voice steady and reassuring.

"You're not listening, Olivia. We don't have time for this!" he shouts.

"I understand, Michael. I want to acknowledge your feelings. Mental illness is no longer stigmatized. Paranoia—believing people are out to get you—is a common experience." The photographs and dossier were compelling, but they could have easily been manipulated with Photoshop.

Suddenly red-and-white flashing lights reflect against the café's front windows. You stand and move toward the entrance, prepared to introduce Michael. Two MPD officers step out of the vehicle, one of them speaking into a microphone mounted on his shoulder. "Dispatch, this is Eight Lincoln Thirty. We're code 10-23. We'll assess the situation and provide an update."

"10-4, Eight Lincoln Thirty," a woman's voice crackled through the speaker.

"Are you the one who made the call?" one of the officers asks you, holding out a small pad and pen.

"Yes, I'm Olivia Davenport. My friend Michael Smith is having a mental health crisis." A small crowd of onlookers begins to gather around you.

"Where is he now, ma'am?" the other officer asks.

You glance back at the spot where you and Michael were seated, but he's nowhere to be seen. "He was just here… He was right here! He's about 5'7", with sandy brown hair and blue eyes, and he weighs around 185 pounds. He was wearing a dark blue suit and carrying a silver briefcase," you tell them, feeling a pang of embarrassment for calling the police.

At that moment, EMTs wheel in a stretcher. "Where is the patient?" one of them asks.

The cops ask you a few more questions while trying not to let you catch them rolling their eyes and sighing at the paperwork they'll have to do later. They radio to have a few cars monitor the area for Michael. The EMTs turn off ambulance's lights and siren and depart as quickly as they came.

Six months later, your smartphone blares with an alert. Emergency ALERT. The CDC is now recommending all citizens shelter in place. You glance at the television, where the same message is being broadcast. News outlets are urging everyone to stay indoors due to a mysterious virus that is sweeping the globe. Dubbed "the zombie virus," it has a nearly 100% mortality rate, and patients' eyes are reported to turn fluorescent yellow before they hemorrhage and die. Two hundred and fifty million Americans are dead, and a reporter on WXYM claims that the CDC in Atlanta is powerless to stop it.

Your stomach twists into knots. Could this be the Pale Horse virus Michael warned you about? Was he telling the truth? Were you wrong?

The End

Go Back to Page 30

Decrypting the Qurman Cipher Wheel

The soft hum of the computers fills the dim room as you gaze at the intricate patterns on the brass cipher wheel. Each symbol seems to taunt you, challenging you to uncover its secrets. Meanwhile, AIDA sifts through pages of historical data at lightning speed.

"We're so close, Olivia," she says, breaking the silence. You carefully try various sequences on a 3D model that Xavier was able extrapolate using photogrammetry and scans before he left. AIDA has concluded that the cipher wheel contains a parchment document.

You nod, your fingers racing across the keyboard as you input another sequence of numbers. The screen flickers with each keystroke, revealing a dizzying array of symbols and codes, the solution remaining elusive.

Hours blend into days as you immerse yourself in the ancient artifact, every failed attempt leading to frustration that gnaws at your resolve.

"It's like trying to solve a puzzle without having the key…" you mutter.

Then a flicker of movement catches your eye. You lean in closer, examining the patterns etched into the cipher wheel.

It hits you like a bolt of lightning.

"The key!" you say, your heart racing with excitement.

Fueled by renewed determination, you start cross-referencing the symbols on the cipher wheel with the historical texts AIDA has compiled. Then, like pieces of a puzzle falling into place, everything clicks.

"The Fibonacci sequence!" you say. "It's the key to cracking the cipher!"

With trembling hands, you input the sequence of numbers into the computer, each keystroke bringing you closer to the truth. Then the 3D mechanism disengages with a soft click, and the computer screen flashes to life in green analog font:

> **Cipher Diagnostics – Successful Result**

You grab the cipher wheel and input the sequence frantically but carefully—for Benji. One end of the cipher wheel tube slides open, revealing a delicate sixth-century parchment map nestled inside.

Your heart races as you gently unfurl the ancient document, scanning its faded markings. It's a detailed map of Jerusalem, adorned with cryptic symbols.

"What does it mean?" you whisper.

AIDA has analyzed the map at lightning speed, processing the information within seconds. "It's a clue," she says, her voice brimming with excitement. "A clue that points to the Ark of the Testimony."

Your breath catches at the mention of the legendary artifact. The Ark is said to possess immense power capable of changing the course of history. Now it seems you're on the verge of discovering its location. Your mind races with the possibilities and the weight of what lies ahead. With this map, you could unveil the truth buried beneath the sands of time and reshape the course of history.

Yet amid the excitement coursing through your veins, a reverence settles over you. You understand that great power comes with immense responsibility, and these secrets are not yours alone to wield.

Thus, with the weight of centuries on your shoulders, you vow to tread forward carefully and honor the past while unraveling its mysteries. In the heart of the desert, amidst the ruins of ancient civilizations, lies the key to humanity's greatest enigma- the Ark. It is now your responsibility to unlock its secrets and ensure they're preserved for generations to come.

Yet the thrill of your discovery is tempered by a growing unease when you glance at the empty desk beside you. Your team has already lost a member in the quest for the truth, Benji, a close friend and intern, leaving behind a primal storm of grief.

You are not alone in seeking the Ark. Dark forces lurk in the shadows, eager to seize its power for their own sinister ends.

The fate of the world hangs in the balance, and you are its last line of defense.

You refocus on the map.

"Our journey is just beginning, AIDA," you say, your voice steady even though a tremor of uncertainty grips you. "Together, we'll find the Ark and save the world!"

Xavier's eyes light up with excitement. "Do you know what was kept in the Ark of the Covenant, Olivia? The breastplate of Aaron! We're going to be rich!"

Maya adds, "The Ark also contained the golden jar of manna, Aaron's rod that budded, and the tablets of the Ten Commandments mentioned in the Bible."

"AIDA, overlay the map's topography with modern maps to pinpoint where the Ark might be found today," Xavier says.

"Yes, of course, Agent Wild Card," AIDA says. "Please draw your attention to this area located on Mount Moriah in Jerusalem. According to the internet, King Solomon began construction of the temple around the four hundred and eightieth year after the Israelites were led out of Egypt by their God Jehovah.

"Construction began in the fourth year of Solomon's reign, during the Hebrew calendar month of Ziv, and the temple was completed in the eighth month of his eleventh year. The project took nearly seven years. It is speculated that the Ark was kept on the Temple Mount (also known as Haram al-Sharif) until its mysterious disappearance. Today, the Temple Mount is home to the Dome of the Rock, an important Islamic holy site, and the local Muslim community prohibits excavation of the area.

"Gear up, team," AIDA continues, "we're heading to Israel!"

When you and your team arrive, the ancient streets of Jerusalem shimmer under the relentless desert sun, casting long shadows across the timeworn stone walls. At the head of your small team, you navigate through the bustling crowds, your senses on high alert. Your mission is clear: infiltrate the Temple Mount and uncover the secrets hidden within its ancient confines.

As you approach the heavily guarded site, tension crackles in the air like static electricity. The IDF and Jerusalem Waqf guards patrol with unwavering vigilance, their sharp eyes scanning the crowd for any sign of trouble. Trouble may be your middle name, but with nerves of steel and a singular focus on your goal, you press forward, your footsteps tapping against the ancient cobblestones. Disguised as awestruck tourists fascinated by the holy site, you move ahead.

Guided by AIDA, you navigate the ancient passages of the underground caves, your senses heightened and your movements precise. Each step draws you closer to your objective, but also deeper into the heart of danger.

At last you reach your destination: a hidden recess in a wall nestled within the depths of the underground tunnels, its shape a perfect cube.

If you want to use a similarly shaped brick to fill the recess, **turn to page 348.**

If you want to use the artifact your team acquired in Lebanon, **turn to page 279.**

 **Bookmark Here**

Look What I Found

Moving with pulse-pounding stealth, you slip through the shadows, entering a structure on the southern side of the site. You evade all the guards and workers, positioning yourself for a better vantage point on the artifact. Here, you feel secure from detection—at least for now.

Your senses are on high alert, each sound magnified in the oppressive darkness, when you intercept a satellite call between Ziad Alhussan and Heinrich Jager. Alhussan reports that they've tested the Pale Horse in Zaire with the anticipated results and confirms that all the dig sites are progressing on schedule.

AIDA isolates and records the satellite call. "Wild Card, can you secure the artifact or at least scan it?"

"Affirmative," you say.

When the area is secure, you carefully descend from your hiding place among the towering stacks of wooden crates. With caution, you approach the artifact. It's a small wooden cube, unexpectedly light, weighing only a few pounds. Intricate, enigmatic symbols are carved into its surface, suggesting its mysterious origins.

Suddenly, at least a dozen armed hostiles storm into the room, their AK-47s aimed at you from every angle. They quickly disarm you and bind your hands behind your back.

The remaining attackers fire their weapons into the air, their shouts of triumph echoing through the room. One of them swings the butt of his rifle, striking you in the forehead. The impact sends a jolt of pain and disorientation through you before darkness overtakes you.

You regain consciousness in a murky room, slumped in a wooden chair with your hands bound behind you by coarse, biting ropes. Your feet are submerged in a corroded bucket half-filled with icy water. Your night-vision goggles and boot knife have been taken, your bag confiscated, and your earpiece is missing, likely lost in the chaos. As you struggle to fully awaken, you catch sight of a man exiting the room.

He returns minutes later, pushing a cart stacked with several car batteries haphazardly wired together, their jumble of connections a chaotic mess. Jumper cables attached to sponges dangle from the cart. His face is set with a sinister smirk, his eyes reflecting a cold determination to extract whatever information from you that he can. Alhussan strides into the room, flanked by two men who exude authority. He glowers at you. "Why hasn't this started yet? Ajal! Ajal!"

The menacing figure dips the sponges into the bucket where your feet are submerged and turns a dial on the apparatus, initiating a low, ominous whirring that fills the room. He presses one sponge against your thigh, the water beading and trickling off your tactical suit. His malevolent gaze meets yours as he gingerly touches the other sponge to your shoulder. A wave of searing nerve pain shoots through your body, causing you to cry out involuntarily, your jaw clenching in response. But the sponge lingers on your shoulder, the agony stretching endlessly.

As he withdraws the sponge, your body collapses into a defeated slump in the chair, exhaustion washing over you. The microphone cap embedded in your molar must have been dislodged when you clenched your teeth against the surge of electricity. You spit it out onto the sand in front of you, relieved to avoid choking on the small, vital piece.

But he isn't done. With a cruel twist of the dial, he increases the amperage and reapplies the sponges. The excruciating pain surges through every cell and nerve ending once more. Your jaw clamps shut and you let out a strained groan through gritted teeth as your body convulses in the chair.

This time, the water bucket is knocked over, and darkness engulfs you as you lose consciousness.

When you regain awareness, the passage of time is a blur. They inject you with adrenaline, jolting you awake. You're immediately assaulted by the agonizing throb of every muscle.

"You know, this place isn't exactly sanitary," you muse, attempting to maintain some semblance of composure.

A burly Iraqi man, his face obscured by a keffiyeh, enters the room. You can't escape the overpowering stench of his unkempt body. He approaches with grim determination, intent on extracting answers from you. Each of his crushing blows sends jolts of intense pressure through your body, though the pain itself is now oddly subdued. You spit out a mouthful of blood onto the sand surrounding you, enduring the onslaught until his strength wanes. He exits the room with a foreboding promise to return as blood drips from your brow.

Hours blend into days, marked only by sporadic sips of water and scraps of torn bread. You feel every bruise, every ache, your body parched and exhaustion settling in. The ropes binding your wrists have constricted your blood flow, leaving your hands tingling with numbness.

Alhussan storms into the room again, his face a mask of irritation, demanding an update on your interrogation.

The one designated to beat you replies in frustration, "Edha kan yaarof ai shaya bolkan qud akhbarna alan. linh ytuhodte. jeageb an naqtalah winenthi minh."

Translation: "If he knew anything, he would have told us by now. He's not going to talk. We should just kill him and be done with it!"

Alhussan's fury erupts as he upends a small table cluttered with horrifying torture instruments. His eyes burn with rage as he glares at his subordinate before storming out of the room.

Several hours later, the door creaks open once more. You hear the uneven footsteps of another prisoner being dragged in. They position him in a chair directly behind yours, his hands similarly bound behind him. In the oppressive darkness, you strain to communicate with the new arrival.

"Name's Wild Card. You?"

A brief pause stretches before a woman's voice finally answers, "Desert Lotus."

The name rings a bell, but you can't recall why. Then it clicks. Desert Lotus was the code name for the analyst Michael Smith revealed to you in the dossier aboard Mother. You were hoping for backup, but instead, you've got an analyst.

In the darkness, you exchange whispered words, feeling a flicker of hope despite your dire circumstances. With your combined intellect and resilience, you might just find a way to escape your captors and reach the exfil point.

A few hours later, you hear the clatter of your captors entering the room once more. They slice through the ropes binding your ankles and force you to your feet.

One of them barks in Arabic, "Get up! Today's not your lucky day."

He seizes you by the neck and propels you out of the room, a gun pressing into your back. You hear the girl being dragged along behind you.

"Where are we going? Where are you taking us?" you ask, your voice trembling with inescapable fear.

"We're taking you to die!" one of them retorts.

They lead you to a dark area outside and force you to face them. "Do you have any last requests?" one of them demands.

You request a cigarette, and one of them strides over and shoves it into your mouth.

Turn to page 196.

Move Over, Harry Houdini

You enter the stall with utmost caution, acutely aware of the guard waiting just outside. Your heart races. As you sit on the toilet, you turn your attention to the handcuffs before you. They're the standard double-lock design, presenting a significant challenge.

With urgent focus, you unscrew the pen's cap, your fingers trembling as you extract the nearly empty metal tube. There's no room for error. You flatten the tube and insert it into the keyhole, your breath hitching in your throat.

The guard's footsteps echo outside, a relentless reminder of the imminent danger. With each twist and turn of the makeshift key, the tension mounts. The key has to be turned counterclockwise first to disengage the double-lock bar.

As you apply pressure to the first lock bar, adrenaline surges through you. Every movement must be precise. With bated breath, you turn the makeshift key clockwise, the ratchet teeth clicking into place.

Finally, with a silent prayer, the cuffs on your wrists spring open, their metallic clack masked by the guard's footsteps outside.

With newfound freedom, you act swiftly, forcing open the small window with safety glass, adrenaline pumping through your veins as you climb out onto the building's ledge.

"Mr. Washington, are you almost finished? Wrap it up!" the guard demands.

You're precariously suspended thirty feet in the air, your slippered feet barely balanced on a narrow strip of brick. As the guard enters the restroom, the old decorative brick beneath you starts to crumble. With nothing to use as a hold, you're soon free-falling toward the concrete termination point at the end of this fall.

The End

Go Back to Page 37

The Mask of Tutankhamun

In 2024, you acquire a map from a grave robber in Thebes, leading to an uncharted area in the Valley of the Kings. The relentless sun scorches the arid landscape, creating an inferior mirage over the ancient tombs. Following the map's directions, you venture deep into the valley under the cover of night. Legends say the remains of Egypt's greatest pharaohs are hidden here, their tombs protected by ancient traps and secrets lost to time.

Guided by the map, you discover a concealed chamber deep within the valley. With trembling hands, you sweep away centuries of dust, revealing the entrance to a long-lost crypt. Holding your breath, you step into the darkness, wary of the dangers that might lie in wait. As you venture forward further, you're met with a breathtaking sight—a magnificent golden mask perched upon a stone pedestal at the heart of the cavern.

For a moment, you stand spellbound, your gaze fixed on the ancient artifact before you. It's the second golden mask of Tutankhamun, a twin to the one that's mesmerized the world for generations.

As you reach out to seize the mask, the ground beneath you trembles, signaling the presence of ancient traps lying in wait. With lightning-fast reflexes, you spring to the side, narrowly evading the deadly arrows that shoot from the walls, their razor-sharp tips glinting in the dull light.

Heart pounding, you race against time, skillfully navigating the treacherous maze of traps. When you finally emerge into the blinding sunlight, you clutch the golden mask to your chest.

Your representative delivers the mask to the Egyptian Museum in Cairo, where he strikes a deal with the curator to sell it. The true significance of your discovery is deemed too valuable to reveal, as it might diminish the worth of the original mask of Tutankhamun on display.

Actually, that's not when you met Michael. It was a different time. Ms. Chamberlain is displeased, and soon you find yourself locked in a cell. You suspect they will obtain what they need from one of the others, as you never see them again. Eventually, you're sent to Cuba to spend the rest of your life as prisoner 1678914.

The End

Go Back to Page 56

You Won't Find This on YouTube

Within two weeks to a month, death claims those infected. Individuals with compromised immune systems succumb even more quickly. The village, once vibrant and alive, transforms into a grim tableau of death, the air heavy with the stench of decay and the haunting echoes of suffering. The Pale Horse weapon proves devastatingly effective, leaving only silence and desolation in its wake.

The bodies are piled into a deep, hastily dug pit and sealed in black cadaver bags. The Pharisees douse the bodies in gasoline and set the macabre pyre ablaze. The wailing of mothers, fathers, sons, and daughters pierce the air day and night, each anguished cry seeping into the atmosphere, creating an insidious grief that clings to the village like a persistent curse.

With chilling precision, they evacuate the remaining Pharisee operatives before deploying two 750-pound fuel-air bombs to secure the most devastating biological weapon the world has ever known. Any contact with body fluids guarantees infection.

The video is horrifyingly compelling, and as the silence lifts, the hangar erupts with urgent discussions and strategies. It's evident that the threat has to be contained and eradicated immediately. If this virus escapes, it'll pose an existential threat to humanity. You have to end this once and for all—for the world and for Shira.

Shortly afterward, you're back aboard Mother with a new mission. AIDA has identified you as having the highest probability of success for infiltrating a warehouse in the rebuilt Port of Beirut. Your objective is to acquire a sixth-century puzzle box that the Pharisees unearthed at Hillah.

The plan seems straightforward: a high-altitude low-opening (HALO) jump to infiltrate the facility and retrieve the artifact. For exfiltration, you have two options. The first, code-named Coyote, involves rendezvousing with Seal Team Six and then boarding a Mark 8 submersible, which will take you to the USS North Carolina, a Virginia-class nuclear submarine waiting for you two hundred meters off the coast.

The second option, code-named Road Runner, is for situations where you're being pursued. In this scenario, you'll deploy a self-inflating balloon connected to a 500-foot steel cable, part of the Skyhook system (the Fulton surface-to-air recovery system). Mother will swoop in, snag the cable, and winch you back on board. You've heard of Skyhook before but you've never actually seen it in action.

You prepare your gear, don your tactical suit, and secure your helmet, determined never to let the bad guys get away with it—not again. Everywhere you go, the memory of your lost sister persists, urging you on with a clear sense of purpose. You're not naïve to the evils of this world, nor are you afraid to venture into the darkness to confront them.

Next you inspect the parachute gear. A flight crew member hands you a chute, ready for deployment. You scrutinize it, ensuring there are no signs of wear or damage.

If you want to use the chute they gave you, **turn to page 31.**

If you want to insist on packing your own chute, **turn to page 322.**

 **Bookmark Here**

I Want to Come In

In preparation for your upcoming meeting with the CIA, you dive into the murky depths of the dark web to acquire essential gear. The process is anything but straightforward, especially in Azerbaijan. After a few tense days, you secure a silenced Glock-19, a karambit, and an Mk13 sniper rifle, as well as a few critical communication devices.

Once everything is in place, it's time to make the critical call.

"Central Intelligence Agency, how may I direct your call?" the operator asks.

"I need to speak with David Pernas. Inform him that Aphrodite is calling."

"Please hold..."

A moment later, the operator returns. "David is unavailable. Is there a number where he can reach you?"

"Yes, please have him call me at +994-12-565-48-48, room 2015. Thank you."

"Have a wonderful day, ma'am."

After hanging up, you wire the hotel phone to a burner, pull the curtains open as wide as they go, and gather your gear. Thirty minutes later, you check into an ideal room at the Four Seasons Baku, offering a perfect line of sight into your room at the Fairmont.

Using a diamond cutter, you cut a small hole in the windowpane, just large enough for your purpose. You then rearrange the furniture to create a stable perch and position your Mk13 sniper rifle at the back of the room, ensuring everything is ready for what's to come.

Two hours later, the phone rings. It's David.

"Aphrodite. Someone's come back from the dead. Did you kill Abelman?"

"I didn't have to. The IRGC took care of it after he tried to kill me. He must not have realized I'd removed the firing pin from his Colt. Funny how fast he confessed to the kill order. I made a neat little audio recording—he sounds a bit shaky, but you can clearly tell it's him. Anyway, I've taken precautions to keep Operation Cleopatra hidden. Unless, of course, something happens to me."

"We would never do anything like that, Aphrodite."

As David speaks, several armed men with silenced handguns storm into the room at the Fairmont, inspecting the phone connected to the burner. One of them, clearly the leader, speaks into a microphone sewn into his sleeve.

"As you can see, I'm not foolish enough to be waiting for them at the Fairmont. Tell your man to sit on the bed and let him know the little red dot on his chest isn't from a laser pointer. Have them all holster their weapons."

"Let's play nice, David. You made certain commitments to me, and I expect you to honor them."

"How do I know you even have a recording?"

"Well, you'll just have to trust me, I suppose."

"What do you want?"

"I want to be flown to the US, granted US citizenship and a passport, and given a house in Los Angeles."

"And for that, we get the recording?"

"In exchange for that, nobody will ever hear a word about Operation Cleopatra. I'll keep the recording to ensure you stay honest. Do we have a deal?"

"Fine. Be at the airport in Baku tonight at 2300 hours. In hangar B7, a G900 will be fueled and ready to take you to Los Angeles. A car will pick you up, Ms. Avraham, and drive you to a hotel where we will arrange for a set of keys to be delivered for a home in Beverly Hills. On the counter, you'll find your citizenship document and passport. That will conclude our business."

"That sounds perfect, David. I'm glad we could reach an agreement. If you need me in the future, just give me a call. I'll be at the airport. Ask your team to behave, won't you? I wouldn't want anyone to get hurt."

You adjust to your new life in Los Angeles with surprising ease. The city's vibrant energy captivates you, and before long, you're enjoying its luxuries, picking up chic handbags on Rodeo Drive and marveling at the iconic Hollywood sign up close.

Your professional life takes an intriguing turn when you secure a position with Black River PMC. The role spans various covert missions and protective details for high-profile clients, which, due to a strict nondisclosure agreement, you cannot discuss. Despite the secrecy, the job offers steady, well-paying work and state-of-the-art equipment. It's the pinnacle of careers for a tier-one operator.

In 2033, while on assignment in Bolivia, you miss your exfiltration window. The PMC quickly arranges an alternative: catching a ride on a private jet departing from Peru. During this unplanned detour, you meet Michael Smith from the CIA for the first time. He's transporting Peruvian antiquities to the United States. As you fly back, you strike up a conversation, exchanging stories about your respective professions and backgrounds.

Upon landing in the US, you thank Michael for the lift and gather your gear. A PMC vehicle is waiting at the airport to take you back to the office for debriefing.

You never expect to hear from Michael again, but in early 2034, you receive an unexpected call. Michael is assembling an off-the-books team called the Ghost Operations Division. Curious about the name, you ask him why he chose GOD. He pulls a coin from his wallet and points to the inscription: IN GOD WE TRUST. "When no one else can help, people can count on us to get the job done."

Michael informs you that you're one of three tier-one operators who have been selected for an urgent mission. Your task is to protect an analyst named Olivia Davenport and lead the mission alongside a treasure hunter named Xavier Washington. Given that the Ghost Operations Division acronym is GOD, you choose the call sign Gabriel, after the archangel.

Everything is cleared through Black River, and soon you're preparing to return home to Israel. A new threat to the national security of both the United States and the world has emerged: a terrorist organization called the Pharisees, led by a figure known only as "the Prophet." His second-in-command is Ziad Alhussan, infamously known as the Butcher of Metula, a biological weapons expert and notorious assassin.

In 2029, Alhussan orchestrated a horrific attack on an Israeli settlement, resulting in the deaths of 1,750 Israelis. The assault began with an unusual missile intercepted by the Iron Dome. However, this missile carried no conventional explosive payload. Instead, it contained Bacillus anthracis, which released anthrax bacteria over the unsuspecting population. The disease devastated everyone—men, women, children, even animals.

The international community, led by the ICC in The Hague, condemned this act as a war crime and a blatant violation of the 1925 Geneva Protocol, the 1972 Biological Weapons Convention, and several other international humanitarian laws. At the time, prevailing wind gusts also caused the deaths of several hundred Lebanese civilians and Pharisee operatives.

The World Health Organization managed to contain the outbreak, but the incident confirmed the sinister and sadistic nature of the Pharisees' threat. It reminded you of why you became an operator: the tragic loss of your aunt and sister to a Palestinian suicide bomber when you were young. That loss has affected you deeply, and you carry it with you on every mission.

As you prepare for your current mission, the gravity of the situation sharpens your focus. The stakes are unimaginably high, but you're determined to confront evil with righteous discipline. Alhussan is number two on the FBI's Most Wanted Terrorists list, while the head of the organization, the Prophet, holds the number one spot.

If you want to make a quick visit to your family home in Petah Tiqvah before the mission, **turn to page 44.**

If you want to meet Michael Smith on the tarmac at Ben Gurion **turn to page 273.**

 **Bookmark Here**

The Long Goodnight

Michael's stories are always fascinating, but what you desperately need is a few hours of shut-eye. You head for your quarters, the anticipation of rest guiding your every step. But as you enter, you notice a folded flight suit and a pair of USA-embossed slippers waiting on a small table by your futuristic rack. A gift from the Ghost Operations Division.

You draw your Sig Sauer from its shoulder holster, release the magazine, and catch it with your other hand. With practiced precision, you remove the round from the chamber and reinsert it into the magazine before placing both the gun and magazine beside your clothes. After removing your boots, you crawl into your pod. Fully reclined, it's surprisingly comfortable, and you feel your body start to unwind.

Just as sleep begins to take hold, the unmistakable sound of gunfire erupts through the hangar. Your heart races as you grab your weapon and exit the pod. Moving silently, you clear each compartment of the plane, your nerves on high alert. But there's no one on board.

Suddenly a voice with a Hispanic accent barks orders outside the ramp. You inch forward to find a vantage point where you can observe without being detected. The crew is on their knees, still in their flight suits, with their hands bound behind their backs with zip ties. One of them has a deep gash on his forehead, a clear sign of a brutal pistol-whipping.

Twelve hooded gunmen in all-black attire brandish AR-15s, encircling the crew. The air is thick with tension as you catch fragments of their heated exchange. It appears there's a dispute over the cocaine Michael smuggled into the US, and the Mexican drug cartel is seeking to renegotiate the deal.

Adrenaline surges through you as you stealthily descend the ramp. You position yourself behind one of the cartel members, your gun aimed at him. In a steely voice, you demand they release the crew. The situation hangs by a thread.

But the cartel leader has other plans and callously shoots your human shield, as though the man is worthless. As he collapses to the floor, you realize you're standing there, gun in hand, clad only in your boxer shorts. They apprehend you, securing your arms behind your back and forcing you to kneel beside the rest of the crew.

Negotiations must have collapsed at some point, frustration boiling over as they ransack the hangar, searching for what they believe to be two hundred kilos of illicit narcotics worth twenty-four million dollars. What they don't realize is that the antiquities are crafted from claylike cocaine and are hidden in plain sight. Out of frustration they open fire on you and the crew.

The End

Go Back to Page 131

Free the Slider

In near-total darkness, Gabriel plummets through the silent void, a mere silhouette against the starry expanse. With steely resolve, she staves off panic, grappling with the tangled lines, her fingers deftly working over the fabric to untangle the snag. Time slips away like grains of sand in an hourglass. Amidst her struggle, she fails to notice her altimeter spinning erratically as the earth looms closer and closer at a terrifying speed. The wind whispers a deadly lullaby of calm, leading to a moment of stark clarity.

Gabriel realizes her efforts are in vain. The slider remains obstinately jammed, refusing to yield.

As she plummets below the 2,000-foot mark, where safety is no longer an option, Maya's fate is sealed. A "no-pull" is logged, marking the silent end of a woman who has repeatedly defied the odds. In the pitch-black night, her spirit soars one final time before being engulfed by the abyss below.

The End

Go Back to Page 321

Decoding the Files

You and Benji return to your room, ready to decrypt the Pharisees' secret messages. Splitting the files between you, you hand him some while keeping the rest for yourself.

After hours of silent frustration, Benji finally breaks the silence. "This is insane! I've tried everything. My decryption algorithm just isn't working." He removes his glasses, rubs his tired eyes, and lets out a weary sigh, stifling a yawn.

"Take a break, Benji. Get some sleep if you're tired." As he considers your words, an idea strikes you—a sudden epiphany. It's a long shot, but could this be just a simple substitution cipher? Would the Pharisees really use something so rudimentary?

"Sometimes the simplest solutions work best in a complex world," Benji muses.

A few minutes later, you exclaim, "I've cracked it!"

Benji springs up. "You solved it?!"

The two of you go over the decoded messages.

The Pharisees speak in Farsi, discussing the tightened security at the Hillah dig site. Guards are now rotated every four hours. One voice asks why there's so much commotion, and another says they believe they're close to discovering the khubz alhayaa —the panis vitae, or "bread of life." The phrase lingers in your mind, its meaning unclear.

Benji raises an eyebrow. "What's so special about a loaf of bread?"

You send your findings to AIDA, eager for her input. Her response is swift: your team should investigate the dig site at Hillah to gather intelligence, especially since it aligns with your existing plans.

A wave of satisfaction washes over you as you plant a light kiss on Benji's forehead. "Take that, NYU scholars! And Professor Alnaemi, who had the nerve to give you a B on your term paper!" Then it hits you. "You really should call your mom in New York, let her know you're okay."

If you want to call your mom in New York, **turn to page 331.**

Or…

Solve this simple substitution cipher. Use the letters and numbers you do know to fill in the other letters, and use the clues to add to it and figure out what page to turn to.

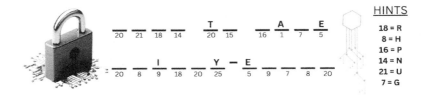

```
__ __ __ __     __T __      __ __A __ __E
20 21 18 14     20 15       16  1  7   5

__ __ __I __ __ __Y - __E __ __ __ __ __
20  8  9 18 20 25    5      9  7  8 20
```

HINTS
18 = R
8 = H
16 = P
14 = N
21 = U
7 = G

260

Recon in Iraq

AIDA informs you that you'll be traveling under the cover of darkness to Najaf, Iraq. From there, you'll undertake a seventy-eight-kilometer journey through hostile territory to Hillah, a route ominously dubbed the Triangle of Death. The trip will take approximately an hour, depending on traffic and checkpoints. Tactical body armor and weapons are essential. AIDA also notes that your passports and papers are stored in the lockbox in your quarters, and that Desert Lotus and Benji must be fitted with tactical throat mics and earpieces, followed by a thorough briefing on their use.

Olivia protests accompanying you into the field, despite Michael's assurance that her role will be limited to acting as an analyst. With Wild Card already deployed, you're short a person. You have eleven hours to reach Najaf, giving you ample time to equip Desert Lotus and Benji with their throat mics and bulletproof vests. After loading your gear into the Gurkha CIV, you drive off the ramp and into the Iraqi night.

The first thirty minutes of your drive take you through dark farmlands, AIDA's voice guiding you through your earpiece. The tension mounts as you approach a makeshift checkpoint. You instruct Olivia and Benji to stay calm and let you handle the negotiations, keeping your Glock-19 within easy reach in case things go south.

As you bring the vehicle to a halt, several members of the Iraqi Army come into view, armed with AK-47s. One soldier restrains a German shepherd on a tight leash, another uses a mirror to inspect the underside of the vehicle, and a third shines a large flashlight inside. The leader, a stern-looking man, approaches the CIV and asks in Arabic, "Where are you folks headed?"

You flash a coy smile. "I'm escorting these archaeologists to the Hillah dig site."

The officer eyes you, trying to mask his interest, and then requests your papers and passports. You hand over a small envelope containing thirty 50,000 Iraqi dinar, worth over $1,100 USD—almost a month's salary for an Iraqi officer. His demeanor shifts immediately, and he smiles and says, "Alright, you're clear to proceed. Enjoy your stay in Iraq." He waves you on and you continue your journey.

The darkness of the Iraqi night envelops you as you drive towards Hillah. The checkpoint encounter went smoothly, but a sense of foreboding lingers. This is just the beginning, and with each passing kilometer, the stakes grow higher and the shadows deepen. The mission ahead is fraught with danger, but you're prepared—or as prepared as one can be in a land where the unexpected is the only certainty.

Shortly after passing the checkpoint, you arrive at the secure, unsanctioned dig site at Hillah. You park the CIV about a quarter mile away, ensuring the vehicle is positioned in a relatively safe spot while remaining close enough for effective reconnaissance.

"Olivia, I'll be back," you say. "I need to find a vantage point for overwatch. You and Benji stay with the vehicle. If you need me, use your throat mics like I instructed. From now on, let's use our code names in case anyone is monitoring our communications. If anyone approaches, remember to act as though you're Americans on vacation."

With that decision made, you set out to find the perfect vantage point. Your silenced Glock-19s are securely holstered on your shoulders and your VKS sniper rifle is strapped to your back, the familiar weight both reassuring. The desert night is hauntingly quiet, the endless sand stretching beneath a sky dotted with stars.

After a brief hike, you discover a dune that provides an ideal view of the dig site. You shape the sand into a makeshift perch with your hands, striving to make it as comfortable as possible. Once settled, you engage your night-vision scope and scan the area, observing the movements of the Pharisee security patrols through the green-tinted lens.

"GOD, this is Gabriel. How copy?"

"We read you five-by-five. Can you provide a sitrep? Over."

"I've identified approximately twenty armed Pharisees and ten civilians. I'm still unable to determine their objective. I'll call out the targets, AIDA, and you mark them with the drone so we don't lose track."

"Affirmative."

One by one, you call out their positions while AIDA marks them, assigning each a designator. The scene below is tense. The guards move with purpose and the civilians work under the watchful eyes of their overseers.

"We need to send someone in to gather intelligence firsthand, you said. Didn't you say Wild Card was on-site AIDA?"

"Wild Card's transdermal transponder has gone dark. He missed his last check-in. Can you ascertain his whereabouts?" AIDA inquires.

"Not without resorting to wet work and leaving a trail of bodies."

"I can do it!" Olivia says.

"Desert Lotus are you sure?" you ask, concern evident in your voice.

"I've got this, Agent Gabriel. I'll sneak in and, if caught, claim I'm a lost tourist. Wearing a hijab should keep me under the radar, but I'll need to remove the tactical vest."

"Okay. Be careful. If you hit a roadblock, let me know, and I'll handle it. I'll keep my eye on you until you're inside. After that, AIDA will track your movements. See if you can find out what they're looking for. You've got this."

You watch as Olivia adjusts her attire, shifting from a semi-trained operative to an innocent tourist. Her confidence is inspiring, and as she begins her approach, you experience a surge of both pride and apprehension.

From your vantage point, you track her movements, prepared to provide cover if necessary. This mission is delicate, and a single misstep could escalate the situation. Still, Olivia is capable, and you trust her judgment. As she nears the site, the tension is palpable.

"Okay, Desert Lotus, I'll guide you through this," you say. "Continue on your current trajectory toward the site. You're doing great!"

"Thanks, Agent Gabriel. I hear voices ahead."

"Copy that. Can you make out what they're saying?"

"It sounds like they're torturing a prisoner. That's not a good sign," she whispers.

"Keep moving, there's an entryway just ahead."

Desert Lotus proceeds with her approach, her steps measured and deliberate. The night air is heavy with tension, every shadow concealing a potential threat. As she reaches the doorway, a guard appears. He lights a cigarette, the flare of the lighter casting a brief, flickering glow. For a moment he doesn't see her, but as he looks up, realization dawns upon him.

His gaze fixes on Desert Lotus, his posture becoming rigid with suspicion.

Your heart pounds as you watch from your vantage point, your finger poised on the trigger of the VKS. Time seems to slow, the silence pressing in all around you. One wrong move could blow her cover, escalating the mission into a deadly firefight.

If you want to take out the guard, **turn to page 57.**

If you want to wait and see what happens, **turn to page 214.**

 **Bookmark Here**

A Secret Passage

A surge of adrenaline courses through you as you prepare to clear the floor. Silently, you move through the monastery, opening doors with bated breath. Inside, you find monks sleeping, their faces serene and undisturbed by your presence. You leave them in peace and proceed to the main chamber.

The vast room exudes solemnity. Your gaze is drawn to the platform where monks deliver sermons. On the floor, you notice strange arched scratches, as if a massive object has been dragged across the stone. Yet no such object is in sight.

Nearby, a wall adorned with intricate designs and a large crucifix catches your eye. Beneath it, an Amharic inscription glimmers. AIDA's translation reads: Trust in our Lord and follow His way. You observe that the crucifix is securely fixed at the top, but the bottom displays signs of wear. Acting on instinct, you grasp the legs of Christ and pull. A deep rumbling echoes as a section of the wall swings open, revealing a hidden passageway with stone walls and flickering candles.

Gripping your tranquilizer gun, you descend into the passage. The sound of each step trembles through the narrow corridor. At the bottom of the stairs, a purple curtain hangs, adorned with a golden inscription above: Holy of Holies. Heart pounding, you draw back the curtain and enter a darkened chamber.

Suddenly, two monks dressed in white and wielding golden daggers spot you. Their faces are set with fanatical determination. The first monk lunges, his blade glinting in the candlelight. You evade his attack, but his follow-up thrust sends your tranquilizer gun skidding across the floor. Unarmed, you seize his arm and slam it against the wall until the dagger falls.

Before you can catch your breath, the second monk charges at you. He throws a wild punch, but you're prepared. You respond with a roundhouse kick, connecting with his chin. He stumbles backward, collapsing to the floor unconscious.

The first monk retrieves his dagger, now visibly enraged, and lunges to stab you. Time seems to slow as your training takes over. You surge forward, intercepting his knife arm with your forearms. Wrapping your arm around his, you pin his forearm against your body, securing his bicep with your free hand to gain leverage. Then you execute an arm-bar, pulling his head down while driving your knee up. The impact is solid. He drops the dagger and collapses.

Huffing for each breath, you stand among the fallen monks, the thrill and relief of victory surging through you.

With trepidation, you retrieve your tranquilizer gun and step into the rear chamber, its walls made of brick. The air is heavy with the scent of aged stone and faint candle smoke.

Another guardian monk emerges from the shadows, his eyes widening in surprise. Without hesitation, you shoot him with a tranquilizer dart. His eyes widen in shock before the potent sleeping agent takes effect, and he crumples to the ground.

And then you see it. The Ark of the Testimony, resplendent atop a slab of rock, rests on a luxurious red fabric trimmed with gold. The magnificent gold cherubs on its lid reach toward each other, their wings nearly touching. The Ark's intricate carvings and gold poles on either side are breathtaking. For a moment, you stand here, awestruck and breathless, blinking repeatedly, unable to believe your eyes.

Compelled by reckless and unbound curiosity, you reach out to touch it, disregarding the dire biblical warnings that death awaits those who dare lay their hands on it.

But there is no ominous sound, no spirits unleashed. No lightning bolts or dazzling lights. Nothing. Carefully, you push the lid aside and peer inside, your suspicion growing. The craftsmanship is flawless, but everything about it feels out of place. This artifact is not from the sixth century. Based on your observations, it dates back to the sixteenth century. The presence of a carved crucifix on one side only deepens your suspicion. The original Ark of the Testimony vanished long before Christ was born, and the concept of a crucifix would have been entirely unfamiliar to its creators. In fact, such a symbol might have been perceived as offensive, or even pagan to them.

While this Ark appears convincing at first glance, it's not the genuine artifact. Inside, it's empty, lacking the golden jar of manna, the budding rod of Aaron, the tablets, and the breastplate of Aaron.

Before you can fully process this revelation, you hear footsteps approaching. Quietly, you take cover, preparing to potentially ambush whoever enters.

A ruthless terrorist—one of the Pharisee henchmen, armed with a rifle—steps over the unconscious monk and investigates the Ark, clearly expecting to find something. As he leans over it, you approach from behind and grab him.

"What are you looking for? Why are you here?" you demand, your voice low and intense.

"Don't hurt me," he pleads. "I'm here for the panis vitae."

"The what?"

"The golden jar of manna! We need it. It cures any illness known to man. My boss wants it to develop a biological weapon. Without the cure, the virus is worthless. But with the panis vitae, we'll be rich."

"You mean this isn't about the Ark?"

"The Ark? What? No. It's about the golden jar of manna inside the Ark. Name your price and my boss will pay."

"You can't afford it," you say coldly, firing a tranquilizer dart into his neck.

He crumples to the ground as the full weight of your discovery begins to sink in. The chamber, once a place of ancient mystery, conceals secrets of a much-darker nature than you once thought.

"Did you get all that, AIDA?" you whisper.

"Affirmative, Wild Card. I suspected they might be targeting the Ark, but the golden jar of manna? Now it all makes sense—the virus tests, the dig sites. These locations were all suspected Ark resting spots. We need to find it first, whether it's an artifact of otherworldly origin or simply a priceless antiquity. Wrap it up before you're caught. Leave everything undisturbed. Agent Gabriel, provide overwatch and exfiltrate with Wild Card. Yohannes is waiting."

"Roger that, AIDA. Gabriel out," Maya says.

"I'm on my way out, Agent Gabriel," you say, heading toward the rendezvous point.

Just as Yohannes comes into view, gunfire erupts. The Ethiopian National Defense Force, alerted by the Pharisee operatives' sloppy entry, is determined to eliminate all intruders, including you.

You dive for cover as Yohannes shouts for you to hurry. Keeping low, you sprint toward the waiting vehicle. Safety seems within reach, but bullets shatter the illusion, striking the windshield and sides.

You race away, the engine roaring, tires screeching, and your adrenaline surging. Sirens blare and lights flash as roadblocks materialize out of nowhere.

But Yohannes skillfully maneuvers through the chaos, veering into a narrow alley barely wide enough for the car. You speed down the cramped passage, the brick walls tearing off the side mirrors.

Your heart pounds, knowing that capture—and likely death—await you if you fail.

In the tense silence that follows, it seems you've shaken your pursuers. You're now just hours away from rendezvousing with Mother. AIDA's voice crackles through the comms, guiding you the rest of the way with satellite directions to avoid any remaining threats.

"Turn left at the next junction and drive straight for two kilometers," she instructs. Yohannes nods, steering around the corner.

"Stay sharp, Wild Card. We're not out of the woods yet," Maya retorts.

The road ahead is dark and foreboding, the city's mazelike streets twisting around you at every turn. Your eyes dart to the rearview mirror, half expecting another roadblock to materialize as Yohannes maneuvers you through tight spots and sudden obstacles. You pass shuttered shops and sleeping neighborhoods, the wail of distant sirens gradually fading into the night. Tension coils within the car, every second stretching out painfully, every shadow a lurking threat.

"Take the next right, then an immediate left," AIDA's says.

Yohannes follows AIDA's instructions to the letter, until the outskirts of the city finally emerge, the road opening up before you. The cool night breeze rushes in through the open window, carrying with it a fleeting sense of relief.

"We're almost there," Yohannes murmurs, his voice steady and quiet but edged with urgency, as if he doesn't want to jinx your getaway. "Just a bit further."

Escaping the city's clamor, you merge into the quiet countryside. The tension lifts, though only slightly. You remain vigilant. The mission isn't over, and the stakes couldn't be higher.

AIDA's voice cuts through the tension. "Stay sharp."

As the first light of dawn creeps over the horizon, you spot Mother waiting on the tarmac, her silhouette barely visible through the early-morning mist. Yohannes drops you and your gear off, vanishing into the fog with a sense of both relief and haste. You toss your gear onto the rear ramp, the hum of Mother's engines stirring the air around you.

"We made it," you exhale, the weight of the night finally lifting from your shoulders.

"For now," Maya says, her voice low and grim. "But it's far from over. Let's move."

With renewed resolve, you strap down your gear and brace for takeoff.

Mother powers up, lifting smoothly into the night sky, her camouflage systems fully engaged. Below, a convoy of technicals swarm the tarmac, their flashing lights shearing through the darkness. Gunfire erupts, tracer rounds cutting jagged lines through the night, desperate but ineffective as you climb higher. The chaos below diminishes, the flashing lights and roaring engines swallowed by the vast sky as you soar beyond their reach.

Turn to page 350.

Meeting His Mother

Arriving at Ben Gurion International Airport a day early feels like fate has taken the wheel. Fortuitously, Michael is already here, his presence signaling the start of something remarkable. He's teased a surprise, and the anticipation swells within you.

In a vast hangar, he reveals it—a stealth aircraft he's christened Mother. The massive black bird, with its strange, scalelike exterior, exudes an indescribable awe. Michael explains that it's equipped with an advanced active camouflage system called InvisiScale. Tiny cameras on the aircraft's upper surface capture its surroundings and project them onto the underside, making it virtually invisible.

This is no ordinary aircraft. It's an experimental marvel, born from a collaboration between DARPA and Northrop Grumman. Despite the affectionate nickname, Mother is a converted B-23 Eclipse Stealth Bomber, powered by a cutting-edge cold-fusion nuclear reactor. It moves with an unsettling silence and can traverse unimaginable distances on just a gallon of seawater.

Originally designed as a first-strike weapon, it can approach targets undetected, delivering its payload with devastating precision—offering little to no warning before it strikes. The aircraft represents a quantum leap in military technology, the kind of over-the-horizon weapon capable of granting air superiority to any government.

The ramp is down, beckoning you closer, and you don't hesitate. Michael leads you inside, and what you find is far beyond anything you've seen at the PMC. In the cargo bay, a Little Bird helicopter and an armored tactical rapid patrol vehicle (RPV) are strapped down securely.

The technological marvel continues as you enter the tactical war room. At the heart of it all is a next-gen computer hub, operated by a quantum artificial intelligence known as AIDA—Artificially Intelligent Dynamic Assistant. She can project herself as a foot-tall hologram from a stand-up tabletop screen, and watching her manifest is nothing short of mesmerizing.

AIDA can scrub the worldwide web for intelligence, scan mobile networks using voice recognition software, and locate anyone on the grid within minutes. Her capabilities are as advanced as the aircraft itself.

A conversation with AIDA quickly reveals the unnerving depth of her knowledge. She can sift through every social media post, algorithm, and online footprint, predicting your preferences down to your favorite brand of toothpaste or shampoo. AIDA is a formidable intelligence resource, and you're grateful she's on your side.

Michael's next mission is to take Mother to the States to pick up your analyst, Olivia Davenport, code-named Desert Lotus. As you wish him a safe journey, a sense of anticipation stirs within you. Tomorrow night, you'll see them again, and you can't shake the feeling that this is only the beginning of something far greater than you ever imagined.

The following evening, around six, you meet Mother on the tarmac at Ben Gurion with your gear. The ramp is already down, and Michael Smith steps out to greet you.

"Shalom, Maya," he says as you shake hands. He inquires about the customary greeting—one kiss on the cheek or more? You share a laugh and he gives you a peck on the cheek. He then informs you that he won't be joining you on this mission, as other business demands his attention. However, Ms. Davenport is already aboard with an unexpected guest—her intern, Benji Hiroshi. After wishing you well, he departs, and you turn to face the ramp, ready to board and settle in.

Rolling your luggage cart up to the ramp, you start stowing your gear in the cargo bay. The interior of Mother feels almost like home now, with its familiar hum and state-of-the-art design. As you make your way to the war room, AIDA greets you.

"Good evening, Agent Gabriel. How can I be of service? I was just helping Agent Desert Lotus and Benji become familiar with the aircraft."

"All good, AIDA. How's everything on the home front?"

"Agent Wild Card is currently conducting advanced recon at a Pharisee dig site in Hillah, Iraq, approximately fifty miles south of Baghdad. While the specific objectives of the Pharisees remain unknown, I am actively monitoring their online and cellular communications for any insights. I've traced several payments through shell corporations but consistently lose the trail once the money enters the hawala network. Nevertheless, I'll persist in monitoring the situation closely."

"Stick with it."

With that, you go to introduce yourself to Ms. Davenport and Mr. Hiroshi. They look a bit mesmerized as you walk in.

"Hi, I'm Maya. You must be Olivia, the one Michael can't stop talking about. He's quite taken with you," you say, shaking her hand. Olivia appears to hide a smile at the compliment.

Before you can turn to her intern, Olivia introduces him. "This is my intern, Benji. Think of him as a mini-me," she says with a smile.

You shake his hand and the initial awkwardness dissipates. They both seem agreeable and competent. Olivia, shorter and more attractive than you pictured, radiates intelligence and poise, while Benji's eager demeanor suggests a sharp mind ready to absorb everything.

AIDA has assigned them translation work, which keeps them occupied. You decide to return to the hangar to clean your weapons, preparing for any mission that might arise. The maintenance task is oddly soothing—a moment of calm before the inevitable storm.

You start with your Russian-made VKS silent sniper rifle, methodically disassembling and cleaning each component. The VKS is a marvel of engineering, crafted for stealth and precision. Next you turn to your Belgian-made FN P90, its tritium sight and infrared laser glinting under the hangar lights. Each weapon in your arsenal serves a distinct purpose, optimized for various scenarios.

Next you turn to maintaining your dual silenced Glock-19s, the familiar weight of the pistols reassuring in your hands. Finally, you focus on your Mk13, ensuring each component is in perfect condition.

As you work, AC/DC's "Thunderstruck" blasts through the hangar, its raw energy electrifying the space. You can't resist dancing around the cargo bay, twirling your karambit in fluid, practiced motions. The curved blade slices through the air as you practice offensive maneuvers, each movement a blend of precision and power.

Lost in the rhythm, you're caught off guard when Olivia pokes her head in. You pause mid-twirl, offering her an awkward yet reassuring smile.

"Don't worry, Olivia," you say, your tone warm and confident. "You're in good hands. I'll keep you safe."

Olivia nods, a flicker of relief in her eyes, before leaving you to your work. Her sudden appearance reminds you that despite the high stakes, a sense of camaraderie is forming—a crucial trust for what lies ahead.

Turn to page 261.

It's a Key

Wild Card hesitates, a flicker of trepidation in his eyes as he carefully places the cubed artifact into the recess. The ground shudders beneath your feet, followed by the low groan of stone shifting. Slowly, a segment of the wall slides open, revealing stairs descending into darkness.

A shiver creeps down your spine as you step inside. You stumble, tumbling with the others into a long-forgotten chamber, the air thick with dust, grime, and the weight of centuries. Laying on your belly, the walls feel like they're closing in, darkness pressing in from all sides. Suddenly the door slams shut behind you. Your fingers brush against something unsettling on the floor —an odd, hairy texture. Then, from the shadows ahead, a series of hisses ripple through the air.

"Is everyone alright?" Agent Gabriel asks through the oppressive gloom.

There's no time for reassurances. Wild Card wipes and adjusts a round, reflective golden shield. In an instant, a beam of light shoots across the room, illuminating ancient artifacts scattered across the floor.

With bated breath, you scan your surroundings, eyes wide with a mix of awe and dread. You loose a blood-curdling scream as the hairy texture under your hand is revealed. Tarantulas skitter across the floor, their hairy legs a grotesque contrast against the cold stone. Venomous snakes slither in the darkness, and you freeze, coming face-to-face with an enraged black cobra, its hood expanded and white markings stark against its scales while its eyes gleam with a malevolent intelligence, tracking your every move.

Then Maya grabs the cobra by its head and hurls it across the room. "Thanks for the save," you manage, your voice quivering with shock.

As the immediate danger passes, a sense of curiosity and wonder begins to seep into the room, and one object emerges as a beacon of ancient power and significance: the breastplate of Aaron. Its golden surface gleams in the dull light, drawing your gaze with a tantalizing promise of hidden riches and forbidden knowledge. Twelve distinct gemstones are embedded into its surface. And six other large beautiful gems lay loosely on each side of it.

As Wild Card reaches for the breastplate, a deafening rumble shakes the chamber, then ports hidden in the ceiling and walls open and a torrent of sand cascades into the room, rapidly beginning to fill the space.

"What did you do?" Maya asks, her voice tinged with panic. As fear grips you, you desperately search for a way out, the escape route seemingly impossible to find.

Agent Gabriel, however, spots something crucial. She gestures toward cylindrical recesses set into one of the walls. "Quick, Olivia, we need your expertise!"

You wipe the dust from the recesses, revealing that each one is designed to hold six small objects. "The gems!" you shout. "They have to be placed into the slots on each side of the wall!"

With no time to lose, Xavier leaps into action, collecting the gems from beside the breastplate so you place them into their designated slots. As the final gem clicks into place, a blinding light erupts, illuminating the chamber. The wall begins to rise, and you use the surge of sand to propel yourself to safety, narrowly escaping the danger.

You slide out of the darkness, panting and coated in sweat and sand, overwhelmed by a wave of relief. As you glance back, you see Wild Card making a daring leap, clutching the breastplate just as the exit slams shut behind him. AIDA analyzes the breastplate, uncovering its true purpose: a crucial clue to locating the Ark of the Testimony's final resting place. With this revelation, you realize your journey is only beginning.

With the Ark in sight and the world's fate hanging by a thread, you step into the unknown again, armed with courage and determination. In the world of espionage and intrigue, there are no second chances. Only the boldest and sharpest can survive.

You return to Mother in a hangar at Ben Gurion, eager to hear AIDA's results from the breastplate scans. The knowledge that the breastplate was kept in the Ark with the panis vitae and other sacred artifacts intensifies the surreal feeling that you're on the verge of humanity's greatest archaeological breakthrough.

Uncertain of Maya and Xavier's whereabouts, you retreat to your quarters to freshen up and catch some much-needed sleep.

And it is a deep, restful sleep. Thirteen hours later, AIDA's voice cuts through the intercom, summoning all agents to the war room. She has information on Heinrich Jager's location.

Interpol's facial recognition flagged Jager a week ago under the alias John Naysmith upon his arrival at Pearson International Airport in Canada, accompanied by thirty of his top operatives. Reports from CSIS and the RCMP confirm they've taken control of the entire 51st floor of the Ritz-Carlton Toronto.

Jager's plan centers on a meeting with Jean-Jacques Francoeur, a notorious logistics mastermind known as "the Frenchman."

"What do we know about the Frenchman, AIDA?" you ask.

AIDA displays Francoeur's image on the screen. "Francoeur stands at six feet tall and weighs 195 pounds. His angular face is marked by high cheekbones and a prominent nose. His eyes are striking—intense and unsettling—radiating both intelligence and menace. His expression is cold and calculating, aligning with his ruthless, manipulative reputation. His dark brown hair is neatly styled but has a touch of disheveled charm. Dressed in an elegant, well-tailored suit, he exudes wealth and influence, his demeanor commanding confidence and control, projecting an aura of authority and danger.

"Known associates include Patrick Hayden, a fentanyl supplier based in Vancouver; Joseph Bousalame, a Lebanese national in Calgary with ties to Hezbollah; Scott O'Neil, a former IRA veteran-turned-mercenary living in Peterborough, Ontario under the alias Bobby Begh; Malek al-Assad, an ISIS operative in Damascus; and Saudi Crown Prince Danny Bin Salman in Riyadh, believed to be the financier behind their operations.

"Where is the Frenchman now?"

"That's why I called you here," AIDA says, offering a detailed update on the situation in Canada, describing events with precision as if she were on the ground.

As the sun sets, a midnight-black 2044 High Country 2500 HD pickup races down Highway 400 toward Toronto, the Frenchman inside. His eyes are sharp and calculating, reflecting a man who thrives on danger. The RCMP follow closely, the tension palpable, aware that this could be their only chance.

The Frenchman's arrival sets off the RCMP's operation. Heavily armed officers prepare to storm the Ritz-Carlton, breaching the building with military precision. The air is thick with the crackle of gunfire. Seven Pharisees are killed and twenty-three, including Jager, are taken into custody.

Amid the chaos, the Frenchman escapes. Despite the RCMP's best efforts, a judge's refusal to issue a warrant allows him to slip through the cracks. His alibi is as polished as his demeanor—he claims he was merely scouting the hotel for an anniversary dinner and denies any connection to Jager. He does, however, acknowledge knowing John Naysmith, a purported construction worker from Brampton. The real John Naysmith was implicated in a massive cyber breach of a popular drugstore brand on April 28, 2024, during which his identity and those of 300,000 others were stolen and sold on the dark web.

Determined to keep Jager behind bars, the RCMP begin transporting him to Kingston Penitentiary along Highway 401 East. The convoy, comprised of three unmarked black SUVs, moves like shadows through the night: four officers in the lead vehicle, three guarding Jager in the middle, and four more bringing up the rear.

But danger lurks. Just outside Picton, Ontario, approximately 160 kilometers (99 miles) east of Toronto, the convoy is ambushed. Twenty members of the Hells Angels Motorcycle Club, armed with automatic weapons, open fire. The night erupts into chaos. CTV News reports ten RCMP officers dead and two others fighting for their lives at Kingston General Hospital, their chances slim.

Jager has disappeared into the night. Alerts flash across Ontario and Quebec as officials initiate a frantic manhunt in Ottawa, Montreal, and Quebec City. The clock is ticking, tension rising. Every second counts.

"Setting Jager aside," Xavier asks AIDA, "have you found anything from the scans of the breastplate?"

"Only the location where the Hebrews concealed the Ark of the Covenant—Mount Nebo."

Maya smiles. "Should have led with that."

AIDA displays a collage of files, photos, and maps related to Mount Nebo.

Xavier leans in with excitement, playfully flipping an ancient gold Babylonian coin, acquired from the Temple Mount, through his fingers. The coin, engraved with cryptic symbols and weathered by centuries, glints faintly in the dim light.

His eyes track the coin's path as it glides from thumb to forefinger to middle finger. There's a rhythm to his movements, a mesmerizing dance of metal and flesh that reflects both skill and casual enjoyment. The coin appears almost weightless, its historical significance overshadowed by its effortless spins and flips.

"With Jager still at large," Maya says, "we need to concentrate on locating the Ark and neutralizing the Pale Horse virus. We also can't overlook the potential implications of discovering the panis vitae, should its healing properties be confirmed."

"I have the coordinates," AIDA says. "Latitude: 31° 46' 2.39" N, longitude: 35° 43' 18.59" E. Mother's engines are powering up now. We'll enter Jordanian airspace in about an hour and land in Queen Alia International Airport in Amman thirty minutes later."

"Your team can take the CIV for the thirty-seven kilometers to Mount Nebo. I discovered an inscription on the back of the breastplate that initially seemed like random marks but could be a topographical map. Considering erosion and geological shifts over the past 2,612 years, I've pinpointed a likely area for the cave mentioned by the prophet Jeremiah.

"Using maps, geological indexes, and satellite imagery, I've also pinpointed a limestone-rich area characterized by disappearing streams and significant erosion. Follow the karst line to the locations where my scans reveal several voids below the surface. It's time to gear up, GOD team!"

Mother touches down at Queen Alia International Airport as the sun sets, the hum of the engines resonating in your ears. You glance at your team, Wild Card and Gabriel, their faces etched with determination. This mission is unprecedented—you are on a quest for the golden jar of manna, the panis vitae, believed to be housed within the Ark of the Covenant.

If you want to take the Boeing MH-6M Little Bird (helicopter) to Mount Nebo (an eight-minute flight), **turn to page 14.**

If you want to drive to Mount Nebo in the Gurkha CIV (a thirty-two-minute drive), **turn to page 226.**

 **Bookmark Here**

It's a Man's Job

You hold the straws while Maya and Xavier draw their picks. Xavier ends up with the short one.

"Looks like it's my turn to save the world," Xavier says with a wink and a smile. "I'll get suited up!"

In the clandestine world of espionage, where shadows dance with secrets and danger lurks around every corner, Agent Wild Card is a rare breed. His real name, Xavier Washington, is buried deep within classified files, obscured by layers of subterfuge. But tonight, he must become a ghost, a phantom moving through the world unseen and unheard.

Soon, Wild Card is prepared for a HALO jump over the Port of Beirut. Darkness envelops him like a shroud as he prepares to descend into the heart of the unknown.

As he leaps into the void, thirty-five thousand feet in the air with no moon to guide him, a solitary figure against the vast expanse of night sky, adrenaline surges through his veins, blending with the thrill of the mission. However, as he plummets toward the earth below, something goes terribly wrong. The thin air at such altitudes distorts his perception, and hypoxia sets in, clouding his thoughts and dulling his senses.

Overcome by dizziness and confusion, Wild Card's vision blurs, his movements grow sluggish, and his consciousness slips away like smoke through his fingers. In just forty-five seconds, he plummets thirty-one thousand feet, failing to deploy his parachute.

"Deploy, deploy, deploy!" AIDA's voice blares through his tactical helmet.

At two thousand feet, he crosses the point of no return.

The relentless pull of gravity claims him, dragging him down into the darkness below at terminal velocity.

The world mourns Wild Card's loss, yet his fate remains shrouded in mystery. His body is never recovered. Some whisper that he vanished into the shadows, continuing his work as a phantom of the night. Others believe he met his end in the darkness, a tragic casualty of the perilous games he played.

The End

Go Back to Page 113

I'll Cooperate

"Please continue, Ms. Chamberlain. I have nothing to hide," you say. "Where would you like me to start?" You feel unnerved yet steady. Your life had become too routine and safe, to the point of boredom, before this adventure. It was your choice to spread your wings, and no one is going to confine this little dove again.
"Why don't you start at the beginning?" Ms. Chamberlain asks. "What does GOD stand for? How were you recruited? And what was your mission?"

The deputy director of the CIA, Keith Atkins, steps into the light and takes a seat at the opposite end of the table. Mr. Atwell from MI6 takes his place as well. Meanwhile the polygraph monitor records a series of erratic peaks and valleys on the paper.

Your memory drifts back to a cozy enclave in Washington, DC in 2034, where a picturesque scene unfolds. A spring breeze rustles through the lilac blossoms and mingles with the scent of freshly cut grass. You sit outside the Rise-n-Shine Cafe, basking in the sun, your rich brown hair cascading in gentle waves around your shoulders while the birdsong of playful chickadees serenades you. Today, the cafe's charm is particularly enchanting as you sip a mimosa and admire the chef's artfully plated Cobb chicken salad.

As you idly survey the tranquil, parklike oasis, absorbing the rhythms of the patrons, an unexpected encounter shatters your carefree reverie. A charming stranger approaches your table, a man with rugged good looks and an air of confidence. His dark hair is artfully tousled and his blue eyes sparkle with mischief and warmth, his tailored suit freshly pressed and his perfect smile underscoring his self-assured demeanor.

"Would you mind if I joined you?" he asks, his voice smooth, exuding a confidence that suggests he's accustomed to being welcomed rather than turned away.

Initially his bold approach and disregard for cafe etiquette take you by surprise. However, your hesitation melts away in the warmth of his inviting smile. "Sure, I suppose," you reply.

He takes a seat opposite you and the air between you crackles with an unexpected electricity. "I hope you don't mind my intrusion," he says, his eyes twinkling with interest. "I couldn't help but notice such ethereal beauty sitting alone."

You chuckle, drawing your hair behind one ear as you check your makeup in a compact. "And you thought you'd rescue this lonely damsel in distress from her solitude?"

His smile widens, revealing a set of perfect white teeth. "Something like that. I'm Michael Smith," he says, extending his hand with a charming flourish, "and I work as a lobbyist. But today, I'm simply a curious observer. This may sound a bit cliché, but I'm certain I've seen you here before."

You shake his hand, feeling a spark of magnetism from the brief touch. "Olivia Davenport," you say. "I work at the Museum of the Bible, just a few blocks away. I suppose I'm a creature of habit, coming here for my lunch breaks. I do enjoy it though. It's a pleasant place, and the staff always remember my name."

Michael leans in, his gaze unwavering. "The Museum of the Bible, you say? That sounds intriguing. I've always believed that the best stories have a way of shaping our lives. And speaking of stories, it seems we might be writing one of our own, Olivia. I can't imagine anyone forgetting you."

Your heart flutters at his flirtations. There's something captivating about his presence, something that draws you in to a world made just for the two of you. "Is that so?" you ask, your tone teasing. "And what sort of story do you think we're in?"

He leans back with a confident grin. "Well, considering how beautiful you look today and how fortuitous our meeting, I'd say we're at the beginning of something special."

The warmth of the sun and the effervescence of the Mimosa creates a perfect moment of lightness alongside the amusement and interest swirling within you.

"Then it must be serendipity. I suppose there's no harm in seeing where this goes," you say.

As you continue the conversation, the world around you seems to fade away, leaving only the playful mystery of your connection. With each shared laugh and teasing glance, the promise of a budding new season and the allure of a burgeoning romance unfolds before you.

"Ms. Davenport, could we please get to the point?" Ms. Chamberlain asks. Mr. Atkins, seated beside her, buries his face in his hands. Mr. Atwell, on the other hand, is barely concealing a smile.

"I apologize," you say, feeling flustered. "I have an eidetic memory and tend to ramble when I'm nervous."

Ms. Chamberlain glances at the polygrapher, who nods and says, "No signs of deception so far, ma'am."

"Very well," Ms. Chamberlain says, her tone softening. "Let's proceed."

You take a deep breath, trying to recall the details with the clarity of that afternoon. "Where was I? Ah, yes. Michael Smith was undeniably handsome. Our dates were filled with laughter and effortless conversation, but it was the last one that stands out most vividly. Perhaps because of our first kiss."

You see, on that day, your car refuses to start. You ask Michael for help, and ever the gentleman, he comes to your rescue. With a few deft movements under the hood, he has it purring like a kitten. "Just a loose wire," he says. His chivalry is genuine as he suggests following you home to ensure you don't face any more trouble.

You invite him in but he declines, citing an early morning the next day. As he's about to leave, you can't help but notice how his pants fit his profile perfectly. Your thoughts wander as you bite your lower lip, caught up in an unexpected surge of desire. Just then, he turns back with a playful expression and asks if you can assist him with a last-minute translation.

Your curiosity is piqued. The voice from the device is unmistakably British, speaking in Arabic to another man. Michael doesn't hand you the phone directly, but the way he subtly adjusts it for you to hear, combined with the shared curiosity of the moment, creates an invisible yet palpable sense of connection.

The man with the British accent says: "هل كل شيء في الموعد المحدد؟"

Translation: "Is everything on schedule?"

A native Arabic speaker with a Palestinian accent replies: "لدينا حصان شاحب. سنختبره غدا في قرية صغيرة نائية في زائير."

Translation – "It sounded like he said, 'We have a pale horse,' or, 'We have Pale Horse. We will test it tomorrow in a small remote village in Zaire.'"

British man: "ها ، ها تقصد جمهورية الكونغو الديمقراطية ، أليس كذلك؟ اسمحوا لي أن أعرف النتائج"

Translation: "Ha, you mean the Democratic Republic of Congo, don't you? Let me know the results."

British man continues. "هل كل شيء يتقدم في موقع الحفر؟"

Translation: "He is asking if everything is progressing at the dig sites."

Palestinian man: "كل شيء في مكانه."

Translation: "Everything is in place."

Then the recording stops. Michael seems to drift into thought, and his demeanor becomes more serious.

"Do me a favor, Liv. Don't tell anyone about this. It's sensitive," he says softly, drawing you closer.

"Sure," you reply. The moment is shrouded in mystery. All the teasing and flirtation seems to dissolve, giving way to a deeper connection. Your lips come dangerously close, his gaze locked on yours. You close your eyes as he gently kisses you, his touch soft and lingering. When he pulls away, the embers of your desire flare into a passionate flame, and you draw him back to you. After a fervent kiss and a quiet moment of intimacy, you both compose yourselves. It feels as though you've crossed an unspoken boundary that kept you at a teasing distance. As Michael leaves, you savor the euphoria of the encounter.

A few days later you receive a text from Michael.

Unknown Caller

(Michael Smith)

> Hey Liv, are you free? I haven't stopped thinking about you. I really appreciate your help the other night. There's something important I need to discuss with you, but it's too sensitive to discuss over the phone. Can you meet me at the place where we first met

If you want to meet Michael Smith at the café, **turn to page 27.**

If you want to play hard-to-get, **turn to page 224.**

 **Bookmark Here**

I Got the Shaft

Maya makes a split-second decision, veering right into the darkest path. It's a daring move but she hopes it'll provide her with the element of surprise.

Ahead, just as AIDA predicted, Maya spots the elevator doors, a beacon of hope in the unlit hallway. In the elevator, she removes the ceiling tiles, climbs up into the ceiling, and carefully replaces them to conceal her presence in the shaft.

Balancing precariously on the frame of the elevator car, the main cable rising into the darkness, her senses sharpen as she hears the telltale click of boots on metal. Members of the Pharisees, their faces obscured by scarves, board the elevator below her, their AK-47s ready for action.

WE WILL FIND THEM AND WE WILL KILL THEM!" Their Arabic voices echo menacingly through the confined space, sending a shiver down Maya's spine.

As the elevator jolts into motion, her heart pounds harder in her chest. The counterweight whizzes by, marking their ascent toward the roof. She has to act quickly.

With a surge of adrenaline, she braces herself, ready to make her move. But in the darkness of the shaft, disaster strikes. The space above the elevator car ends abruptly, about to crush her against the cold metal.

Maya's thoughts race back to her mission and the artifact she's risked everything to protect. As darkness closes in, she whispers a silent prayer.

Back on Mother, AIDA reports that she's no longer detecting any vital signs from Agent Gabriel. The eerie coding of a heart monitor is all that fills the otherwise silent war room.

The End

Go Back to Page 177

Stop, Drop, Roll

With the breastplate firmly in your grasp, you recognize there's no room for greed. The ancient chamber is collapsing around you at a frenetic pace. The air is choked with dust and the rumble of shifting stones. Your heart pounds as you dive for the base of the door and roll beneath it.

"What were you thinking?" Maya says, her voice, edged with frustration, piercing through the haze as you scramble to your feet.

"I don't know," you reply, catching your breath. "Figured we might need it. Think about it—this breastplate is our only piece of evidence that we're on the right track to finding the Ark and the golden jar of manna. Or, if you prefer Latin, the panis vitae."

She shakes her head, clearly exasperated. "Don't do that again!" "Yes, ma'am. Admit it, you'd miss me." You laugh and grin, attempting to lighten the mood. "But next time I'm trapped in an ancient treasure chamber filling with sand and a ten-ton slab threatens to seal me in forever, I promise I won't go back for the treasure."

Olivia steps forward and gives you a quick, relieved hug, reminiscent of that of a younger sister. As you turn to Maya, she too embraces you. Her warmth overtakes the chill of the surrounding stone walls. When the embrace ends, your eyes lock, and for a fleeting moment, time freezes. You can feel the charged air, your lips a mere inch apart. Your heart races as you battle the impulse to close that small gap.

However, professionalism prevails. With a shared, unspoken acknowledgment, you pull away, acutely aware that she felt it too. The adventure continues, but the spark between you remains undeniable, a fluttering flame just beneath the surface.

You hand the breastplate over to AIDA, who begins her analysis even before you return to Ben Gurion. Along the way, she mentions that she might have uncovered a clue to the final resting place of the Ark of the Testimony.

You're eager to return to the hangar at Ben Gurion. AIDA's cryptic clue is tantalizing, suggesting a potential revelation about the lost Ark. The anticipation is intense, and your imagination races with possibilities. However, upon arrival, AIDA's update is disappointing. She's on the right track but hasn't pinpointed the exact location yet. She needs more time.

As you absorb the news, you spot Maya in the cargo bay, cleaning her weapons. It seems like an ideal moment to follow suit. You head to your quarters, feeling the reassuring weight of your Sig Sauer P226 MK25 in its shoulder holster. The familiar maintenance routine offers a welcome distraction.

You begin by drawing the weapon from your holster and ejecting the magazine, then pulling back the slide to ensure the chamber is empty. The satisfying click and smooth movement of the slide are almost therapeutic. You rotate the takedown lever ninety degrees and lift the slide off the frame. The guide rod and spring come out and leave just the barrel. A swift spray of Rem Oil down both ends of the barrel prepares it for a thorough cleaning.
As you clean your gun, your thoughts wander to the mission ahead. The scent of the oil and the rhythmic brushing provide a calming respite, a stark contrast to the chaos and uncertainty of your usual encounters.

You brush the slide rails and the frame, focusing on the ejector and the ramp where dirt frequently accumulates. Using a Q-tip, you carefully clean along the frame rails and around the hammer. The barrel demands the most attention, so you spend extra time cleaning it with the barrel brush, ensuring it's thoroughly spotless.

Once the cleaning is complete, reassembling the gun is quick and satisfying. The barrel slips back into the slide effortlessly, followed by the guide rod and spring. You ease the frame back into place, turn the takedown lever, and release the slide. A trigger pull and slide cycle confirm that everything is functioning smoothly. Finally, you clean the magazine and return the gun to its shoulder holster. A clean weapon is an effective weapon, you think to yourself.

With your Sig Sauer reassembled and ready, your mind feels clear. Now it's time for a shower and some rest to prepare for whatever challenges lie ahead in your quest for the lost Ark.

You're jolted awake by AIDA's voice over the intercom, summoning all agents to the war room. She delivers urgent news about Heinrich Jager. Interpol, CSIS, and the RCMP had captured Jager, operating under the alias John Naysmith, during a sting operation in Toronto, Canada.

However, the victory was fleeting.

En route to Kingston Penitentiary, a brazen attack by the Hells Angels Motorcycle Club facilitated his escape. Several officers were killed in the chaos, and authorities are now desperately searching for the notorious arms dealer.

In addition to pursuing Jager, they're monitoring his logistics manager, JJ Francoeur, in the hopes that he might lead you to the Pale Horse. Jager and Francoeur were scheduled to meet, but the takedown occurred before they could make contact, leaving Canadian authorities without sufficient grounds to detain Francoeur.

"Putting Jager aside for now, have you discovered anything from the breastplate scans?" you ask.

"Only the location where the Hebrews hid the Ark of the Covenant on Mount Nebo!" AIDA says.

Maya quips about AIDA burying the lead, eliciting laughter from everyone.

Suddenly AIDA projects a flurry of files, photos, and maps related to Mount Nebo. As the information flashes onscreen, your attention shifts to an ancient Babylonian gold coin that you found in your boot after the Temple Mount mission in Israel. As you flip the coin between your fingers, it catches the light, casting a shimmering glow. Olivia, sitting nearby, appears entranced by it.

Maya shatters the silence, emphasizing the urgency of your mission. You must locate the Ark and prevent the release of the Pale Horse virus. She speaks fervently about the panis vitae, or the bread of life, and its potential to revolutionize medicine. If scientists can harness its healing properties, it could potentially cure diseases ranging from cancer to Alzheimer's. The golden jar of manna signifies more than just a solution to the Pale Horse threat: it embodies the promise of a medical breakthrough with the potential to benefit all of humanity.

"I've got the coordinates," AIDA says. "Latitude: 31° 46' 2.39" N, and longitude: 35° 43' 18.59" E. Mother's engines are spooling up now, and we'll enter Jordanian airspace in about an hour. We'll touch down at Queen Alia International Airport in Amman thirty minutes later. Your team can then drive the thirty-seven kilometers to Mount Nebo.

"The inscription on the back of the breastplate, which initially appeared as random marks, actually represents a topographical map. Taking into account erosion and geological changes over the past 2,612 years, I've estimated a probable location for the cave mentioned by the prophet Jeremiah.

"Using maps, geological references, and satellite images, I've pinpointed a limestone-rich area characterized by disappearing streams and significant erosion. Upon arrival, you'll follow the karst line to a location where my scans indicate several underground voids. It's time to get ready, GOD team!"

As the sun sets over Jordan, you touch down at Queen Alia International Airport. The golden light drags long shadows across the runway, heralding the arrival of dusk. After retrieving your gear, you, Maya, and Olivia pile into the CIV. A brief debate ensues over who should drive, with Maya eventually handing you the keys.

You have two routes to Mount Nebo, each with its own advantages. The first option is the most direct: take Airport Road and then turn onto Zaid Bin Haritha Street. This route covers approximately thirty kilometers and is estimated to take about thirty-nine minutes.

The second route offers a scenic detour. From Queen Alia International Airport, head towards Madaba via Madaba Al-Gharbi. This path winds through some of the region's most picturesque areas. The distance to Madaba is roughly thirty kilometers (nineteen miles), which takes about forty minutes to drive. From Madaba, it's a short six-mile drive to Mount Nebo.

If you want to take the most direct route, **turn to page 42.**

If you want to take the less common route, **turn to page 87.**

 **Bookmark Here**

Into the Creepy Cellar

You creep down the stone stairs, your tranquilizer gun aimed ahead. The cool damp air brushes against your skin as you descend. Upon reaching the base, you find the Ark missing. Instead, metal bars with pointed barbs crash down from the ceiling, sealing off any chance of escape. As you spin around, another set of bars slams down in front of you. Trapped. A sudden sharp pinch on your neck sends you into darkness.

When you awaken, you find yourself in an entirely unfamiliar environment. This isn't Ethiopia. The smell is all wrong. The humidity and temperature are different. You can hear the bird song of gulls which suggests you're now by the sea. Hovering over you is an older man dressed in an unusual red hat, a red buttoned cloak with intricate white sleeves, and a large gold cross hanging from his neck.

He introduces himself as Gianfranco Corleone, a cardinal from the Vatican in Rome. Beside him stands a stern guard, scowling and armed with a Beretta M12 submachine gun. The guard is wearing a navy-blue uniform, a black tie, and a distinctive flat-topped hat, indicating his position in the Vatican Gendarmerie. Nearby, several members of the Pontifical Swiss Guard, dressed in their iconic striped uniforms, stand at the ready.

"Hello, young man," Cardinal Corleone begins. "It was unwise of you to break into a church. What were you doing there?"

"Where am I?" you ask.

"You were brought to the Vatican overnight. It seems you were drugged. Now, who are you? Did you think you could steal the Ark?"

"No. I was there to protect the Ark."

"From what?"

"I can't say more. But I was not trying to steal it!"

"As you can see, we have our own security and are more than capable of protecting our property. Unfortunately, we cannot simply release you. I have consulted with His Eminence, and you will not be charged with trespassing. However, you will need to sign nondisclosure agreements, confirming that you will not speak about, write about, or discuss anything you may have seen or witnessed at the site in Axum."

Reluctantly, you sign the forms and are released after offering a sincere apology. You're then entered into the Vatican database and instructed to say ten Hail Marys and twelve Our Fathers. Cardinal Corleone warns you that this is your final chance and emphasizes that it's up to you to reform your life.

The End

Go Back to Page 144

Phase Two

Identifying Sneaky Pete, you carefully place the C-4 in the engine's air inlet, ensuring it's secure and concealed. The tension is palpable, with every sound amplified in the stillness of the night. With the explosive in place, you slip into the shadows, knowing that your mission is only half-complete.

The return journey will be just as perilous, if not more so. The reality of being deep in enemy territory, surrounded by the elite Quds Force, weighs on you. There's no turning back now.

You reach the edge of the brush line just as a patrol approaches, your heart racing and tight all at once.

"Don't move, Aphrodite," Eagle Eye's urgent whisper crackles through your earpiece.

You freeze, kneeling, the foliage barely concealing you in your ghillie suit. The voices of the patrol grow louder, their conversation in Farsi chillingly close.

"آماد، باورتان می‌شود رئیس‌جمهور برای افتتاح سد اینجاست؟"

"Amad, can you believe the president is here for the dam inauguration?"

"احرف نزن و کارت را بکن، بهروز!"

"Stop talking and do your job, Behrooz!"

For some reason, the patrol halts at that precise moment. You can see their boots through the underbrush, mere inches from your face. They peer into the forest. Every muscle in your body tenses as you remain perfectly still, making not a single sound. Your heartbeat pounds in your ears, so loud you fear it might betray you.

Time seems to stand still. Your entire existence narrows to this moment of absolute stillness. The patrol lingers, their quiet conversation a cruel reminder of how dangerously close you are to discovery.

After what feels like an eternity, the patrol finally moves on, their voices fading into the distance. Your lungs burn as you exhale the breath you've been holding. Eagle Eye's voice crackles back into your earpiece.

"All clear."

You rise slowly, trying to control the adrenaline still surging through your veins. The immediate danger has passed, but the mission is far from over.

Burdened by the weight of your mission, you retrace your steps, covering the single kilometer back to the site where you previously landed via zip line. There, you retrieve the M107, a .50 caliber anti-materiel rifle—an instrument of both precision and immense power—before Eagle Eye updates Looking Glass on your position and progress over the comms.

"Looking Glass, this is Eagle Eye," he says, his voice steady despite the tension. "Sneaky Pete is green. We're en route to Objective Charlie and will assume position shortly."

"Affirmative, Eagle Eye. Good hunting, you two."

"Eagle Eye out."

Your next objective is to reach higher ground—a vantage point from which you'll set up the reverse zip line for your escape into Azerbaijan. Eagle Eye works to load another cable cartridge as you trek. After ten grueling kilometers, you arrive at the designated coordinates: a spot with a clear line of sight, perfect for the critical shot you need to make.

Eagle Eye climbs to the top of a nearby hill, tying small strips of red tape around specific trees to gauge the wind. Meanwhile, you prepare for the long wait ahead, laying out a pad, extending the bipod legs on the M107, and settling in. Eagle Eye, focused, jots down elevation and windage settings in his notebook. The hours crawl by, each one stretching into what feels like an eternity.

At ten in the morning, a nomadic tribe drifts across the horizon, their small flock of goats trailing behind. They pass just a hundred yards from your position, but you remain invisible, a phantom blending with the landscape. Hours later, at 1320 IRST, intelligence relays that Sneaky Pete is preparing for takeoff. You remove the lens cap and bring the scope to your eye, your focus narrowing.

Eagle Eye feeds you markers, elevation and windage data. The challenge is immense: striking a moving helicopter in formation, using an anti-materiel round traveling at 2,799 feet per second. Mist clouds your view while the helicopter's downdraft disturbs the air, multiplying the difficulty. It's a near-impossible shot—one that you're determined to make.

The minutes crawl by, each one thick with tension. You regulate your breathing, forcing your heart rate to slow, your aim steady as steel. The helicopter emerges from the mist, its rotors slicing through the air, whipping up a swirling fog around it. Tail number EP-ZYX—confirmed. Eagle Eye's voice remains calm, guiding you through the final adjustments.

"Elevation plus three, windage minus two. You've got this, Aphrodite."

Your breathing steadies as you exhale slowly, finger poised on the trigger. The world compresses into the tight confines of your crosshairs, the moving helicopter locked in your sight. Time stretches, the seconds drawn out in silence.

You squeeze the trigger. The rifle bucks against your shoulder, sending the round screaming towards its mark.

The anti-materiel round, carrying deadly kinetic energy, cuts through the air, leaving a faint vapor trail in its wake. It slams into the Bell 212's rotor assembly, striking the pitch change link, a vital component that controls the rotor blade angle. The impact is surgical, the consequences catastrophic.

The damaged pitch link immediately plunges the rotor blades into chaos, their once-rhythmic rotation turning wild and erratic. Violent vibrations tear through the helicopter, shaking it to its core. The pilot fights to regain control, but the damage is too severe. The imbalance worsens and the Bell 212 plunges into a rapid descent—Sneaky Pete is going down.

Thick black smoke billows from the rotor assembly, curling into the sky. Eagle Eye, ever calm, confirms the situation with Looking Glass, raising the antenna on the long-range detonator, his finger hovering just above the switch.

"Looking Glass, this is Eagle Eye. Sneaky Pete is down. Permission to engage?"

"Affirmative, Eagle Eye. You're cleared hot."

Eagle Eye flicks open the switch protector, then presses down on the detonator. A split second later, the C-4 ignites, and a massive fireball erupts into the sky, followed by a thick plume of black smoke.

The mission is complete—what seemed nearly impossible is now a reality.

You move quickly, disassembling your rifle and packing up your gear. Every second matters. The adrenaline from success surges through you, but the mission isn't over. A perilous journey lies ahead as you prepare to evade the Islamic Revolutionary Guard Corps (IRGC) and make it to your Azerbaijani CIA contact. Time is against you, and every step toward the extraction point carries the risk of a deadly encounter.

Just then, a familiar and chilling sound breaks the silence—the click of a Colt M1911's hammer cocking behind you. Your blood runs cold. You've heard that sound too many times not to deduce the lethal intent that follows.

Before you can react, Sergeant Abelman's voice crackles over the radio.

"Looking Glass, this is Eagle Eye—I'm about to tie up that loose end."

A deafening click echoes as the sergeant pulls the trigger, anticipating a bullet in the back of your head. Silence follows. His stunned reaction grants you the crucial moment you need. In a flash you pivot and disarm him, knocking the gun from his grasp as he desperately attempts to fire again. With your karambit pressed to his throat, you murmur in his ear, "I removed the firing pin, you fool. Radio in and report that it's done." You tighten the blade against his skin.

"Looking Glass, this—this is Eagle Eye. Do you r-read?" he stammers.

"Affirmative, Eagle Eye. Status report?"

"Aphrodite is down. I repeat, Aphrodite is down!"

"Acknowledged, Eagle Eye. Secure the scene and exfil as planned. Over and out."

"Good," you say after turning off the radio, shattering it into pieces.

Suddenly a bullet whizzes past your shoulder and hits Abelman in the head, killing him instantly. Your heart races as you grab what you can and sprint deeper into the forest, bullets zipping through the air around you. The gunfire reverberates, a deadly symphony in the heart of the Azerbaijani wilderness.

In the distance, dogs bark as they close in on your position. Thinking quickly, you dive into a nearby stream, the icy water biting at your skin as you move downstream to throw off their scent. The forest around you blurs into shadows and moonlight, each step a frantic bid for survival.

After two grueling hours, drenched and exhausted, you finally reach the CIA rendezvous point. The relief is fleeting as the harsh reality of your situation sets in. You've narrowly escaped death but the danger isn't over. The struggle extends beyond enemies in the shadows, encompassing the betrayals from within.

Then you see her—a woman in her mid-twenties, draped in a wine and gold Arkhaluk standing beside a car with its hazard lights blinking. You approach cautiously and catch her from behind.

"It's a great night for a walk," you whisper.

"You must see Martuni," she says, her voice trembling.

"I'm Adila. We don't have much time. Get in."

You release your grip, and she hurriedly takes the driver's seat while you jump into the passenger side.

"My code name is Eagle Eye," you say, deciding to use your deceased spotter's identity for safety.

"Yes, I've been instructed to take you to Martuni, and then onward to Baku."

"I should call in and let them know we're en route."

"Don't! We must remain radio silent until Baku. The IRGC will be monitoring all communications."

"Yes, of course. Let's get moving then."

On the way to Martuni, a sharp pain flares in your shoulder. You unzip your tactical suit and discover blood. The shot that took out Sergeant Abelman grazed you. It isn't a penetrating wound but it will require stitches.

You arrive in Martuni, a quiet town cloaked in shadows. Adila slips into a small market and emerges with honey, a needle, and some thread, as instructed. You drive on toward Baku, the road stretching endlessly before you. Partway there, you pull over and build a small fire off to the side, its flames flickering in the encroaching darkness.

You heat the honey until the thick golden liquid boils. "Adila," you say, handing her a wooden spork you picked up at a gas station, "apply it to the wound."

"Isn't that going to hurt like hell?"

"It'll help cauterize the wound and prevent infection."

Adila applies the hot honey to your shoulder and a searing pain shoots through you. You can't suppress a cry of pain. The initial agony gives way to a welcome numbness. She works with steady hands, threading the needle and stitching up the gash. Her touch is gentle yet efficient. Within minutes the wound is closed, a neat row of stitches holding the skin together. There's still an ache, a reminder of the night's violence, but the bleeding has stopped.

You sit by the fire, the silence between you heavy. The road to Baku awaits, fraught with danger, but for now, you have a brief respite, the warmth of the fire a fragile shield against the cold uncertainty of your future.

During the journey to Baku, you manage to catch five hours of sleep in the car. Upon arrival, you instruct Adila to take you directly to the Fairmont Jaipur in Baku, bypassing the airport where assassins are most likely lying in wait.

On the morning of May 20, 2024, ARB-24 Azerbaijani News repeatedly covers a significant incident: the crash of an Iranian Air Force helicopter near the village of Uzi in East Azerbaijan, Iran. This tragic event results in the deaths of several high-ranking officials, including the President of Iran, Farhad Ebrahimi; Foreign Minister Dariush Azar; Governor-General of East Azerbaijan Abtin Ahmati; the Representative of the Supreme Leader in East Azerbaijan, Javion Mousavi; the head of the president's security team; and three flight crew members. The helicopter was part of a convoy of three, traveling from the Giz Galasi Dam to Tabriz.

Notably, one day before the crash, the Iranian Meteorological Organization issued an orange weather warning for the region, indicating severe conditions that could lead to damage or accidents.

At approximately 1330 IRST, the helicopter crashed in Dizmar Forest, about two kilometers (1.2 miles) southwest of the village of Uzi. The exact coordinates of the crash site are 38°43′8″N, 46°39′17″E.

If you want to contact David Pernas at the Central Intelligence Agency, **turn to page 249.**

If you want to go dark and disappear forever, **turn to page 204.**

 **Bookmark Here**

Quick, Nobody's Looking

The three of you duck under the Do Not Cross tape that marks the forbidden area. The air is thick with dust and the scent of ancient stone. You proceed cautiously, your footsteps echoing off the walls as you venture deeper into the earth's depths.

After what feels like an eternity, you arrived at the location indicated on the map where the Ark of the Covenant might be concealed. All that greet you are bare stone walls. Frustration mounts until Olivia notices a small recess in the wall. Her eyes widen with realization, and she turns to you and Xavier.

"The cube," she says, referring to the cube-shaped artifact you discovered earlier.

Xavier nods in understanding as Olivia hands him the cube. He inserts it into the recess and it fits perfectly. A deep rumbling reverberates through the tunnel. You watch in astonished silence as a substantial section of the stone wall slides open, revealing a staircase that descends into the darkness below.

You exchange nervous glances, steeling yourselves for what lies ahead. Then you begin your descent. The door rumbles shut behind you, sealing you in a pitch-black chamber. As you reached the bottom, the final step gives way, sending you tumbling into the abyss.

"Is everyone alright?" you call out, your voice echoing in the cavernous space.

"Yeah, I'm okay," Olivia replies, her voice trembling.

"I'm fine as well," Xavier adds, sounding somewhat winded.

A hissing pierces the silence, sending a chill down your spine. Xavier, ever observant, notices a gold disc among the debris and wipes it clean with his keffiyeh. As he does, a beam of light catches the disc, casting an eerie glow that partially illuminates the cavern.

Olivia's scream pierces the darkness, laced with terror. You whirl around to find her sprawled on the ground, face-to-face with a black-hooded cobra, its hood flared and fangs bared. Now the hissing makes sense. Driven by sheer instinct, you seize the snake just below its head and fling it across the room, far from her.

As the light casts its eerie glow over the chamber, piles of treasure come into view: gold coins, glittering gems, and ancient artifacts scattered haphazardly. But the opulence is marred by the grisly presence of human skulls, serpents slithering across the floor, and tarantulas creeping in the shadows.

At the heart of the chamber, perched on a stone pedestal, stands the magnificent artifact: the breastplate of Aaron. Its regal brilliance shimmers with an otherworldly light that beckons you closer. The air around it crackles with a sense of ancient power and imminent peril, marking the precipice of a monumental discovery. Around the Breastplate sit six precious jewels on each side.

Compelled by the breastplate's allure, Xavier steps cautiously toward the pedestal and gingerly reaches out for the artifact. The moment his fingers make contact, a hidden mechanism is triggered, and sand starts cascading from concealed vents in the ceiling, rapidly filling the chamber and threatening to engulf you.

"What have you done?" you shout, panic edging your voice as the sand climbs around your ankles.

"I—I didn't do anything!" Xavier says, his face pale and eyes wide.

Frantically, you search for an escape as the sand encroaches. Your hands graze two small recesses in the wall, hidden beneath thick cobwebs.

"Olivia, we need your expertise now!" you say. "Find a way out before it's too late!"

Olivia scrutinizes the recesses with the precision of a seasoned puzzle solver. "These look like they might hold the gems over there. Xavier, grab those stones and hand them to me!"

Xavier picks up the gems from around the breastplate and rushes them to Olivia, who slots each one into its corresponding holder. As the final gem is placed, a deep rumble shakes the chamber, and a different section of the wall starts to ascend.

The sand continues to cascade, and all three of you ride the rising tide through the emerging opening. As the wall begins to descend again, Xavier makes a desperate move, diving back into the chamber, seizing the breastplate, and rolling beneath the wall just as it crashes shut.

"What were you thinking?" you admonish, your voice quivering with frustration. "You nearly got yourself killed!"

Xavier, breathless and coated in sand, flashes you a defiant grin. "I wasn't about to leave it behind. It's the only evidence we have that we're on the right track to finding the Ark and the golden jar of manna."

"Don't ever do that again."

Olivia wraps Xavier in a hug. "We're lucky to have made it out alive."

Despite your frustration, a deep sense of relief washes over you at his safety, and you join in the hug. The bond between you and Xavier has always been special, and as you hold him close in this brief, chaotic moment, the intimacy of your connection is palpable. Your eyes meet, and he softly reassures you, "I'm okay."

"Let's get out of here," Olivia says, pulling you back to the present. "Did anyone see the Ark?"

None of you did, but discovering the breastplate of Aaron reaffirms that you're on the right path. Unfortunately, the answers that might have been uncovered in the chamber are now forever sealed away.

As you exit the underground tunnels, Xavier clutches the breastplate of Aaron. The progress you've all made in your mission boosts your spirits. While the path ahead remains uncertain, you're united and prepared for whatever challenges may come next.

If you want to turn the breastplate of Aaron over to the Israel Antiquities Authority (IAA), **turn to page 06.**

If you want to take the breastplate back to AIDA for analysis aboard Mother, **turn to page 333.**

 **Bookmark Here**

It's Nappy Time

You sneak up from behind the guard, subduing one of them while shooting the other with a tranquilizer dart. His body wavers before collapsing, and you tighten your grip on the remaining guard, sucking him into the shadows. Your heart races as you whisper urgently, "Where are you keeping the artifact?"

His eyes widen in confusion and fear. "Mae kata athiriaus?"

Translation: "What artifact?" he replies shakily.

You increase the pressure on his neck and say in Arabic, "It takes only ten pounds of pressure to break the bones in your neck. So, let's not play games. WHERE ARE THEY KEEPING THE ARTIFACT?"

"Die, American pig!" He spits in defiance. "I will die before I tell you anything. Allahu Akbar! Allahu Akbar!"

You apply pressure with your forearm, cutting off blood flow on the left side of his neck while flexing your bicep—your elbow positioned under his chin—without pressing on the trachea. He falls unconscious in your arms, and you drag him and his sleeping friend to the tent and conceal them in the shadows with the others.

Like a phantom, you slip from shadow to shadow, inching closer to the heart of the Pharisee operation. Your senses are on high alert, every sound amplified by the oppressive darkness. As you approach, you overhear a tense satellite call between Ziad Alhussan and Heinrich Jager (aka the Prophet). Alhussan mentions that they have tested the Pale Horse in Zaire and confirmed that all the dig sites are on schedule.

You creep closer, straining to hear more, when suddenly you feel the cold steel of a rifle barrel pressing against your shoulder. Your blood runs cold.

"Drop your weapon and stand up, dog!" a harsh, aggressive voice commands from behind you.

Time seems to freeze as you slowly raise your hands, your mind racing for a way out of this dire situation but coming up short. You try to disarm him, but he's too fast on the trigger and too far away. His bullets tear through your heart and other organs in succession even before you can manage a word.

The End

Go Back to Page 173

Ladies First

This mission is more perilous than any before it. A striking American operative, her appearance inconspicuous in all black, is set to leap from a cutting-edge stealth aircraft at thirty-five thousand feet. As she plunges into the darkness, she'll face the risks of frostbite and hypoxia. Her objective: to infiltrate a heavily guarded warehouse at the Port of Beirut. What could possibly go wrong?

Maya equips herself and spends thirty minutes breathing pure oxygen to prepare for the jump. She carries dual silenced Glock-19s, a silenced P90 strapped to her back, and a karambit. Her gear includes a black Gentex PM HALO helmet with a heads-up display and night vision, paired with a tactical black flight suit. On her left forearm, a slim computer screen encased in her gear interfaces with AIDA. With her custom black Icarus World X chute packed, Maya stands poised for the ramp to open. She signals her readiness with a thumbs-up as the cargo bay door lowers and the bitter minus forty-five-degree temperatures envelop her.

Without a word, she tumbles backward out of the cargo bay. AIDA reports that Agent Gabriel has reached terminal velocity—126 mph—and will free-fall for approximately forty-five seconds before deploying her chute. Visibility through her bodycam is minimal due to the near-total darkness. AIDA also reports an elevated but steady heart rate, with all systems functioning normally.

In the heart of the night, high above the shimmering lights of Beirut's bustling port, Agent Gabriel descends like an eagle on the hunt. Her sleek black silhouette cuts through the darkness at over 100 mph.

The frigid air whips past her as adrenaline surges through her veins. She plunges through the thin veil of clouds with reckless precision.

As she plummets, the altimeter on her wrist ticks down rapidly, the numbers dwindling as she approaches her target altitude. At four thousand feet she yanks the rip cord and is jolted as the parachute deploys above her.

But as the chute deploys, a terrifying problem arises. The main chute has malfunctioned, caught in a dangerous slider hang-up. With precious seconds slipping away, Maya knows she has to act quickly. The HUD confirms she's still on course, but death seems intent on claiming a victim tonight.

AIDA's voice, which has been counting down from ten thousand feet, now commands, "Deploy, deploy, deploy."

If you think Maya should cut her main chute free, **turn to page 65.**

If you think she should try to free the slider, **turn to page 257.**

 **Bookmark Here**

DIY

You prepare your equipment, your fingers moving with practiced precision to ensure everything is in place. Then you take deep breaths and inhale oxygen for thirty minutes before the jump as a precaution against hypoxia. A sense of calm determination settles over you, sharpening your focus.

Your silenced dual Glock-19s are snug in their holsters, ready for action. The silenced P90 is strapped to your back, a reliable companion for the chaos ahead, and your trusty karambit is sheathed at your side. You're clad in a sleek black tactical suit that fits well. Your HALO helmet, equipped with a heads-up display and night vision, is securely fastened. On your left forearm, a thin, flexible computer screen in a protective sleeve serves as your interface for AIDA, your mission's lifeline.

With your custom black Icarus World X main chute packed, you stand ready for the ramp to open. You give a confident thumbs-up to the crew as the cargo bay door lowers and the frigid air rushes into the bay at 35,000 feet.

Without hesitation, you fall backward into the darkness, swallowed by the void.

AIDA's calm voice cuts through the wind, announcing when you've reached terminal velocity. The rush of free fall is exhilarating, the wind roaring around you as the ground becomes a distant shadow below. You feel like an eagle, poised to strike its prey, your arms tucked against your sides. Your eyes flick to your altimeter, preparing for the deployment of your chute.

At four thousand feet, you pull the rip cord and feel the jolt as the canopy deploys. But panic strikes as the main chute malfunctions, leaving you in a perilous slider hang-up. Precious seconds tick away as you focus, recalling your training with sharp clarity. You draw your karambit and cut through the tangled lines of the main chute.

AIDA's voice has been counting down from 10,000 feet, a steady reminder of your altitude. At 2,000 feet, her voice turns urgent. "Deploy, deploy, deploy." Then it cuts out.

In these heart-stopping moments, you plummet to 1,500 feet. With only seconds to spare, you yank the cord for your backup chute and feel a reassuring tug as it rapidly fills with air, slowing your descent from a frightening 126 mph to a steady 17 mph. As you glide toward the port, you tap your helmet to check for comms issues. The city lights below sparkle like terrestrial stars, offering a fleeting moment of beauty amid the tension.

Touching down on the rugged terrain, you waste no time, gathering your chute into the shadows and disengaging from the harness. The successful HALO jump is just the beginning of your mission. Adrenaline pulses through your veins as you scan your surroundings, preparing for the challenges ahead. Your senses are on high alert, every nerve attuned to the surrounding silence. In the distance, the city lights flicker, unaware of the storm about to unfold. You take a deep breath, the weight of your mission settling heavily on your shoulders. This is your world now, and you're ready for whatever comes next.

"GOD, Gabriel has touched down at the LZ. Do you copy?"

"We're reading your traffic, Gabriel," AIDA's familiar voice crackles through your earpiece. "We lost communication for a few minutes. Good to hear your voice. What's your status?"

"I've stowed my backup chute and am approaching the warehouse now. Any intel from the eye-in-the-sky?" you whisper, activating your night-vision goggles.

"There's an enemy combatant one hundred feet southeast of your position. He appears to be alone. Use the dumpsters to conceal your approach."

Staying low, you slink toward the warehouse. The darkness conceals your approach as you near a patrolling guard, scanning for any threats.

"GOD, I have a visual. Permission to engage?"

"Gabriel, you are cleared to engage Tango One."

You bring your P90 into position, the butt snug against your right shoulder. Your left eye narrows as you focus through the holographic sight. Taking careful aim, you fire a single round. The silenced shot is barely a whisper against the ambient noise of the shoreline.

The combatant falls without a sound.

You grab his body and drag it to a nearby dumpster. His dead weight is cumbersome, but once his upper body is in, hoisting his legs over the edge is straightforward.

"Did you see that, Xavier? That's how a real operator gets it done," you say.

"Just keep your head on a swivel and come back to us in one piece," he says with a chuckle.

You press on, your senses alert and your heart pounding as a bead of sweat trickles down your brow.

"There's another guard ahead, smoking a cigarette near the entrance," AIDA says. "I've detected a biometric door lock. Maybe you can persuade him to let you in, Agent Gabriel."

"And how do you suggest I do that?"

"I don't know. I'm sure you'll figure something out."

Ordinarily you would just shoot him, but AIDA's challenge piques your curiosity. You remove the elastic from your ponytail, letting your blonde locks cascade over your shoulders while unzipping your tactical suit just enough to reveal a hint of cleavage.

As you slowly approach, the guard's eyes lock onto you.

"What are you doing here?" he asks. "This is a restricted area. You can't be here."

"I was looking for a big, strong, handsome man to sweep me off my feet. I just can't resist a man in uniform."

You flash a bewitching smile, flipping your hair as the breeze adds to the effect. He's drawn in by your seduction, his eyes roaming over you like those of a man starved for affection.

His surprise is palpable as a sudden thrust to his throat leaves him breathless. He grasps his throat, choking and unable to speak while you deliver a powerful double ear-slap that disorients him. Sliding behind him, you snap his neck with precise, resolute force.

Then you drag his lifeless body into the shadows, your breath steady despite the adrenaline coursing through your veins. With a practiced motion, you twirl your hair and put the elastic back from around your wrist. You briefly consider dragging the dead guard to the biometric sensor but decide that using your karambit to remove his thumb is more expedient. The blade's edge shimmers in the dim light as you make a clean cut, preparing to use the severed digit on the sensor.

You shrug on your dual shoulder holster, the familiar weight of your silenced Glock-19s reassuring against your sides. Concealing your P90 to avoid unnecessary bulk, you take a deep breath and prepare to move.

"GOD, this is Gabriel. I'm in."

"Affirmative, Agent Gabriel."

You storm through the shadows like a ghost, unseen and unheard. AIDA is your lifeline, feeding you real-time intel as you navigate the labyrinthine warehouse. The maze of corridors, crisscrossed with overhead piping, offers few places of concealment. Each step is calculated, each movement deliberate.

Suddenly muffled voices of unknown combatants grow nearer. Your heart quickens as you realize you're only halfway down a dim corridor with no cover. The walls seem to close in and the shadows aren't deep enough to offer sanctuary. You press yourself against the cool concrete wall, every sense on high alert.

The voices grow louder, their footsteps tapping against the concrete, echoing through the corridor. You glance around frantically, your mind racing for a solution. The flickering overhead light casts eerie, shifting shadows.

Just as their voices reach a crescendo, you spot a narrow gap between two ceiling pipes. It's a tight squeeze but you know you can manage it. Silently, you run up the wall, leap to the pipes overhead, and hoist yourself into the gap, holding your breath as the combatants stroll beneath you. The air is thick with the scent of oil and metal, the quiet punctuated by the murmur of their conversation.

Your hand rests on the grip of your Glock-19. The seconds stretch into what feels like hours as they pass by. Your pulse pounds in your ears but you remain perfectly still.

Once their voices fade into the distance, you exhale slowly and deploy the nano-UAV you brought with you, courtesy of DARPA. The danger has passed but the mission is far from over. For now, you remain concealed among the pipes running along the corridor's ceiling.

You operate the nano-UAV with surgical precision. The tiny drone buzzes through the air with near-silent efficiency, revealing enemy positions without betraying your presence. The live feed is displayed on the screen wrapped around your left wrist while AIDA's calm voice provides real-time analysis, integrating the data with her ongoing reconnaissance.

Through the drone's camera, you spot a figure emerging from a decontamination room—a woman of similar build to yourself, clad in a hazmat suit. She moves with purpose toward a changing area. Your interest piqued, you maneuver the UAV to follow her, noting that she's alone.

Turn to page 71.

Swim for Your Life

Despite your fear, a daring impulse drives you to leap from the safety of the canoe and Don Miguel into the unknown depths below.

The water envelops you in a cold embrace, swallowing you whole as you kick and thrash through the murky currents. Panic sets in as you grasp the enormity of your impulsive decision.

But there's no turning back.

With each stroke, you plunge deeper into the darkness, shadows swirling around you like specters of the night. You quicken your pace, desperate to reach the shore before it's too late, but just as you near it, a force grabs you from below with unimaginable strength.

You're yanked under, your lungs burning for air as you struggle against the crushing grip of the monstrous predator. The beast, a massive black caiman, thrashes and rolls, its jaws clamping down on you with a viselike grip, snapping several ribs with sheer force.

Desperation fuels every movement as you fight against the caiman, your survival instinct fully engaged, but to no avail.

Eventually, you're forced to gasp for air, inhaling the icy river water instead. It slithers into your lungs like liquid knives. The death roll pulls you deeper, and everything fades to black.

The End

Go Back to Page 135

Calling Home to Momma

There's something comforting about reaching out to your mom to reassure her of your safety. You pull out your phone and dial her number.

"Hello? Is that you, Liv, dear?"

"Hi, Mom, it's me. Just wanted to let you know I'll be out of town for a few days on a work assignment. Could you do me a favor and check on my orchids? Only water them if they're bone dry by soaking their bark overnight. Then drain any excess water. They should be fine until I return. The spare key is in the usual spot."

"Alright, Livy. Take care and stay safe. And don't forget to watch your carb intake. You don't want to gain weight if you want to find a partner. I'll look after the orchids so you can focus on your work. By the way, do you remember Eunice Flaman? She mentioned her nephew, who's around your age and single. Apparently, he's both handsome and a dentist."

You roll your eyes and try to let go of your mom's antiquated outlook on food. "Mom, is that the one from Bingo or the one who's been widowed five times from bridge club? Oh, never mind. This isn't the best time to discuss my love life. It'll happen when it happens."

"What about that guy from your work? You're always spending time together. I've noticed the way he looks at you. Your mother has a keen eye for these things."

"Do you mean Benji?" you ask, surprised. "No, Mom, he's just my intern. There's nothing going on. We're just colleagues. Give Daddy a kiss for me and let him know I'll be over for dinner when I get back."

"Alright, Livy. We love you. Muah!"

"Love you too, Mom. Bye."

The plane suddenly loses altitude, and you scramble to steady yourself. The captain's voice crackles over the speaker system. "Better strap in, folks. We've got two Bavar 373 surface-to-air missiles tracking us, launched from Baghdad just over two minutes ago. We have no radar signature, and the active kinetic camouflage is engaged. I don't understand how this happened."

AIDA's voice cuts in. "I believe they've traced an unencrypted cellular signal from our location."

An intermittent beeping alarm pierces the air, slowly merging into a continuous tone reminiscent of a hospital code alert.

The End

Go Back to Page 260

It's In AIDA's Hands Now

You have AIDA scan the breastplate, eager to start the analysis, even before you can return to Mother at Ben Gurion. During the journey, AIDA mentions she might have found a lead—a clue that could point you to the final resting place of the Ark, which heightens your urgency to return to Mother and regroup.

Upon your arrival, AIDA is still processing the data, so you use the time to clean your weapons in the cargo bay. Although you have a personal quarters like the others, the cargo bay has become your unofficial hangout. Afterward, you enjoy a hot shower and get some much-needed rest.

Five hours later, AIDA summons you to the war room with urgent news about Heinrich Jager. According to the latest reports, Jager has been spotted in Canada with several associates, operating under an alias. He was taken into custody by the Canadian RCMP in a joint operation with Interpol and CSIS.

However, during his transfer to Kingston Penitentiary, a notorious biker gang ambushed the convoy, allowing Jager to escape. The RCMP sting operation had been triggered prematurely, and Jager's logistics contact also managed to evade capture.

"Setting Jager aside," Xavier says, "have you found anything from the scans of the breastplate?"

"Only the location where the Hebrews hid the Ark of the Covenant on Mount Nebo!" AIDA replies.

"Nice job burying the lead," you quip.

AIDA then pulls up a flurry of files, photos, and maps related to Mount Nebo.

Xavier fiddles with a gold coin that fell into his boot at the Temple Mount chamber while Olivia tries to ignore him and you focus on the intel.

According to Apocryphal documents—historical writings of disputed authenticity that some consider part of the Biblical canon—the Ark of the Covenant was hidden in a cave on Mount Nebo by the prophet Jeremiah. He instructed the exiles not to reveal its location until Jehovah reunited His people. While no archaeological evidence has confirmed the Ark's presence there, the site is revered as the place where Moses glimpsed the Promised Land before his death.

Preventing the Pale Horse virus from being weaponized and sold is crucial. When combined with the historical significance of the Ark, the prospect of finding the panis vitae—a purported cure for everything from the common cold to cancer, if the Pharisees' claims about its power are accurate—is astounding.

"I have the coordinates," AIDA says. "Latitude: 31° 46' 2.39" N, longitude: 35° 43' 18.59" E. Mother's engines are spooling up now. We'll enter Jordanian airspace in one hour and land at Queen Alia International Airport thirty minutes after that."

What initially appeared to be innocuous etchings on the back of the breastplate turn out to be a detailed topographical map of Mount Nebo, marking the location of a hidden cave. Fearing that failing to document the Ark's location might result in its loss forever, the exiles chose a discreet spot to inscribe the information before relocating the breastplate.

AIDA had to factor in 2600 years of erosion and shifting terrain to locate the cave entrance, now buried two meters underground. By analyzing maps, geological indexes, and satellite imagery, she is confident she can guide you to the Ark.

As you touch down at Queen Alia International Airport in Jordan, the sun begins to set across the tarmac as they usher in the evening. Xavier jumps into the driver's seat and you hand him the keys. Mount Nebo is just a thirty-minute drive away. You call shotgun and slip into the passenger seat while Olivia takes the back.

As Xavier speeds toward Mount Nebo, you remain focused on your mission: to locate the Ark and neutralize the Pharisee biological threat once and for all.

As you arrive at Mount Nebo, the sun hangs low in the sky, casting cool shadows that envelop the landscape. AIDA is on the line, guiding you with instructions to follow the karst formation. After a final scan of the area, she identifies a geological feature that leads to an underground shaft entrance.

"Could I get a cup of coffee?" you ask back in the interrogation room. "I'm parched and running low on energy."

Mr. Atkins stands and stretches his legs. "Why don't we all have a cup?"

Ms. Chamberlain purses her lips but signals a nearby attendant, and soon the oppressive atmosphere of the interrogation room is eased by the comforting aroma of fresh coffee.

"Could you remove these?" you ask, gesturing to the handcuffs that make it difficult to add sugar and cream.

Chamberlain's cheek twitches but she nods again, and the attendants remove the cuffs from your hands. Freed, you tear open three sugar packets and dump a generous amount of cream into your coffee, stirring it with a worn single-use plastic stir-stick, despite the cutting-edge technology in the interrogation facility. It's a paradox. You wouldn't be surprised to find an old rotary phone somewhere in this place.

The coffee is hot and soothing, allowing you to resume your story.

"Now, where was I? Ah, yes—Mount Nebo."

You retrieve shovels from the back of the CIV and strap on headlamps to illuminate your work. Olivia, preferring not to disturb her hair with the headgear, uses the light from her phone instead. The sand and soil yield easily, as if an unseen force is helping you uncover a secret that's been hidden for nearly three thousand years. Your heart pounds with a mix of anxiety and excitement, the air thick with a palpable blend of fear, adventure, and reverence.

Your digging soon uncovers a shaft shrouded in darkness, leading to a narrow corridor lined with jagged stalactites that appear to warn you to turn back. But turning back isn't an option in your dire quest to save the world. You forge ahead, more determined than ever to discover where this path leads.

After a brief trek into the unknown, you come upon a sudden drop-off. There's no way around it. The other side is a sheer rock face plunging into darkness. Xavier cracks some glow sticks and drops them into the abyss, hoping to gauge its depth. From your vantage point, the pit seems bottomless, with your headlamps failing to penetrate the inky void. You watch, breathless, as the glow sticks tumble down, eventually revealing a floor about fifty feet below—unless it's merely a ledge or outcropping.

You return to the CIV to retrieve ropes and harnesses. You and Xavier secure cams and bolts into the ground at the edge of the drop-off, and then you begin the cautious descent into the abyss. As you slowly sink, you hammer pitons into the rock face for added safety. Above you, you notice the fear in Olivia's eyes as she hesitantly positions herself at the top, her back to the drop-off, leaving the safety of solid ground and testing the strength of the rope and her harness.

The descent is fraught with tension. The cold, damp air clings to you as you carefully navigate the narrow shaft, each step down the rock face deliberate in the dim glow of your headlamps. The walls seem to close in around you, the silence punctuated only by your breathing and the occasional clink of metal against stone.

When you finally reach the bottom, the glow sticks illuminate a vast cavern that seems to stretch endlessly into the shadows. You pause, catching your breath and steadying your nerves. The air is thick with the musty scent of ancient earth, and a profound sense of solemnity envelops you as you prepare to delve deeper into the heart of Mount Nebo and find the secrets of the past.

As your eyes adjust to a nearby torchlight, both you and Olivia stand in awe, overcome by shock. The flickering flames cast creepy profiles that dance across the ancient walls. Xavier, lost in mutterings about the mission, remains unaware of what looms just behind him.

Xavier notices the look in your eyes and turns around just in time to see what looks like—though it can't possibly be—an elderly angel sitting like a sentinel before two heavy doors. His wings are folded extraordinarily behind him, absorbing the torchlight from the wall, while his eyes exude a timeless, weary wisdom.
The angel identifies himself as a messenger, sent to guard the Ark since its arrival. His voice, raspy and strained, bears the weight of centuries. This revelation is the last thing you anticipated on this mission. You've encountered many extraordinary phenomena in your life, but nothing as enigmatic and inexplicable as this. Could the Bible be more than just a book of fables and myths?

"Behind me stand two entranceways—two doors," the angel says, his voice resonating with cryptic gravity. "One will lead the righteous to the city of Zion, while the other will bring certain death. I will unlock only one for you. But only if you brought the armor."

Sensing the immovable obstacle, you start to release the clasps on your dual silenced Glock 19s. However, Olivia places a reassuring hand on your arm, her gaze signaling that she has the situation under control. The air is charged with tension, and for the first time, you feel completely out of your depth.

Xavier quietly moves to the side of the angel to look closer at his wings. Looking back toward us, he manages to mouth, "I think those are real..." his eyes wide in amazement.

Xavier begins to bow, but the angel rebukes him. He wouldn't tell us his name, but he said that all worship should be directed to his Father.

He's talking with Olivia about allowing access to the Ark only if we have some sort of spiritual armor. Olivia says he's referencing the book of Ephesians 6:14. Xavier, who was an altar boy when he was a kid, doesn't even know what they're going on about.

Then the old guy calls you by your full name, despite you never having given it to him. He knows things he couldn't possibly know about you. He says you're wearing the belt of truthfulness, and since the loss of your sister, you've been wearing the breastplate of righteousness. He knows things about all of you, and it's unnerving.

The final test is a riddle.

You stand at a fork in the road. One path leads to the city of Beelzebub, where everyone lies. The other leads to the city of Zion, where everyone tells the truth. A guardian stands at the fork, but you cannot discern which city he represents. You may ask him only one question to determine the correct path."

As Olivia ponders the riddle, you briefly consider whether shooting the messenger might be a quicker solution. However, you aren't sure such a thing would even work. However, Olivia remained confident she could solve the puzzle without resorting to violence. The minutes stretch interminably, but finally, Olivia faces the angel and asks, "Which city do you live in?"

Her rationale appears solid. If the guardian is from the City of Zion and always tells the truth, he will indicate the correct passage. Conversely, if he is from the City of Beelzebub and always lies, he will still point to the safe path.

The angel's response comes as a near whisper: "Clever girl."

He produces a massive skeleton key, the sort that looks like it can unlock a colossal door. The key glints with a menacing gleam as he inserts it into the lock of the left door, which opens up to reveal an ominous darkness. As the door creaks open, the angel's form becomes enshrouded in golden light, and the ceiling of earth opens up to reveal a bright light among the clouds. A golden orb appears from his chest and he rises into the sky. The form that remains transforms into clay and then dust, disintegrating into a pile on the ground, with only the key ring resting atop it.

You venture into the dark corridor, with Xavier leading the way, holding a torch he retrieved from the wall near where the angel sat. The corridor walls are adorned with ancient Hebrew symbols and depictions. One mural illustrates the Levites transporting the Ark across the Jordan River while an unseen force holds back the waters. Other scenes depict rams' horns heralding a triumphant cry. The torchlight casts eerie shadows, causing the symbols to seem as though they're writhing.

The corridor soon opens into a vast cave, where, resting on a stone altar in the center, is the Ark of the Covenant. It radiates an otherworldly power that defies description. Although you studied the Ark extensively in the Bible, nothing could have prepared you for this moment, the reality far surpassing any written description.

But as you move closer, an inexplicable force holds you back. The gold glints as though it has just been polished, and the craftsmanship is unparalleled. Majestic golden cherubs with outstretched wings crown the top while gold-encrusted acacia poles adorn the sides, giving the impression that the Levites only recently placed it upon the altar.

Suddenly the sound of boots echoing from behind herald the arrival of Heinrich Jager, Ziad Alhussan, and a group of armed mercenaries. Their shadows loom, distorted in the flickering torchlight, casting monstrous shapes that dance across the walls.

"Step aside!" Jager barks, his authoritative scowl cutting through the tension in the air. His men spring into action, moving to seize the Ark.

Olivia desperately lunges forward. "STOP! YOU HAVE NO IDEA WHAT YOU'RE DOING!"

With a callous disregard Jager shoots Olivia in the stomach. She staggers back, her face a portrait of shock and fear, before collapsing to the ground. You dash to her side, ripping a strip of fabric from your shirt to staunch the bleeding, desperately trying to soothe her. Xavier drops to his knees beside her, his face twisted with rage and helplessness.

Meanwhile, as Jager's men lay their hands on the Ark, chaos erupts. One of them suddenly convulses, his body writhing in a violent seizure. He and his companion collapse, their eyes glazed over with white cataracts. The scene is a waking nightmare, the torchlight casting ghastly silhouettes over their twisted bodies.

Jager orders additional men to proceed with a different tactic. They insert crowbars into the gaps around the lid, grunting as they pry it open. The deafening screech of metal on metal shatters the silence, tearing through the cavern.

Then a deafening roar of wind and thunder erupts in the cave as a specter rises from the Ark. It hovers, its gaze locking onto Xavier before shifting to Jager, Alhussan, and their men. In that instant, you're no longer the formidable Maya—you're a terrified child. Clutching Olivia to your body, feeling the air grow cold and seeing an ethereal mist and jagged bolts of blue lightning crawl and crackle across the room before you shut your eyes. Xavier turns away, pulling both of you into a protective embrace.

Panicked gunfire and desperate screams reverberate through the cavern as Jager and his men scramble for a way out. The unleashed power of the divine rages uncontrollably, and it feels as if nothing can contain it.

The howling winds and ominous roars gradually diminish, leaving behind an unsettling silence. As you open your eyes, you see that Olivia has tragically succumbed to her injuries.

You hasten to the open Ark and retrieve the golden jar of manna. Inside, you find what appear to be glowing, ethereal crackers. Carefully, you break off a small piece and place it on Olivia's tongue, praying that the Pharisees' claims about the panis vitae are accurate. You and Xavier watch with bated breath.

Initially, there's no visible effect. Then, Olivia's pallid cheeks slowly regain their color. Moments later, she sneezes and opens her eyes, as though awakening from a deep, restorative sleep. The gravity of the situation dawns on you as Olivia lifts her shirt, revealing that she is fully healed—no trace of the gunshot wound remains. The only remnants are the bloodstains on her clothing.
Any remaining doubt about the Ark's authenticity evaporates. The Ark has to be safeguarded—or perhaps the world needs protection from it.

Before the full impact of recent events can settle in, the sound of approaching boots reaches you again. This time, it's the United States military, led by stern men in black who flash their credentials and bark orders. Their authoritative presence is palpable as they crate the Ark and its contents. You're escorted to a lift they installed on the rock wall where you descended. The lift carries you fifty feet to the surface, and upon reaching the top, you're directed back to the shaft entrance.

Outside, the scene grows increasingly chaotic. Soldiers flood the area, erecting lighting towers and stringing up Do Not Cross tape. Flashing lights and the intense spotlight of a circling helicopter bathe the area in a blinding glare, heightening the frenetic activity. Additional soldiers fast-rope in, bolstering the already substantial presence. You're escorted to an EMS truck for a thorough medical checkup and clearance.

Olivia, persistent and anxious, repeatedly asks where the Ark is being taken. Her pleas are initially ignored, but eventually, a soldier with a semblance of authority answers her. "The Ark will be well protected, ma'am. We're transporting it to a secure location."

Much later, you're briefed on the global economic upheaval that would be triggered by the discovery, and you're informed that the Ark poses a significant threat to US national security.

"Where has it been taken?" Ms. Chamberlain demands.

"I can't say for certain, Ms. Chamberlain. This is beyond my scope," you say. "I'm an operator, not a policymaker. You might want to consult higher-ups. Someone must know where it's been taken. I noticed a few airmen with patches from Edwards Air Force Base, which manages Area 51. If I were you, I'd start there —assuming you can obtain the necessary clearance."

Ms. Chamberlain leaned forward, pressed a button, and said, "Remove all references to the angel and the specter from the record, and redact them from her statement. We found traces of black mold from Stachybotrys chartarum, which has known hallucinogenic properties. It's clear that her team was suffering from its effects."

"This interview is concluded," Chamberlain says. "Please sign here. You'll be flown back to the US afterward. This is a CIA nondisclosure agreement. Be aware that any discussion of this interview or the information you've provided will result in charges of treason, which is a capital offense punishable by life imprisonment or death."

"I have a question. How did we get here? I don't recall much from the time we were cleared by medical until we arrived."

"It doesn't matter. You were brought here for your own safety."

Atkins and Atwell stand up and exit the room, followed by Chamberlain. Their voices, muffled, drift down the corridor.

A few hours later, they remove the shackles from your feet, return your clothes, and transport you to Andrews Air Force Base in Washington, DC. Once there, your personal effects are handed back to you and you're officially released.

You book a commercial flight back to Los Angeles and experience an overwhelming sense of relief as you unlock the front door and step into the sanctuary of your home. You remove your boots and pour yourself a glass of red wine from Ménage à Trois, a local winery in St. Helena.

Months pass, and the memories of the mission that ended the Pale Horse biological threat fade. While lounging by the pool on a sunny afternoon, an Amazon drone buzzes overhead, delivering a small package. Inside is a GOD-team earpiece and mic. As you place it in your ear, AIDA's voice crackles to life once more.

"Agent Gabriel, you are being activated."

"I thought the GOD team was disbanded."

"We operate above traditional clandestine services, Agent Gabriel. We respond to existential threats that demand a unique form of rapid response. It benefits us if traditional government branches believe we don't exist. All records concerning you and your team have been systematically erased. The truth is, we don't exist. We are the ghosts—the 'them'—the 'they.'

"Please pack your gear and prepare. Arrangements with the PMC have been made. You will be contacted again."

"Wait, where are we headed?"

"I can't disclose the details at the moment, but do you enjoy Chinese food?"

"Yes, definitely."

"Perfect, I foresee some dim sum in your near future."

And with that cryptic promise, the line goes dead. The thrill of the unknown stirs a familiar excitement within you, and you smile as you contemplate the new adventure that awaits.

The End

All That Glitters

Despite the breastplate now being secure in your hands, the surrounding treasures prove impossible to ignore. Gleaming gold coins, shimmering jewelry, and sparkling stones practically beg to be taken. Lucky for you, your cargo pants have deep pockets. But as you begin to shove the treasures inside, sand clings to the gold. Soon, half your pockets are heavy with both treasure and gritty sand that refuses to be shaken off.

The treasure pulls at you, a tantalizing whisper in your mind, urging you to grab more. Time is slipping through your fingers, but the gleam of gold is maddeningly irresistible. The heavy rock door grinds closer and closer to the ground, and soon it will trap you inside. Panic surges through your veins as you lurch toward the exit, yet the burden of gold and sand slows your every step, turning your escape into a sluggish, desperate struggle.

What felt like plenty of time vanishes in an instant. The sand floods the chamber, rising at an alarming rate, inching higher with every heartbeat. Desperation grips you as you hurl the breastplate beneath the descending door, fully aware that you're not going to make it.

Maya reaches out for your hands, her eyes wide with a mix of terror and fierce determination, but it's too late. The stone door crashes down with a deafening thud, sealing away your final chance at freedom. Helpless, you watch as the snakes and tarantulas slip through cracks in the walls, leaving you alone in the suffocating chamber, the sand rising relentlessly around you.

Time distorts into an endless moment of dread. As the minutes drag by, the light fades, swallowed by the encroaching sand burying the golden shields that once bathed the room in warmth. What was once a vibrant treasury is now a cold, quiet tomb. Fatigue sets in as the air thins, each breath harder to take, the weight of the sand pressing down on your chest.

You collapse onto the sand-covered treasures, your body weighed down by exhaustion. The once-irresistible pull of the gold and jewels feels distant, overshadowed by an overwhelming sense of finality. As the sand creeps higher, you reflect on all the narrow escapes, knowing now that no one's luck lasts forever.

The End

Go Back to Page 356

Just Another Brick in the Wall

True to his name, Wild Card strides toward the ancient device with reckless confidence, pressing an arbitrary brick into the cube-shaped recess, his eyes narrowing as if daring fate to respond.

A deep rumble reverberates through the corridor, and without warning, a razor-sharp circular blade shoots out from the wall, slicing through Wild Card's jugular in one brutal motion. Blood sprays from his neck as the blade buries itself in the stone with a deafening clang.

You and the rest of your team stand paralyzed in horror as the blades slowly retract, leaving you trembling but alive.

As you survey the walls for more potential threats, something unsettling catches your eye. Carvings that once appeared benign now seem to conceal a more sinister purpose, their true nature emerging from the shadows.

Before you can shout a warning to Maya, a series of wall-mounted vents erupt with a menacing hiss. Poison darts fly, their tips gleaming in the dim light. You lunge to push Maya to safety, but the lethal projectiles find their mark.

Pain sears through your body as the darts penetrate your flesh, their toxic venom coursing through your veins. Darkness encroaches as you fight to remain conscious, the world spinning out of control. Through the haze, you watch in horror as Maya collapses, a cluster of poisoned darts embedded in her bloodied torso. Nearby, Wild Card slumps to the ground, clutching his throat as blood flows freely from his wounds.

Israeli news later reveals the discovery of three American treasure hunters at a secret location on the Temple Mount. Speculation mounts as rumors circulate that the hunters inadvertently triggered ancient traps designed to fend off Babylonian invaders in the sixth century.

The End

Go Back to Page 237

What's Next

The state-owned Ethiopian Broadcasting Corporation announces that an unspecified number of Muslim extremists have desecrated Our Lady of Zion Church, where the Ark of the Testimony is housed. They report that these attackers attempted to steal the Ark but were thwarted by the courageous Ethiopian National Defense Force, which allegedly eliminated all intruders. According to the guardian monks, the Ark chamber was not breached and the Ark remains securely in their possession.

"Ethiopian tax dollars hard at work," you muse.

As your plane ascends into international airspace, the weight of Benji's loss begins to settle in. Olivia, her eyes brimming with tears, is more resolute than ever to solve the cipher wheel and locate the panis vitae before the Pharisees do. Maya, recognizing Olivia's distress, offers her a comforting embrace. You remain silent, unsure of what to say, the gravity of your mission crushing down upon you.

But Olivia manages to stifle her emotions and tells AIDA to display a map of the dig sites. It becomes evident that the Pharisees have been in pursuit of the golden jar of manna, the panis vitae, for some time now. Olivia needs to confirm whether Jager would indeed hold off on deploying the Pale Horse virus without securing the cure first. Maya's response is chilling: without the cure, the virus could potentially devastate the entire planet.

You propose locating the virus and securing it, though you're uncertain where to begin. The entire operation hinges on Olivia deciphering the cipher wheel. What initially feels like endless hours soon stretches into days, with AIDA and Olivia working around the clock to crack its code, until finally, a breakthrough occurs—Olivia applies a Fibonacci sequence, successfully unraveling the cipher wheel's mystery.

Inside it, you find a meticulously detailed map of Jerusalem on ancient papyrus, adorned with cryptic symbols and intricate annotations. AIDA's advanced core analyzes the map, pinpointing the precise locations of both the Ark and the panis vitae.

"Do you grasp the significance of this?" you say. "Do you realize what's housed in the Ark? The breastplate of Aaron—crafted from solid gold and encrusted with twelve precious gems, each representing one of the twelve tribes of Israel. I know my treasures!

Let's do this!"

The thrill of the hunt has commenced, and you're racing against the clock and elusive adversaries to uncover ancient treasures and avert a global catastrophe.

You tell AIDA to superimpose the ancient map onto contemporary topography to pinpoint the Ark's present location. Her analysis confirms that the Ark is situated on Mount Moriah in Jerusalem. Armed with this crucial information, you proceed to Ben Gurion International Airport in Tel Aviv. From there, you travel overland in the Gurkha CIV to the Temple Mount, an area fiercely guarded by the local Muslim community, which staunchly opposes any excavation attempts. Olivia and Maya choose to accompany you on this high-stakes mission under the glaring light of day.

As you approach the heavily guarded site, the visible presence of the IDF and Jerusalem Waqf guards is undeniable. You blend in by posing as tourists, leveraging the Temple Mount's status as a major attraction for both Christians and Muslims. Olivia deems it prudent to bring the cube and cipher wheel, anticipating they might prove useful.

With AIDA's guidance, you navigate through the labyrinthine tunnels beneath the Temple Mount. The air grows cooler and the darkness more oppressive as you delve deeper. Finally, you reach your destination: a hidden wall recess deep within the underground maze. At first, you're perplexed by what appears to be a concealed doorway. The recess bears a striking resemblance to the cube. You turn to Olivia, requesting the cube in hopes that it might be the key.

You place the cube into the recess and it fits perfectly. The wall rumbles and slides open, revealing a narrow staircase that disappears into the darkness below. As you begin your descent, the door slides shut behind you, plunging you into pitch blackness. Suddenly a worn or missing step cause all of you to tumble deeper into the unknown.

"Is everybody okay?" Maya asks.

A sudden hissing fills the air, but you can't see a thing. Your hand brushes against an object that feels like a shield on a stand that allows it to articulate. It's caked in dust and cobwebs. You remove your keffiyeh and polish the device until it gleams like a mirror, and a beam of light catches its surface, partially illuminating the chamber.

That's when Olivia lets out a bloodcurdling scream. She's lying on her stomach, face-to-face with a hooded black cobra, her hand flinging a tarantula away in disgust. Without hesitation, Maya lunges forward, grabbing the cobra just below its head and hurling it across the room. Olivia rolls onto her back, taking a deep, relieved breath.

One by one, you all polish the other golden shields scattered around the room. As each one catches the incoming sunlight, the chamber slowly brightens, revealing its ancient splendor. The suspense of your descent, the danger lurking in the dark, and the discovery of the golden shields has added layers of intrigue and mystery to your quest. You're now deep within the bowels of the Temple Mount, on the brink of uncovering secrets that have been buried for centuries.

All around you, mounds of treasure glitter under the reflected sunlight, casting a mesmerizing glow that dances on the ancient stone walls. Piles of gold coins, their edges worn smooth by time, lie heaped together like shimmering dunes. Precious gems, each one a marvel of nature's artistry, sparkle with an inner fire, their colors a symphony of reds, blues, and greens. Ornate jewelry, crafted by hands long gone, lies scattered amidst the riches, its intricate designs telling silent tales of lost civilizations and forgotten artisans.

But as breathtaking as this display of wealth is, your eyes are irresistibly drawn to the center of the room. There, on a raised stone platform, stands the most magnificent treasure of all. Elevated on that stage, bathed in an ethereal light that seems to come from nowhere and everywhere all at once, is a sight that steals your breath and fills your heart with awe: the breastplate of Aaron.

Its presence is otherworldly, as if it harbors the very essence of divinity within its fabric. Each gem embedded in the breastplate gleams with a brilliance that outshines everything else in the room. The facets catch and command the light in a mesmerizing dance. The gold framing the gems pulses with a life of its own—warm and inviting yet also solemn and reverent.

You stand transfixed, unable to move as your senses are overwhelmed by the sheer majesty of this ancient artifact. Time seems to have stopped, the air around you thick with history and the weight of countless generations who have sought and revered this sacred relic. A silent energy crackles in the air, imbuing the atmosphere with a tangible sense of the divine that makes each breath feel like a privilege.

In this moment, enveloped by treasures beyond imagination, you realize you're in the presence of something truly unparalleled. Before you stands the greatest treasure mankind has ever uncovered—the breastplate of Aaron—a testament to human devotion, craftsmanship, and the eternal quest for the divine. Around it is six gems on each side.

As you reach out to grasp the breastplate, a deafening rumble echoes through the room. Your heart races as you glance around, a growing sense of dread overtaking you as sand pours into the chamber from concealed ports at a frantic pace.

"What did you do?" Maya cries, her voice tinged with panic.

You all scramble to find an escape route, but hope seems to be slipping away. Your eyes race from wall to wall, desperate for a solution. Then Maya spots a wall with peculiar cylindrical cutouts, each featuring unique claws that appear designed to hold something. But what could it be?

"Olivia, do that thing you do!" Maya urges, her eyes wide with both fear and determination.

Olivia quickly assesses the devices, her fingers tracing their contours. "The stones around the breastplate!" she suddenly exclaims. "Hurry, and bring them to me!"

You watch with trembling hands as Olivia places each gem into its designated holder. With every stone that clicks into place, the tension in the room mounts, until finally, the last gem fits into its slot. A blinding light fills the chamber, and a section of the wall begins to rise. Without hesitation, you ride the surge of sand—your only escape route—as it gushes out of the chamber.

As you're swept away, you glance back at the chamber. The breastplate, rests atop the rising sand, still a potent symbol of historical significance. The wall section that facilitated your escape is gradually lowering back into place. How can you let the breastplate of Aaron be swallowed by the sands of time? You can't. It remains one of the most historically significant artifacts ever discovered.

"What are you doing?" Maya's voice vibrates with alarm as she sees you duck under the descending door.

The wall grumbles, its ominousness intensifying as it descends. You have only seconds left. Your heart pounds in your ears as you seize the breastplate, its weight heavy into your hands.

If you want to dive for the space that's left and roll underneath before it closes, **turn to page 296.**

If you want to fill your pockets with a little more treasure before you dive for the exit, **turn to page 346.**

> **Bookmark Here**

There's Going to be Fireworks

You descend the ramp with Benji to meet Agent Gabriel as she boards. Up close, she looms over you. You barely come up to her chin. Her athletic build is striking, with defined biceps hinting at impressive strength. Her hair is pulled back into a tight ponytail and she's dressed in a tactical vest over a white sports bra paired with skinny jeans.

"Hi, Agent Gabriel, I'm—"

"Olivia Davenport, code name Desert Lotus. You're an expert in cryptology, languages, biblical studies, and Middle Eastern affairs. I've reviewed your file. Don't worry, I'll ensure your safety. I have a strong track record. Could you assist me with my gear?" Agent Gabriel asks, brushing past you on the ramp.

You intended to make a sharp introduction, but her friendliness has disarmed you. Her hands were too full for her to notice your hesitation anyway. When she smiles, you melt like a warm lava cake with a gooey center. In just under a minute, the shift from strangers to feeling like old friends is almost magical. That's her charm. Everyone warms to her, unless she's kicking your butt.

You pick up some of her items while Benji, either boldly or recklessly, grabs a case marked Explosive Ordnance – Handle with Care. You follow Agent Gabriel onto the plane, noting with a mix of concern and disbelief that Benji seems oblivious to the warning as he carries the case with careless ease.

Agent Gabriel, turning to collect more items, spots Benji swinging the case around playfully. "Could you please ask your friend to handle that more carefully?" she asks you. "It contains explosive ordinance."

But it's too late. The handle slips from Benji's grip and the case tumbles down the ramp, landing on the tarmac with a jarring thud. Time seems to stretch as you shout at Benji to be careful. Adjusting the shoulder strap on one of Agent Gabriel's cases, you descend the ramp and watch as Benji retrieves the fallen case.

"Everything's fine, Olivia!" he assures you with a grin, his glasses fogging up in the humidity.

Suddenly a deafening explosion erupts and Benji is violently torn apart and the blast hurls you backward.

As darkness encroaches, you lose consciousness. When you come to, Agent Gabriel is kneeling beside you, urgently unzipping your jumpsuit and cutting through your blood-soaked shirt. She presses the defibrillator paddles against your bare chest and she shouts, "Don't you dare die on me!" right before your heart beats for the last time.

The End

Go Back to Page 164

We Need Our Gear

In the cover of darkness, the forest becomes a shadowy labyrinth, illuminated only by the faint glow of the moon filtering through the canopy. You spot the supply case, tangled in the branches of a beech tree, suspended high by the parachute lines. Every rustle and crackle seem magnified in the still night air, and your heart races as you approach the tree.

You start your ascent, the rough bark scraping against your gloved hands. Each movement is deliberate, your senses attuned to every creak and rustle. When you reach the top, you draw your karambit, its blade shimmering in the moonlight, and slice through the chute lines with precision. The supply case drops to the forest floor with a muffled thud, its impact absorbed by the thick underbrush.

You descend rapidly and rush to the case. After keying in the code, you hold your breath. The green light that flashes back at you is a welcome relief. Everything is in place. You're ready to complete your mission.

You and Eagle Eye don your ghillie suits, the fabric blending with the forest shadows. With rifles in hand, you gather your supplies and he initiates the sitrep, his voice a steady whisper in the still night.

"Looking Glass, this is Eagle Eye. We have reached the Big Red Balloon. Over."

"Affirmative, Eagle Eye. We copy."

"We are proceeding to Objective Alpha. Eagle Eye out."

You get your bearings, every sense on high alert. The Aras River crossing is your next objective, demanding both caution and speed. The forest holds its breath, every rustle and snap suggesting a potential threat. The two of you move purposefully, through the encroaching darkness in the humid night air as you push through the underbrush. Ahead lies your destination, shrouded in both mystery and danger.

Through the underbrush, you and Eagle Eye glide like shadows through the forest. The fourteen-kilometer trek through the dense woods to reach the Aras River, Objective Alpha, is a grueling test of endurance and stealth. Upon reaching the river's edge, you climb to a higher vantage point, scanning the surroundings for the ideal anchor.

From your vantage point, a solitary tree on the opposite bank stands tall and resolute. Eagle Eye retrieves the Helix REBS Launcher, its titanium tip gleaming in the narrow beam of moonlight that filters through the canopy. He takes precise aim, the quiet intensity of his concentration palpable in the still air. With a sharp hiss, the grapple soars through the darkness, embedding itself into the tree across the chasm of the Aras.

You lean back and give the line several firm tugs. Satisfied with its hold, you secure the steel cable to a robust tree on your side and ready the metal slide plates for the zip line. Below, the Aras River churns, a swirling torrent that offers no mercy. With your equipment fastened securely, you launch onto the zip line, soaring over the river with the wind whipping past and the roar of the water filling your ears.

Upon reaching the far side, you conceal the .50 Cal M107 at the base of a tree, marking the location with a symbol only you can decipher. The rifle will be crucial on your return, but for now, you'll only carry the essentials.

Your mission has just begun, and the thrill of adventure pulses through your veins. With each step taking you deeper into the shadows of Iran, you draw closer to your objective. You advance with a mix of caution and excitement, prepared to confront whatever awaits. The night wraps around you and the forest seems to whisper primal secrets as you venture into the unknown, your resolve unwavering.

"Make no mistake, Aphrodite, we're now in harm's way," Eagle Eye whispers.

"Understood, Eagle Eye. Let's get it done," you say, bracing yourself for what's to come.

Having successfully crossed the Aras River, you now find yourselves deep within the Islamic Republic of Iran. The shadows here are denser, the air heavier with tension. You're just one klick north of your next objective, Bravo—a Bell 212 helicopter from the Islamic Republic Air Force, tail number EP-ZYX, code-named Sneaky Pete.

Your target lies near the Giz Galisi Dam, a new infrastructure project currently being brought online by Iran. Intelligence indicates that high-ranking officials will be present, making this leg of your journey the most perilous yet. Every rustle in the underbrush and every distant sound heightens your anxiety. You know that the next kilometer will be fraught with danger.

Your mission is to place a small brick of C-4 on the designated helicopter within a three-chopper convoy. These aircraft will be closely monitored by the Quds Force of the Islamic Revolutionary Guard Corps, known for their ruthless efficiency and cunning.

As you navigate through the dense foliage, the forest feels alive with unseen eyes. Moonlight barely penetrates the canopy, casting eerie shadows that flicker around you. Every step is a calculated risk, every breath deliberate. The stakes are higher than ever, with no margin for error.

As you reach the outskirts of the dam, you hunker down and scan the area. The helicopters come into view, their dark shapes looming ominously in the night. Guards patrol with disciplined precision, their silhouettes a sharp contrast against the dim light. "Looking Glass, this is Eagle Eye. We've reached Objective Bravo, and the fox is in the hen house. I repeat, the fox is in the hen house."

"Roger that, Eagle Eye. Hourglass out."

"We've got this," you whisper to Eagle Eye, trying to reassure yourself as much as him. He nods, his gaze fixed on the target.

You lie flat on your bellies, waiting for the perfect moment as the seconds stretch into what feels like hours. At last, a gap in the patrols appears. You advance with swift, silent precision, every sense heightened.

The helicopters stand in a row, their imposing forms casting long shadows in the dim light. Eagle Eye covers you with a silenced sniper rifle from the brush line. As you dash for the helicopters, you're fully exposed for the first time, traversing an expansive concrete slab at least 120 yards wide.

Turn to page 304.

Introducing Maya Avraham

Date: July 23, 2034 Location: CIA Black Site, Cairo (Near 30.0444° N, 31.2357° E)

Somewhere between the Nile River and the 6th of October Bridge

Red lights flash as sirens blare with an oscillating wail. "Alert level gamma, asset out of containment. I repeat, alert level gamma, asset out of containment," a voice drones.

In Interview Room Three, a metal table bolted to the floor holds an elaborate origami swan and dragon, a half-used brick of paper, a pen, and a note. The note reads: CIA, meet me at the Trivium Business Complex, North 90th Street, New Cairo, Egypt. Maya.

The door bursts open as Ms. Elizabeth Chamberlain, the CIA station chief in Cairo, storms in. "How did this happen?" she thunders.

"Mmm... Mmm..." The polygraph attendant, held by an unseen force, struggles to respond, his right hand raised unnaturally above his head.

"Speak, damn it!" Chamberlain barks, wrenching his arm down. Instantly the invisible bonds vanished, leaving him free.

"Oh, thank you! I've been stuck like that for five minutes."

"Dare I ask how?"

"Ma'am, she requested paper to make a statement. I had to unlock her handcuffs to connect the polygraph equipment. She was quietly making origami and seemed harmless. But in an instant, she struck me with just two fingers at several points on my chest, neck, and shoulder, and then I was frozen in place, unable to speak. I don't know how she did it, ma'am. I couldn't move!"

"Well that's just perfect! I leave you alone with her for a few minutes and now she's escaped. Gather some men and track her down. NOW!"

"Yes, ma'am! Right away, ma'am!" The attendant hurries out of the room.

"AND SOMEBODY TURN OFF THESE DAMN ALARMS!"

Forty minutes later, twenty armed CIA agents in white overcoats arrive in three unmarked vans, surrounding you while you enjoy a hot dog and cheesy fries outside Nathan's fast-food joint in New Cairo. The three young men who were making advances suddenly look away.

You smile at the burly agent barking orders. "Any chance I can finish these cheesy fries? You arrived a bit early."

"GET DOWN ON THE GROUND AND INTERLOCK YOUR FINGERS BEHIND YOUR HEAD!"

You wipe the cheese from your lips, raise your hands, and kneel, keeping eye contact. The agents move in, forcing you to the ground and cuffing your hands behind your back. Two of them lift you to your feet while a third pulls a black hood over your head.

Half an hour passes and you find yourself back in the cold, sterile confines of Interview Room Three. Shackles dig into your wrists and ankles, a harsh reminder of your predicament. Your writing supplies have disappeared, leaving you alone with your thoughts. This time, there's no polygraph—just a more direct approach. The "bad cop, bad cop" routine is in full force, with Ms. Chamberlain leading the charge. Mr. Atkins, the formidable deputy director of the CIA, and Colin Atwell, the aloof MI6 officer, are also present, their stern faces etched with disapproval. None of them find your spontaneous fast-food detour amusing.

The questions come swiftly and sharply.

"Where is the Ark?"

"How did you join the Ghost Operations Division?"

"Who was your handler?"

They question you as if they already know the answers. The process feels less like an interrogation and more like a formality.

You sit defiantly, remembering who you are: Maya Abigail Avraham, a highly trained and motivated Israeli operator whose aunt and sister were killed by a Palestinian suicide bomber. The conflict in the Middle East isn't just a news byline to you, it's a deeply personal crusade for justice, driven by a need to hold those who commit evil accountable.

The story begins on May 12, 2024, when you are with Mossad. A mysterious invitation brings you to a clandestine meeting with CIA agent David Pernas and his Israeli counterpart Daniel Cohen. They outline a covert sniper mission: a two-man cell tasked with infiltrating hostile territory to eliminate a political figure obstructing sensitive regional negotiations.

They ask you to volunteer for the mission, explaining that it will be entirely off the books. Should you or your spotter be killed or captured, both the US and Israeli governments will disavow any knowledge of your actions. In exchange, you'll be offered US citizenship and the choice of your assignments.

If you want to accept the assignment, **turn to page 17.**

If you want to turn down the assignment, **turn to page 81.**

 **Bookmark Here**

Olivia's Puzzle Solutions

Cryptograph puzzle found on page 260 points to Not Just a Pretty Face on page 38.

Caesar Cipher puzzle found on page 78 points to The Tetragrammaton on page 145.

If you had any difficulty solving Olivia's puzzles, here is the answer key.

Made in the USA
Middletown, DE
13 April 2025